SPECTRUM

2022

The Spectrum Series

SPECTRUM
DIFFUSION
CRYSTALLIZED
COVALENCE
IRIDESCENCE
SCINTILLATE (PREQUEL)

SAMANTHA MINA

SPECTRUM

BOOK I OF A SERIES

The characters, names, and events as well as all places, incidents, organizations, and dialog in this novel are either the products of the writer's imagination or are used fictitiously.

ISBN: 978-0-9991577-0-1

Visit the author's website at **http://www.SpectrumSeries.org**
to order additional copies.

For Tracy Gusukuma,

the first to lay eyes upon the earliest draft of this story, in the spring of 2005. Thank you for encouraging me to strive for my best. Sometimes, tough love is just what a girl needs to reach her true potential.

Cease would certainly agree.

PRONUNCIATION GUIDE

Acci: *"AX-ee"*
Arrhyth: *"AR-hith"*
Ichthyosis: *"Ik-thee-OH-sis"*
Leavesleft: *"LEEV-ssleft"*
Lechatelierite: *"Luh-shaht-LEER-ahyt"*
(rhymes with "light")
Qui Tsop: *"Key Sop"*

NORTHWESTERN HEMISPHERE OF SECOND EARTH

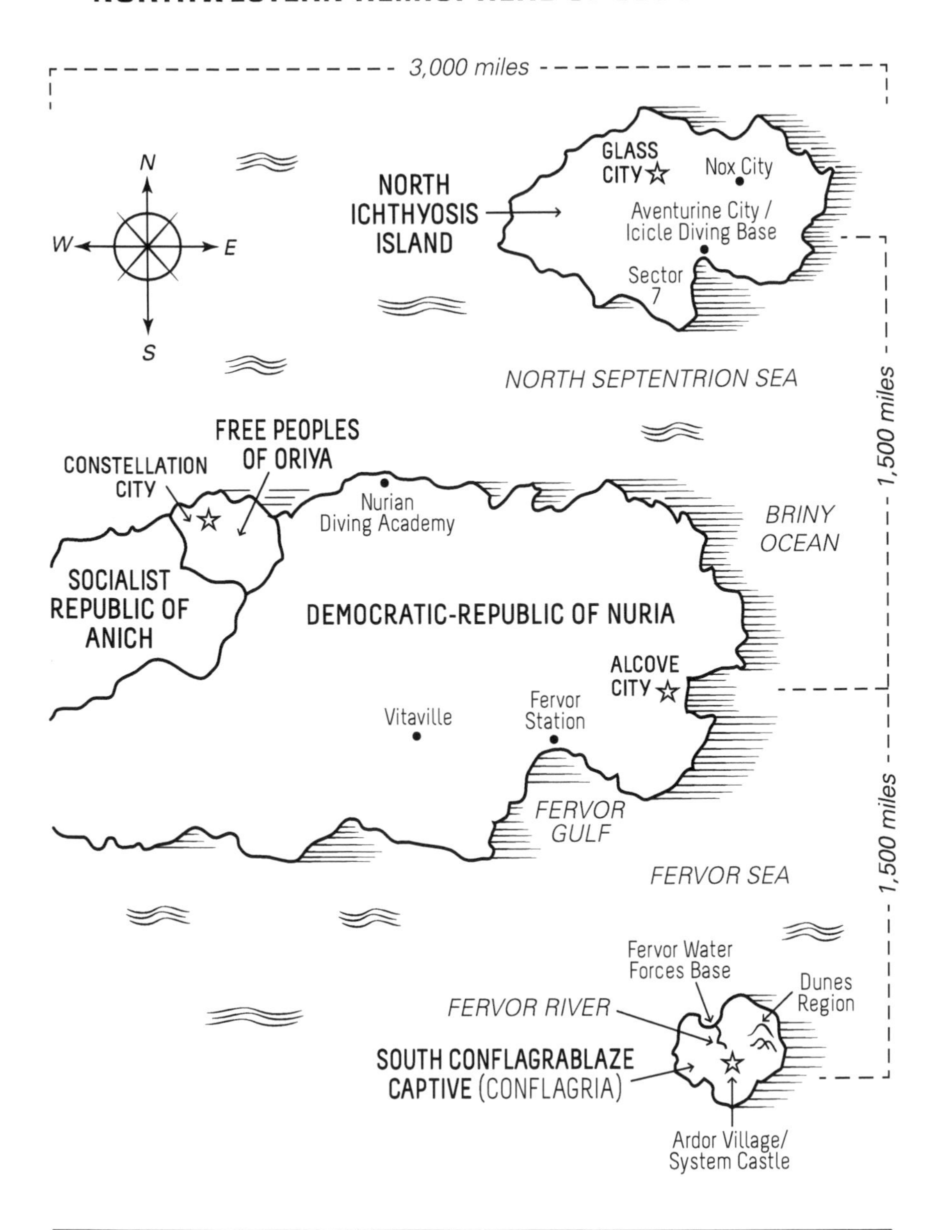

PART I

Eyes of Fire

Some say the world will end in fire,
Some say in ice.
From what I've tasted from desire
I hold with those who favor fire.
But if it had to perish twice,
I think I know enough of hate
To say that for destruction ice
Is also great
And would suffice.

—*"Fire and Ice" by Robert Frost*

SCARLET JULY

Scarlet. What would pop into your mind if you pondered the word? I'd think of blood, lit on fire.

The System named me, 'Scarlet Carmine July.' I was born on July seventh of the seventy-seventh age, seventh era. At fourteen ages old, I weighed about eighty pounds and stood two inches shy of five feet, and everything about me was as crimson as my name—my hair, my permanently sunburnt skin, my robe, my old home… everything except my emerald eyes.

Until age ten, I lived in a nation tiny enough for one to traverse on foot in a couple days: the South Conflagrablaze Captive—or, Conflagria, for short. Fire burned continually throughout the island, hot as the breath of a hobnail dragon. Fire was central to our society because it had many crucial magical uses. The temperature around here rarely dropped below one-hundred-twenty, even at night. But, the heat was nothing. Nothing compared to my past. Everything changed nine ages ago, on my sixth birthday.

"You will come with me to the System Mage Castle today," Mother told me that morning, black eyes alight. Her long, raven hair looked almost blue, in the blazing sunlight. "You will begin your magical education."

"Why do I have to start so young?" I whined. "Amytal and Caitiff started when they were seven." My siblings, the twins, were three ages older than me.

"It's what the System requests." She cast me a hard look. "And, we don't question the System."

Fair enough. The System didn't make mistakes, after all. The System kept our fires burning, the System named us at birth, the System taught us our magework, the System told us who to marry and when, the System told us where to live, the System appointed our jobs, the

System rationed our food and possessions and the System decided whether or not we were worth keeping alive. I regarded the System fondly, like a majestic deity worthy of our praise and obedience. After all, it put scabrous-dragon meat and taro-root on my plate and gave me all the supplies I needed to draw pretty pictures and craft spin-tops and kites. What more could a kid want?

The System named my father, 'Coronet Regal'; my mother, 'Melanize Stygian'; my sister, 'Amytal Angel'; and my brother, 'Caitiff Carpus.' 'Coronet Regal' meant 'majestic purple,' 'Melanize Stygian' meant 'black entirety,' 'Amytal Angel' meant 'blue angel' and 'Caitiff Carpus' meant 'yellow wrist.' So, basically, I had a purple father, a black mother, a blue sister and a yellow brother. Everyone on the island was colorful. Our 'magic' was born from the visible portion of the electromagnetic spectrum, or what we called the 'spectral web.' Every mage's magnetic field peaked at a different optical frequency. There'd been many red children in our land before, but none as red as me.

The System typically chose our names according to our colors or prospective powers. When I was born, the Christeners told my parents they were giving me a name they'd been reserving since the first era—one of few set aside for those whose auras were the pinnacles of their colors. Reserved Names were given to the blu*est*, green*est*, yellow*est*, redd*est*—and so forth—mages in the spectrum. For orange, the Reserved Name was 'Tiki.' For blue, it was 'Azure.' For green, it was 'Jade.' And, for red, it was 'Scarlet.'

Mother told me I didn't open my eyes during my Christening Ceremony. The weird thing was, I actually remembered that day, though I was just a baby. I always remembered everything, without trying. When I thought back to my Ceremony, I recalled a strange sort of fear overcoming me, when in the presence of the Christeners, compelling me to keep my eyes shut as long as they were near. I wasn't sure why, but I knew it was the right thing to do.

"If you did open your eyes," Mother said, "your last name would probably be 'Emerald.'" For long while, I wished my name really was Scarlet Emerald. I thought it sounded more majestic than Scarlet July. But, the Christeners insisted on 'July' because I was 'called to the month,' whatever on Tincture's island *that* meant. They said I was special, that I would do something important in my future. I was the Red One. I was different.

Well, on my sixth birthday, I didn't feel very different or special. I felt like a lost little girl in a huge castle full of strange, colorful people.

I was brought before a ring of System professors who'd decide my course of training. Afraid, I watched them through closed lids.

"Where does her magic originate?" an old woman began, voice scratchy.

I opened my eyes and the circle gasped.

"We won't be able to find a teacher for her," the System Principal—Tiki Tincture, for the color orange—said, gravely. Since I had a Reserved Name, I was 'privileged' to have the Principal himself attend my exam. Not that it felt like a privilege to me, but rather another reason to shake in my sandals.

"Conflagria has never seen a mage with this source before," the old woman said. "I expected to assign her to Magister Risque the Blue—I was sure from her Christening Ceremony that her spectrum would be in her hair."

The circle buzzed in agreement.

"Maybe it's in her hair *and* eyes," said a dark-robed man with a goatee. "Let's not make any rash decisions, here. We should hold her for further observation and testing. Take her to the spectroscopers to be examined."

The Principal laughed richly at that. "Are you suggesting this *little girl* is the Multi-Source Enchant? *She*, the first to possess magic in more than one source?"

Everyone chuckled except the dark-robed man.

"Well, she *is* the granddaughter of Spry Scintillate," he said.

At once, the atmosphere went chilly. What did this mean? I didn't know much about my grandfather. Just that he died the week I was born and was somehow the reason my family—once wealthy and powerful—lost its prestige. To me, any relation to Spry Scintillate sounded like all the more reason to be cast aside. But, the goateed man seemed to be using it to my defense. Why?

"Spry Scintillate was a failure," the Principal spat, icily. "We won't waste our time or resources on any of *his* descendants."

His words were met with widespread cries of affirmation. Only the goateed man remained still, arms folded.

"Her brother, Caitiff Carpus," he argued, "is a wrist mage with a hint of throat spectrum—"

"*Unusable* throat spectrum," the raspy-voiced woman shot. "He's a partial-multi-source mage, like Scintillate." She faced the Principal. "I suppose we have no choice but to leave Scarlet July unschooled."

"Unschooled?" Mother stood up.

Everyone stared at her. Neither the examinee nor the examinee's family were permitted to talk during a Circle Trial. The rule was set in place to preserve the neutrality and purity of the System's decision, since family members often came with biases and incorrect pre-conceived notions.

"I didn't know that was an option, if her frequency isn't infrared," Mother continued.

"A declaration of Uselessness is always an option," the woman said. "Now, sit down."

Mother didn't sit.

"Surely, you know, not just Infrareds are considered Useless, but also those with impractical power-sources that render them unable to adequately contribute to society," the Principal told her, mildly.

"What's impractical or unusable about eye magic, Your Excellence?" Mother breathed.

"Well, since no one has had it before, our economy simply isn't structured to accommodate it. Society has no use for it."

"Then, find one, sir," Mother countered. "She's a smart girl. Teach her anything; she'll learn."

"There's no one to teach her," the Principal answered. "She's the first of her kind. I'm sorry."

Decades ago, Uselesses were permitted minimal instruction at the Castle. But, these days, as the island became more crowded and resources more scarce, the policy changed. Uselesses were left completely uneducated.

"Your Honor," Mother wrung her hands, "what about what the Christeners said when she was born? They told me she's special."

"She is." The Principal looked at her with sorrow in his citrus gaze. "That's the problem. Scarlet is too peculiar for the System. She can't be trained. She's Useless. That's our decision."

"Sir, I object!"

"You can't," another man interjected, coldly. "You can't argue with the System. Nor can you change it."

The Principal then stood for the Final Declaration that followed every child's Circle Examination.

"I, Principal Tiki Tincture, hereby declare eye-mage Scarlet Carmine July—born July seventh of the seventy-seventh age of the seventh era, resident of Ardor Village of the South Conflagrablaze Captive—Useless. July is hereby banned from all training programs and dismissed from the Mage Castle. The System reserves the right to declare July's existence unnecessary at any time and request its termination. All System decisions are final."

Mother started crying as we were escorted from the Castle.

As for me, there were no tears. I could feel a pit of revolution forming in my heart—the seed of the person I was today, at fourteen.

Four aimless ages later, when I was ten, an island-wide depression began. There was a job shortage, a magic shortage, a food shortage and a fire shortage. The System wasn't kind to my family since I was declared a waste of resources. They rationed us less food, took our land and our fire and demanded my parents work harder and the twins train longer. Every day, the torment of being written off smoldered in my heart. I spent most of my time at home, reading my siblings' schoolbooks and drawing pictures in berry-ink on scraps of parchment. When I did venture outside, it was usually to swim in the Fervor River. The water was one of the only places I felt free. I could hide in the warm waves, vanishing from before the judgmental eyes of the village-folk.

On July twenty-fifth of the eighty-seventh age, just a couple weeks after my tenth birthday, I went outside not to dash to the shore and dive into the river, but to find my only friend, Fair Antiquartz Gabardine.

Fair was named for her long, straight, white hair. Back before our Circle Trials, our families believed the two of us would probably study under Magister Risque the Blue. Fair and I spent our first five ages of life excited about the future we'd spend together, facing all the same adventures in hair-mage training.

Even as my declaration of Uselessness shattered our dream, Fair and I still remained the best of friends. The only joy of my childhood was to watch her blossom into a successful, young mage. Our regular Sunday-afternoon hangouts were the highlight of my week. Fair always came to my cabin at exactly seventeen o'clock on Sunday to sit by the fire and chat for hours about her exciting week. Sometimes, her grandfather would come over too, which was always a lot of fun, though his hypersensitive ear-magic made him difficult to talk to (it was safer to whisper). Auricle Capitulum—whom I called Grandpa Auri, since I never knew Spry Scintillate—was the jolliest man I ever met. I admired his courage to be so happy, since the circumstances of his life gave him every reason not to be. Like me, he was declared Useless by the System. But, unlike me, he was sentenced to a life of labor in the taro fields. (If I grew up during his time, I also would've been a field-hand. But, I'd been spared by the Useless Women Protection Act of the Seventieth Age.) Decades of backbreaking fieldwork afflicted him with scoliosis so extreme, he was due to die of spinal-fluid-leak, any day now. But, from the joyful way he carried on, one would think his life was always perfect. I wished I could take my failure so well.

Whenever Fair ran late for our weekly catchup—which wasn't often—I walked over to her place, instead. July twenty-fifth of the eighty-seventh age was one of those days.

The first stranger I passed didn't miss the occasion.

"Is that Scarlet July?" a green woman carrying a bread basket asked her companion.

"Why, yes, I think it is," the other said with a scowl, cradling her purple son in her arms.

"She's still alive! For Tincture's sake, I thought the System would've terminated her already, with the shortages and all."

"It'll happen soon, no doubt. She and that old ear-mage—Auricle is his name?"

"Nah, Auricle is so old and bent, he's about to kneel over soon, anyway. I think they should just go ahead and kill Scarlet, though."

"What a waste of food and fire, that girl. At least she doesn't waste magic."

"That's 'cause she's got no magic. She's a bloody, dragon turd with scary eyes."

"Is it true, the Castle expelled her because of those eyes?"

"Yep. What a waste of a Reserved Name. My daughter was born two days before her and would've gotten that name if the System didn't give it to that scrap of taro root. And, to add insult to injury, they betrothed Scarlet to my son!"

"What? Wow, poor Crimson and Ambrek. I know the System doesn't make mistakes, but what on Tincture's island did your family do to deserve all *that*?"

Any kid would've scurried home in tears upon overhearing such a conversation. But, I just stared, weakness ebbing in anger. My body temperature seemed to rise in parallel to my fury.

One of the women dropped her bread basket and the other, her toddler. The bread withered to ashes on the floor, and the little boy screamed.

I blinked and stepped back, horrified. My gaze only lasted a second—I couldn't be the reason for what happened, could I?

I turned on my heel and ran back down the Dust Path, toward home. And, I rammed right into none other than Crimson's brother—fourteen-age-old Ambrek Coppertus. He was an Iridescent, the only one I knew. Iridescents had two-toned auras. He stared at me wordlessly as I scrambled back to my feet, his amber-gold eyes wide and eerie. His rusted-copper hair always stood upright, as though oiled with dragon fat. Averting his gaze, I scurried right around him, hoping no one else would notice me. Unfortunately, the town freak couldn't fly under the spectrometer for long. In a flash, an olive-green System mage intercepted me.

"Scarlet July," he barked, surveying me from the hem of my tattered red robe to the wiry mess of my hair.

Instinctively, I closed my eyes.

"It is with great pleasure I announce, the time has come. Principal Tiki Tincture has declared a state of emergency; the shortages have gotten out of hand. We can no longer supply rations for deadweight."

The word 'deadweight' sent a prickle of anger through my body, and I felt the edges of my hair begin to curl.

"The System reserves the right to terminate Useless lives," he continued, seizing me with the strength of a hand-mage.

I struggled in his grasp, to no avail. My eyes throbbed under my lids. He hoisted me over his shoulder and began to carry me into the center of town—the 'square'—where most of the island's spectral fire burned. It was gathered in a large and deep pit, continually surrounded by people anxiously awaiting their daily ration. On the verge of tears, I caught snippets of various conversations.

"Is that Scarlet July?"

"It must be time!"

"So glad it is."

"What a waste of rations, that girl."

"She and all those Uselesses and Infrareds."

"How did the System let her live so long?"

"I can't wait to see her thrown into the Pit; that'll help us get more fire."

"I can't believe it's taken the Tincture administration until now to do it."

I kicked and screamed, only succeeding in attracting more attention.

"There's no use resisting, Useless," my captor spat. "When the System decides to do something, it gets done." He tightened his arm around my ribcage, constricting my breathing. "We're here, the Fire Pit."

In appropriate doses, fire from the Pit was soothing. However, as we all knew, too much of a good thing could be dangerous. The System warned the wealthy folk who owned vast 'flame fields' about the dangers of uncontrolled fire usage. Once, a rich man named Ribald Briny decided to adorn his best dinner gown with a fine fire lining. Well, unsurprisingly, *that* got out of hand fast, and he wound up burning alive, right in front of his wife and children, in the middle of the Mage Castle's Annual Summer Solstice Day Feast. After his death, the System passed the 'Ribald Briny Fire Safety Laws,' which forbade everyone from coming in direct contact with more than two gallons of fire at a time, unless specifically authorized and properly outfitted.

And, now, I was about to get thrown into a pit containing millions or maybe even billions of gallons.

"No! That's my daughter! Stop!"

A couple hundred feet away, Mother came running through the packed crowd, hair swinging. She was closely followed by Father, bright purple in the neck, and Caitiff, who was a sick, pale shade of yellow. With one swing of Caitiff's powerful wrist, five unsuspecting men were knocked to the sand. Amytal flew above them, wings a blue blur.

"OUT OF OUR WAY!" called Father's sonic voice. "PUT HER DOWN, RIGHT NOW!"

In an instant, System mages surrounded my family, lassoing spectrally-fortified ropes around each of their power-sources—Mother's hair, Father's throat, my sister's wings and my brother's wrists.

"Decree twenty-five of the System Syllabus strictly forbids the use of offensive magic against innocent townspeople," the Principal said in a cool tone.

"I don't care!" Caitiff yelled, hint of so-called 'unusable' throat magic giving his usually-melodic voice a threatening edge. "You're murdering my sister!"

"It's not murder," the Principal retorted, rather calmly. "The System reserves the right to—"

"You can't kill Scarlet!"

"Resisting the System is punishable by death," he said, viciously.

Flames zipped from his hair to the ropes.

"NO!" I screamed.

Behind closed eyes, I could see the unspeakable unfold. Yes, I could see my family crying, cursing and thrashing, as they burned alive.

Hot rage, unlike anything I'd felt before, swept through my body. Spectrum pulsed through my veins like venom, rippling my hair, burning my eyes, flushing my skin.

The town watched with excitement as the olive-green man held me over the Fire Pit fence. Over and over, my mind—cursed with eidetic memory—replayed the instant my family collapsed in unison, flesh blackened.

"The termination of Scarlet Carmine July will commence on this twenty-fifth day of July of the eighty-seventh age, by order of System Principal Tiki Tincture."

The man's grip loosened and I slid, flames licking the bottom of my robe. My family fell once more in my mind; it was all I could think about. I didn't care if I was about to die. I just wanted revenge.

I opened my eyes, ignited a lock of hair and struck my captor in the chest. He shrieked and dropped me. But, before I could fall to my death, I snagged the fence with another lock and pulled myself over, swooping into the scattering crowd. Then, I spun on the balls of my feet, whipping my hair out, spraying fire in all directions.

And, that was when I learned my flames weren't soothing like a handful of Pit Fire. Apparently, my fire, in any quantity, consumed human flesh. Instantly.

"I told you!" the goateed man from my Circle Trial shouted to the System mages ducking beside him. "Four ages ago, I warned all of you what she could be!"

Chaos surrounded me. People screamed and ran and pushed and shoved. System wing mages dove from above and shot magically-reinforced ropes around my body. My eyes pumped fire up the bindings and burned their hands right off their arms. Another System officer arrived at the scene on scabrousback, a tank of water strapped to his back, a hose in his auburn hands. He shot a powerful stream directly at my face, but—I couldn't believe it—my fire ignited the water itself.

I guessed I wasn't Useless, after all.

* * *

Untrained and young, only about thirty minutes passed before I ran out of photons to keep fighting fire with fire—my eyes went dull and my hair went limp. But, the chase continued for hours thereafter. And, as I ran around, it slowly dawned on me why I was able to hold out for so long, especially when I wasn't a particularly fast runner (I was a lot swifter in the water than I was on land). Sometimes, it seemed like they just… couldn't see me. It was like, one moment, they were hot on my tail, and the next moment, they were turning in circles and yelling that I'd 'vanished.'

I couldn't keep it up forever, though. I was outnumbered and, eventually, too exhausted to take another step. By twenty-one o'clock, they managed to seize me, shackle me and throw me in a cell aboard a submarine.

The System couldn't kill me, so they settled for deporting me. They never deported anyone before. I was the first citizen they weren't able to execute when they wanted to.

The sub headed northeast, across the Fervor Sea and the Briny Ocean, to the peninsular nation of Nuria, a 'democratic-republic,' whatever that meant. The only possessions I had were the two robes I'd put on before going outside to find Fair, earlier in the afternoon—I always wore layers before leaving my cabin, because I got cold so easily.

Nuria. How would I live there? I had no trade and no support system. So, my life would depend on my untrained magic? If so, I was in deep trouble. I clearly couldn't control my powers too well; my fire ignited with emotions. Oh, Tincture. What was I going to do?

Slowly, as the night passed, resolve started smoldering in my chest. No, I didn't need a support network. I didn't need anyone. Not even a magister to teach me. I'd educate myself. I loved to read and could consume books faster than anyone I knew, even the adults. So, I'd go to libraries, laboratories, research centers and most importantly, mage castles. I'd study every day and learn to control my spectrum on my own. And, I'd be content with knowledge as my only possession. I wouldn't let myself get weighed down by anything that could be lost, like friends or items of material or sentimental value. I wouldn't stay in one place either, lest I become attached to my environment. With just the robes on my back and the sundial tied to my wrist, I'd be content. This was my code of life.

On the twenty-seventh of July—after two days and two nights sleeping on the splintered wooden floor, urinating and defecating in the corner of my cell and eating dragon giblets and rotten taro stems the guards threw at me—we arrived at the southeastern shore of Nuria, in a port of a village called, 'Alcove.'

On the way out of the sub, the Captain, whose feet were gnarly and green, read off a scroll: "I, Captain Uncure Livision, declare ten-age-old Scarlet Carmine July, born July seventh of the seventy-seventh age, permanently exiled from the South Conflagrablaze Captive by order of System Principal Tiki Tincture. Such is the consequence of July's violation of laws seven-two-five and seven-eight-seven, committed the twenty-fifth day of July of the eighty-seventh age. All System decisions are final."

And, with that, he kicked me. I wasn't expecting it, at all. His green foot struck me square in the stomach; I cried out and fell backward. I willed my hair to do something, anything, to fight back, but this time, it didn't move. A guard's yellow hands seized me under the arms from behind and dragged me out the door.

Once out of sight of the Captain, the yellow guard let go of me. I looked up into his brown eyes and thought I saw a flicker of sympathy. I wanted to run, to put as much distance as possible between myself and anyone from the System, but his kind gaze froze my feet.

"Take this," he whispered. "It'll keep you strong."

He shoved a rough, ovular, silvery stone into my hands. It caught the light and sparkled like sunlight dancing on water. I'd never seen anything so beautiful before. I stared at it, captivated. I wanted to thank the guard, but when I looked up, he was gone. I watched as the sub sank back beneath the surface of the Briny Ocean.

Doubt punctured my captivated awe for the rock. Material objects, like people, were always temporary, and when they were lost, pain resulted. I knew what I had to do. I had to get rid of the crystal before I became too attached to it. But, as I held it in my palm, I couldn't bring myself to drop it in the ocean. It wasn't just beautiful, it was... well... I felt like it was a part of me. In that wild moment, I decided to break my code, just this once, and keep it. I thrust it into my pocket.

My eyes fell on the rough, wooden dock. Oh, yes. I was all alone on the shore of a strange and new land—a land, the System mages said, as vast as First Earth's United States of America. The hair on the back of my neck stood at attention—not from spectrum, but fear. And, cold. The air was downright frigid. What temperature was this? I'd never felt anything like it before. I shivered and drew my robes tighter around my bony body as I looked in wonder at the sky, which was blue instead of orange. Boy, were the cabins huge around here. As tall as the clouds themselves! And, they were made of some sort of shiny, silver material rather than wood. I 'zoomed in' my eyesight and examined the village. Just as I'd hoped, there were plenty of places to educate myself: I learned later they were called, 'laboratories,' 'libraries' and 'museums.' But, no mage castles. How was this possible? I felt like I swallowed a lump of raw, slimy, scabrous-dragon meat. People here wore black jackets over collared white shirts, pleated pants and tube-like skirts. Not robes. They drove self-propelled, multicolored wagons. How did these wagons go without scabrouses to pull them? What was everything running on, if not spectrum? Was there a different kind of energy source here?

Nuria was no place for a mage.

But, as I stood, back to the ocean, a burning mix of curiosity and ambition slowly replaced my fear. I wasn't going to stay ignorant—I'd start my self-education, right away. The first thing I needed to do was get a closer look at 'Alcove City,' to get some bearings. Get some sense of my environment. I'd take a walk.

Many paths—which I learned later were called 'roads' or 'streets'—were lined with candles *twenty feet tall*. I walked right up to one, staring in awe at the white flame standing perfectly still, at the top. I climbed up the pole, which didn't feel at all like wax, and reached a lock of hair into the glass frame. I touched something solid and somewhat warm. What? This wasn't fire! What was it? Artificial fire? Wow. I couldn't believe it. If only the people of Conflagria could see this!

My excitement wore off as I slid down the pole. I wasn't a part of Conflagria anymore; I needed to stop thinking about my old home. I had to separate myself from my past—even if that meant learning to live without Pit fire, without possessions, and without the only people I loved in this world.

I spent the entire night exploring Alcove City. I was stunned I could just walk around freely without being stopped or questioned by anyone. It felt strange. Exciting. And, terrifying.

When I saw a street-sign for the first time, I realized the Nurian language didn't even share the same alphabet as Conflagrian. Only the number symbols were the same. Great.

At some point in the night, I fell asleep by a giant, smelly, green box of trash behind a big cabin made of rectangular, red blocks. Long snakelike wagons zipped to and from the building, on black, striped tracks. I soon learned this was a 'train station' and the big bin was a 'dumpster.'

The next morning, my stomach hurt with hunger. It took me by surprise. The previous day, I was too emotional to be hungry. Desperate, I climbed inside the bin and unearthed an apple core that still had a few bites left on it. I scrambled out with my find, dry-retching from the stench.

I wandered until I wound up at the entrance of a shiny, metallic cabin full of books. I saw from a short distance the doors had no knobs. How would I get inside? Then, when I was just a couple feet away, the glass panels slid apart, on their own. I gasped. I didn't sense a photon of spectrum in the doors. How did they move by themselves like that? Were they powered by the same stuff as the self-propelling wagons and the hard, lukewarm fire?

A man pushed past me, bellowing a garble of sounds. So, *that* was what Nurian sounded like? Tincture. It was like a mouthful of consonants. There was so much to learn! How was Conflagria on the same planet as this strange country?

It took me twenty minutes just to get past the doorway. I examined the doors as they opened and closed, eyes dissecting their inner workings. And, slowly, I came to understand the basic concept of 'electricity,' the Nordic substitute for spectrum. Of course, I didn't know it was called that until I read the word in a book, later on.

When I finally went inside, I immediately sought out a librarian. I needed to find out when the library closed so I'd know when to leave and sneak back in. But, when I addressed the elderly woman behind the front desk—in Conflagrian—she stared at me for a moment with disgust and confusion in her brown eyes, then shook her head, pointed to the exit and screeched in Nurian. I shrank away from her, feeling her harsh glare on my back.

I spotted something on the wall. It was round and had numbers all around it. A sundial, indoors? How did it tell time without shadows? I stared at the numbers. There were thirty-six of them. Thirty-six? There were twenty-four hours in a day. This was crazy. Nuria didn't even tell time the same way as Conflagria?

Eager to find answers to my questions—any of them, I didn't really care which, at this point—I went to a shelf and randomly pulled out a large volume. Books here were so polished, the pages so white and clean. I couldn't even see weaves in the parchment. Amazing. I stared at the words. Of course, I couldn't understand a thing. Feeling slightly panicked, I yanked open another book. And, another. Unless the library had something in Conflagrian, I wasn't going to get very far in my self-education. I ran up and down the rows, eyes scanning spines, and, sure enough, *everything* was in Nurian.

Heartrate rapid, I plunked down on a puffy chair with much-too-high armrests—nothing like the wicker rockers or wooden stools I was used to, back home—and breathed with an open mouth. I needed a Nurian-Conflagrian dictionary, or something along those lines. But, if this huge building full of books didn't have one, would anywhere?

Conflagria was, what, fifteen-hundred miles away from this country? Nuria was the closest nation to Conflagria on the map, and yet we knew nothing about them, and, apparently, they knew nothing about us. I wondered, why were nations—even neighboring ones—so very ignorant of one another?

I watched as two boys and a woman came in and sat at the table nearest to me. A mother and her children, perhaps? The woman had short blonde hair, dark brown eyes, and wore what looked like a sparkly crystal on her left hand—it glistened a lot like the one in my pocket, but it was clearer and whiter. One of the boys looked a lot like her. He was lanky and had sandy hair and bright hazel eyes. He spoke with a mellow voice and smiled a lot. The other boy was shorter, louder and had buzzed, light-brown hair. They plopped their knapsacks—which I later learned were called 'backpacks'—on the table and pulled out strange-looking books lined with silver coils and featherless quills that were oddly narrow and short—'notebooks' and 'pens,' I soon learned. For a couple hours, I watched, fascinated by the sounds of their language, as the the three of them talked, laughed and read. This was my first clear and prolonged exposure to spoken Nurian. The kids looked, what, twelve or thirteen ages old? Were they doing some sort of school project? But, it was July. Nurians had school in the middle of summer? Well, not on Saturday mornings, apparently, because they were here, in this book-house, instead. In Conflagria, Sunday was the only day Fair didn't train.

"When will Arrhyth be back from Oriya, again?" the buzz-haired one breathed. I figured, by now, the boys were probably friends or classmates, not brothers. "Sucks we have to do all this stuff for our project without him. Not fair. 'Specially since we can't even use his dad's library as long as he's away."

"They'll be back on the ninth, Ecivon," the blonde kid answered. "Arrhyth doesn't get to go on these trips with his dad too often, so they left a week before the Order's meeting, to make a vacation out of it."

Ecivon snorted. "The ninth! The project's due the tenth, Nurtic. Figures the son of the leader of the world government would get away with that. Ugh."

Nurtic just shrugged.

Wait, when exactly did their words start making sense to me? And, how? My heart pounded in my throat. I didn't understand *everything*, maybe every second or third word. But, still, that was incredible.

"We got assigned to the same group as the *son* of the *Second Earth Order Chairman*," Ecivon reeled, "and we don't even get to use his dad's crazy, home library. We're stuck here instead."

"Stuck here?" Nurtic echoed, laughingly. "This is the National Library. The biggest library on the coast. We're not exactly starved for resources. And, I don't think we'd need any of Mr. Link's international stuff, anyway. This is a science fair project, not social studies."

"What 'social studies'?" Ecivon smirked. "Do the Isolationist Laws leave us any social studies to study?"

"Heh, good point."

There was a pause.

"I guess, I was just curious to see what kind of stuff Mr. Link has, you know?" Ecivon piped. "Arrhyth's always bragging about it at school."

I sat up straight, gripping my armrests. World government? Isolationist Laws? Second Earth Order? What? It all sounded very important. How come this was the first time I'd heard of any of this, if it was so important?

The woman looked at the automated sundial on her wrist. "Alright, boys, time to go!" she chimed, smiling the same dimpled smile as Nurtic. "Let's go get ready for your basketball game!"

My mind was swimming. So, Arrhyth Link was the classmate of these two buffoons, and the son of the Chairman of a world government called the Second Earth Order. Mr. Link had a home library with 'international stuff,' as Nurtic so eloquently put it. These resources were special. Not available in regular libraries. Why? Because of the…Isolationist Laws?

"Can we stop by Arrhyth's on the way home, mom?" Nurtic swung his bag over his left shoulder. "I told him I'd leave a copy of the syllabus with his housekeeper, so he can have it as soon as he gets back."

"Sure. Their place is only a couple blocks from here. We can walk over, then take the metro home."

They got up and disappeared out the self-sliding doors.

I stared. They were headed to the Link house. Right now. I slid from my seat and ran after them.

* * *

My understanding of the spoken Nurian word developed almost effortlessly, as days passed. It seemed like, all I had to do was position myself in public places—libraries, cafés, train stations, parks, streets, wherever—and listen to people speak, and over time, their words made more and more sense. Was this ability a facet of my magic, like my eidetic memory? Foreign language was an arena I'd never been exposed to before—Conflagria was mostly monolingual, save for the handful of dialects spoken by the gypsy tribes who lived all the way out in the Sand Dune Region, by the island's northern shore, where I'd never ventured. So, until now, I didn't know I could breathe in a tongue and breathe it right back out.

I didn't, however, have quite as much luck with absorbing the written Nurian language. Staring at pages of books didn't do much for me. I could memorize the shapes of the letters easily, but couldn't draw a correlation between them and the words people spoke.

That is, until I snuck into the massive Link mansion and got my hands on some 'special' books. Books that were stamped as being on loan to the Chairman from the Second Earth Order itself.

Sneaking in wasn't even hard. Nurtic had mentioned when the Links were returning from their trip—August ninth—so, that day, I hid in the bushes by their garage and waited. Sure enough, by mid-afternoon, a long, sleek, black 'flivver'—what Nurians called their wagons—pulled up and four people with big bags on wheels got out: a man with a fuzzy grey cloud for hair; a slender, platinum-blonde woman; a boy who looked about Nurtic's age with a swirly, brown mop on his head (that was Arrhyth, I supposed); and a girl who looked a couple ages younger than Arrhyth, with long, dark-brown ringlets. Politically, the most powerful family in the world.

Looking at them, I decided I wanted to be invisible. And, as the Links lugged their suitcases through their wide-open stained-glass-paneled front-doors, I slipped inside, right before their oblivious eyes.

* * *

I sat down behind the Alcove City train station and began to prowl through the books I stole. The first one I looked at had two titles, one in Nurian and one in Conflagrian: 'The Conflagrian-Nurian and Nurian-Conflagrian Dictionary.' It took me the rest of the day to read and memorize its contents. I paused only once, to dumpster dive for scraps of food. I used the pronunciation-guides to practice the words out loud. Night fell; nevertheless, I proceeded onto the other books, which were about grammar. Thanks to my eye-magic, I could read in the dark. By morning, I was literate.

So, I went back to the National Library to research geology, determined to find out why days here felt insanely long. Sure enough, the first geo reference I checked confirmed the Earth completed a rotation in thirty-six hours! Frustrated, I paged through the book, and my eyes caught sight of the name of my country in a tiny footnote at the bottom of page one-hundred-eighty-seven:

> [7] *Upon its expulsion from the Second Earth Order on the 24th age of the 3rd era, the spectrally-dependent, totalitarian nation of the South Conflagrablaze Captive reacted to its rejection from the world in a rather unique manner. Charged for breaking twenty-four of the seventy original Isolationist Laws, the governing entity of the Fire Island, known as 'The System,' manipulated their 'spectral web' to make a day appear to its habitants to be only twenty-four hours.*

I stared, heat building in my scalp. I had to close my eyes and breathe deeply so I wouldn't set the book on fire.

* * *

Now that I was literate, it was time to search for work. It felt strange to look for a job on my own. I was so used to being a pawn of the System, it took me a while to realize no one was going to hand me my food and fire, and tell me what to do and when to do it. I was completely on my own. For a brief moment, I actually missed the System.

No. I knew I shouldn't feel insecure and unprotected. I should feel free. For the first time in my life, I was in control. I was no longer Useless. The System didn't throw me away; they uncaged me. Suddenly, I wished everyone back home could know what it was like to have such control. They believed they couldn't survive without shepherding. I did, too, before my exile. Why? I didn't understand how the System's dominion was so absolute. How was I the first Useless to escape execution? How come no one before me saw through the corruption and tried to take action? Why did everyone believe so firmly the System never made mistakes? In mage history, there was no mention of revolution. Not even a skirmish in the paths. The population was completely docile. How? It made no sense. It was impossible.

I did know one thing, though: July twenty-fifth of the eighty-seventh age was the day I was reborn. And, my real home was Nuria, now. No one else I met would ever hear of my past or learn I was born on an island where people were treated like scabrouses. Never.

* * *

I got a part-time job as a train conductor. It wasn't the employment of my dreams, but it was enough to get me a night at the Motel Seven whenever it was too cold to sleep outside, and a few meals a week. I was a good employee. I owed that to my eyes—I used them to power the furnace. "She uses a fraction of the firewood we supply, yet she manages to maintain the biggest fires I've ever seen!" my boss, Mr. Eval, once said. The job had a few advantages, like free transportation. When my workday was over, I got off at whatever stop we happened to be at, and there was often a library or lab there for me to sneak into. The last perk was that I got to spend four hours a day in front of a fire, enjoying the warmth. Even as ages passed, I never really adapted to Nurian weather. In the summer, when Conflagria would easily reach one-hundred-forty degrees Fahrenheit in the afternoon, Alcove City only reached eighty-five or ninety. Wintertime was unbearable, with temperatures described by a word foreign to all magekind: 'freezing.'

During the winter in Nuria, soft white crystals called 'snow' fell from the sky. The first time I read about snow—months before I actually got to see it fall, in person—I grew very excited (I should've known better). Since I effortlessly memorized everything I read, I could still recite the encyclopedia entry:

> *Snow consists of ice crystals formed around debris or other small particulates in the air when H_2O vapor condenses at temperatures below 32°F. Somewhat melted particles frequently adhere together to form 'snowflakes' whose unique structures vary according to temperature and other key environmental factors during crystallization...*

Each day, I learned more. I spent every waking minute either working or studying. In four ages, I finished every non-fiction book in every public library in southern Nuria, and had spent considerable amounts of time invisibly snooping at research centers, universities and labs. At fourteen, I'd surpassed the levels of the top colleges. As far as honing my magic, however, I was totally on my own—Nurian literature on spectroscopy didn't help. To an extent, Nurians knew how to manipulate the spectrum for their purposes—they had x-ray machines for medical diagnoses, for example—but they had no organic, biological ability to do so. They had to use external tools. Their bodies didn't have electromagnetic fields in the visible portion of the spectrum; they were all Infrareds, and if they lived in Conflagria, they'd all be considered Useless.

Although I had an eidetic memory, I began revisiting places of study, to make sure I didn't skip over any material and to take a peek at new publications. And, I was able to give more time to my job, hoping to afford more food. In the summer, I slept in the street—usually, by the dumpster near my work. But, during the colder months, I had no choice but to sleep in the motel, skipping food to afford it. Malnutrition stunted my growth. At fourteen, I was still below five feet and weighed roughly eighty pounds. I knew it was spectrum that kept me alive. My body fed off of my aura.

Sometimes, when I lay awake at night, hands numb and heart pounding against my ribcage as though in protest to my dropping blood-sugar, I thought of selling my crystal. But, whenever I took it out of my pocket, it would catch the light and sparkle in my eyes, and I'd feel my attachment to it overcome me like an ocean wave.

Attachment to anything frightened me. But, I didn't know how to make it go away.

CEASE LECHATELIERITE

The subzero North Septentrion Sea was a bold, cobalt-blue, littered with icecaps the size of vitreous silica ships. I kicked my flippered feet and plunged deeper into the water, seventy white-suited bodies tucking their chins, cradling their weapons and following suit.

I'd been a soldier since as far back as I could remember. Two ages ago, when I was fifteen, I was promoted to commander of the elite Diving Fleet, and the Trilateral Committee created a new title just for me: Leader of the Ichthyothian Resistance. My life's purpose was to fight the mage armies who wanted to imperialize my homeland, the North Ichthyosis Island.

Yes, that's right. The barbaric, fire-worshipping, totalitarian state of Conflagria actually dispatched men to fight in the coldest place on Second Earth. While a student at Icicle Diving Academy, I learned all about our enemies, the Conflagrians, and the all-powerful 'System' that dictated their every breath and bowel movement. What a joke. Magefolk were like animals, shepherded by their government, astonishingly ignorant of their own nation's fifteen-age war with Ichthyosis.

I was six when the Childhood Program had me take 'Mage Culture 101.' When I learned of the oppression magekind suffered at the hand of the dictatorial System—particularly, the inhumane treatment and systematic execution of the 'aura'-less—I was stricken with grief. After that first class, I had insomnia every night for a week. I would lie on my cold, cramped bunk, haunted by the idea of an entire country of men, women and children born into total subjugation. It was one thing to learn tyranny existed sometime in First Earth history—back when the human race was an infant of intelligence. But, to know there were people living like that *today*, in the seventh era of Second Earth, was too much to handle. I wondered, how was the System's power so absolute?

How come there'd never been a single revolution in Conflagrian history? The general mage population was impossibly docile. There had to have been a secret behind that. Slowly, as the course went on, my grief turned to anger. If the citizens of Conflagria couldn't help themselves for some reason, why didn't anyone else take some action? Why did the seven-hundred nations of Second Earth just sit back while the Joseph Stalins of Second Earth marauded around? Why didn't anyone care that, somewhere on this planet, human beings were treated like property? The Conflagrians needed to be freed from the System.

I confronted a teacher about it. One day, in the middle of class, I raised my hand and brought up the matter.

My peers stared at me with cold eyes. Colonel Autoero Austere marched to my desk and placed a hand on my shoulder. His grip was so firm, I could feel my skin bruise under his fingertips.

"Have you learned nothing from the fall of First Earth? We may no longer be a part of the Second Earth Order, but we can still learn from their principles: no nation should ever meddle with the welfare of another. The wellbeing of magekind does not negatively impact our lives, so we do not bother with it." My right arm was going prickly-numb beneath his impervious grasp. "Does the ignorance or oppression of the Conflagrian people affect the food on your plate or your bunk in the barracks?"

My throat went dry.

"I asked you a question, soldier!" he barked.

I swallowed. "No, sir."

"Then is it your duty to even sacrifice a salmon-bone from your dinner to the land of the enemy?"

My entire right arm was numb, by now. "No, sir."

"If the general Conflagrian population ever became aware of this war, their loyalties may motivate an even stronger offensive. We actually learn from history at this academy, not repeat it." He released his iron grip and stalked to the front of the silent class. "Lechatelierite, if you feel so inclined to save endangered species, perhaps you should join APO, not the military."

APO. The Animal Protection Organization. The tension in the room broke as everyone laughed. My cheeks felt as hot—not from embarrassment, but anger. I grunted.

"What was that, soldier?"

"I said, the Conflagrians aren't animals, they're people." I realized I was standing. When exactly did I get to my feet?

The silence in the room was thick enough to cut with a glacier-melting lance.

"One more word and you're iced. I don't care if you have the highest test scores in the history of Icicle Academy. With that attitude, you'll never gain command of a single diver in North Ichthyosis. Understood?"

I stared.

"Soldier?" Austere pressed.

My comrades held their breaths.

I wanted justice, but I wanted a shot at command more.

"Sir, yes, sir."

As ages passed, I began to realize the foolishness of my rebellion. I sped through the academy, my mage-sympathies slowly giving way to appropriate loathing of the enemy race, System and citizens alike. The Conflagrians were not to be pitied, but studied, analyzed and brutally countered. I was a fighting machine who wanted nothing less than the complete annihilation of all things magical. It was what the Colonel wanted me to want. It was what I did want.

When I was six, I used to wonder about that. I saw little difference between the way the Childhood Program indoctrinated its soldiers and the way the System brainwashed the people of Conflagria. Now, however, I knew better. Now, as the seventeen-age-old commander of the Ichthyothian Diving Fleet, I realized the world was better without magical presence. Their problems weren't my problems. They didn't need to be helped. They needed to be destroyed.

* * *

Icy seawater fought against my movements as I dove deeper. The water pressure was intense enough to burst a human lung in seconds, but our 'arrhythmic' suits prevented it. Our suits were impenetrable as steel but fluid as mercury. My team of divers soared through the water, in formation, ready to strike. I used my visor's zoom to help me locate the Conflagrian 'dragon ship,' seven-hundred yards below. I initially spotted it without my visor's visual magnifications. My vision broke records, at the academy.

"Units one through six," I spoke into my helmet's intercom. "To the vitreous silica. Buird, you're in charge of that task force."

Inexor Buird's name truly suited him. He was the most unrelenting, shrewd man in my fleet. I'd trust him with the Ichthyothian Resistance. He was my second-in-command.

"Unit seven, you're with me. I hope your oxygen-beads are full; we're riding on the outside of crystalline shuttle seven."

A bead tank was the size of a single marble. However, enough oxygen could be compressed into each to breathe underwater for days at a time. "We're penetrating the dragon ship and taking the pilots hostage. Surface-riders, be ready for the pass. Forty-five-degree launch."

My divers responded beautifully. My men were capable and my battle plans were always ingenious. It wasn't cockiness, only the truth. How could those Conflagrian beasts with their hocus-pocus magic tricks even stand a chance?

INTERLUDE

The Fall of Earth began at the turn of the second millennium, AD.

By this time, the pan-American theory of 'policeman of the western hemisphere' slowly expanded into 'patrol of the entire world.' If there was a nation on the map suffering internal economic or political unrest or facing a dispute with a neighboring state, the United States was ready to reach around the globe with its mighty fist of democracy. The crutch on which this Great Policeman leaned was the military. War was no longer the necessary evil of international development, but simply a necessity. Rather than being the last resort, it became the go-to problem-solving strategy for all the afflictions and ailments plaguing the overpopulated world.

Like a sprinkle of spring rain that slowly progresses into a tumultuous summer thunderstorm, minor conflicts began to pop up across the globe with increasing frequency. Throughout the world, boundaries of individual dispute expanded until they touched corners, then overlapped, then blended so well, seams disappeared. If a nation had a rare or vital natural resource, everyone nearby would hover like fleas before latching onto its skin, piercing its flesh, and sucking it dry. If a small country was imploding, outside forces always dove in and escalated things into a grand, multi-state affair.

An international nuclear-arms-race ensued. Each country cast a fearful eye across its boarders like frightened puppies peeking into neighboring yards. And, the only way to remain safe in the serpent cage that was the world was to continue increasing the volume of one's own venom sacs.

True disaster could only strike once. World War III lasted a single hour. It began at seven-twenty-five in the morning on December twenty-second, in the year '2100.'

Interlude

From space, the planet looked like a disco ball—scattered flecks of light danced across the globe. Or, it could be described as a shimmering crystal, sparkling in the white-hot sunlight. In truth, these points of light were nuclear explosions, each thousands of miles in diameter. Within sixty minutes, the sparkling sphere of ice seemed to ignite into scarlet flames. By the hand of man, the Earth ceased to exist.

It was by the hand of the Creator that something new came to be, three thousand years later, giving mankind a second chance at life. He created this new earth void of plutonium, eliminating the possibility of nuclear weaponry. Then, He bestowed humanity with the gift of free will, and once again, watched as His flocks ran amok, twisting everything they had into tangled knots.

The Second Earthlings had access to the complete history, science, technology, culture and art of their predecessors through the miraculous—indeed, it was protected by the Creator—survival of a three-thousand-year-old First Earth space station. The International Space Station had—also, miraculously—fallen like a meteor into the new Earth's atmosphere and landed in the Briny Ocean where it was soon found floating only miles away from the shore of Nuria, a nation who possessed both the resources and intellectual capital to decode all of its information. Although the majority of the external structure had burned up in the atmosphere during it's decent, all the computer chips onboard had—miraculously—remained intact.

And, so, as Nuria broadcasted the station's information across the globe, the habitants of the new world learned all about their predecessors. They learned that the Second Cold War of First Earth began at the turn of the second millennium, AD, and concluded by '2100' with the destruction of the planet. In commemoration of the century-long ordeal, the people of Second Earth organized their time-keeping system into century-long units known as 'eras.' For example, the year '425' was called, 'the 25th age of the 4th era of Second Earth.' Just as on First Earth, each year—or, 'age,' as the Second Earthlings called it—was twelve months long, and each month was roughly thirty-one days. However, the rotation of the planet was slower than that of First Earth, so a day was thirty-six hours.

Armed with the space station, Second Earth achieved in a few hundred ages what had taken their predecessors thousands of years. Civilization on Second Earth quickly and easily surpassed that of their examples, though the overall population was a fraction of that of First Earth.

But, they did not always learn the right lessons.

As people had the tendency to do, the Second Earthlings became extremists in their desire to avoid the mistakes of the past. The seven-hundred nations of the world each elected or appointed representatives to the global legislating entity known as the Second Earth Order, which instituted the 'Isolationist Laws,' whose goal was to keep each state completely independent from its neighbor and maintain a worldwide status quo. Under the Isolationist Laws, the Order had the responsibility to proportionately collect specialized 'raw and/or furnished goods' taxes from every nation, which they distributed across the globe to each country as needed. The Order thereby eliminated the need for nations to independently engage in trade. Order was usually reasonable in its taxes, accurate in its assessment of the needs of each state, and fair in its distributions. Rarely did a nation find itself in need of a particular resource that wasn't readily available. It was a truly ideal system, or so everyone thought.

The Isolationist Laws did not just forbid nations from becoming involved in each other's affairs, they prevented countries from learning about one another, at all. Schoolchildren only studied the history and geography of First Earth and of their own nation, only vaguely aware of the presence of their neighbors. Libraries carried references only pertaining to their own state. Each land completely minded its own business. A perfect status quo was indeed established.

In the center of Second Earth's northwestern hemisphere was a peninsular nation the size of the United States: the Democratic-Republic of Nuria, the original decoders of First Earth's International Space Station. And, indeed, the Nurians were much like the long-dead Americans; they were a curious people who easily grew discontent and hungered for change. So, Nuria channeled its restless energy into rapid technological advancement and rose to prominence among all the nations of Second Earth in every field of applied science.

However, their technological pursuits were costly. In a month or two, Nuria was liable to expend an entire age's worth of petroleum rations. And, Nuria did not have a single natural oil source of its own. As a result, by the start of the second era, their prominent scientific status had become too costly to maintain; their economy began to decline and their gas prices rocketed into exorbitance.

Nuria requested larger petroleum rations, but the Order was unable to afford it. The rest of the world was not willing to pay higher taxes to compensate for what they considered extravagance. Desperate, the

Nurians began to look north, across the Septentrion Sea, toward a small, uninhabited, ice-covered island. It was located just below the North Pole—barely south enough to be spared the pole's midnight summer sun and thirty-six-hour-a-day winter darkness. Most Second Earthlings were well-versed in the history of First Earth (the Order's educational policies made sure of that) so the Nurians knew that, once upon a time, Alaska was America's oil goldmine. The Nurians hoped that this northern land—which was only about the size of First Earth's England—could be their Alaska.

Immediately, the Nurian representatives to the Second Earth Order applied for permission to send colonies to the new island. Their main goal, they said, was to search for oil and establish mines. The Second Earth Order did not believe colonies would survive the island's seismic instability and brutal meteorological conditions. Almost every day, the ice-land experienced severe snowstorms involving accumulations of several feet and intense winds up to two-hundred miles per hour. The temperatures there rarely reached thirty-two degrees Fahrenheit in the summer. During winter months, it could reach negative seventy. Nevertheless, Nuria's proposition was accepted; as long as they were not bothering another nation, Nuria had the right to dig its own grave, the Order supposed.

Despite all odds, it wasn't long before Nuria established a handful of fairly successful mining colonies. Because salmon was one of the only natural food-sources out there, the colonists christened their land 'Ichthyosis'—a word whose prefix, 'Ichthyo,' meant 'of the creatures of the sea.' Indeed, Ichthyosis was rich in petroleum and salmon, but had little else. And, so, sort of mercantile system was established between Ichthyosis and Nuria in which the Ichthyothian colonies provided their motherland with plenty of much-needed oil while Nuria provided the colonists with everything else they needed to survive.

It was not easy for Ichthyosis to be so helpless. If ships from Nuria were delayed by mere days, colonies literally starved. While the Nurian economy thrived as never before due to the influx of petroleum, life was grueling for the colonists. The imports from Nuria never seemed to cover all their needs. Moreover, Ichthyosis did not receive rations from the Second Earth Order, nor did they enjoy representation. Ichthyosis was not a sovereign state, so it also had no privacy or indemnity from Nuria, as they were not protected by the Isolationist Laws.

The seed of rebellion lay dormant like a sleeping dragon in the hearts of the Ichthyothians for ages. However, as everyone knew, colonial revolution was an inevitable, repeating pattern throughout the history of First Earth. And, so, one day, Ichthyosis rebelled from Nuria, not with armies and guns, but by abruptly halting all export ships.

Nuria surprised Ichthyosis by almost immediately granting its independence. Beneath their loud cries for freedom, most Ichthyothians were only truly hoping to force Nuria to provide them with greater concessions. Instead, Ichthyosis got what it 'wanted' and was kicked out of its mother's home on the twenty-fifth day of the seventh month of the seventieth age, facing the Order's cumbersome, seven-month, new-state application process. Until approved, Ichthyosis could not receive any rations.

The Nurian economy suffered indeed, but no one suffered as much as the Ichthyothian people. With neither the support of Nuria nor the Second Earth Order, seventy percent of the Ichthyothian population fell victim to starvation and hypothermia in mere months. The 'ice-crystal-nation' was nearly wiped out by the time it was accepted into the Order. And, so, the deadly, seven-month period between independence and acceptance became known as the 'Epoch of the Crystal-Land's End.' Historians concluded that the Ichthyothian people would have never survived the seven-month 'Epoch' without the brilliant leadership and resourcefulness of a man whose true first and last name evaded the history books in favor of a nickname. Because Ichthyosis was often called the 'Ice-Crystal Island,' the Ichthyothian people fondly christened their leader after the archaic Nurian word for 'crystal': 'Lechatelierite.' 'Lechatelierite,' who established the first Ichthyothian colony back in the seventeenth age of the second era, was seventy-seven by the time Ichthyosis was granted independence. Despite his old age, he fulfilled his post masterfully, using his intelligence, charisma and prudence to sustain the struggling land until the day he died.

The day Lechatelierite passed away was the same day Ichthyosis was admitted into the Second Earth Order: February seventh of the seventy-first age. Upon acceptance, Nuria and Ichthyosis obtained a special trade license from the Second Earth Order to prevent the Nurians from begging for more petroleum rations and to prevent Ichthyosis from perishing outright.

Eras passed and resentments faded. Nuria and Ichthyosis became an unstoppable pair; their special trade relations coupled with the support of the Second Earth Order enabled the two countries to quickly become the stars of the scientific and technological world. Although

Ichthyosis was Nuria's child, they had become completely different peoples by the turn of the third era. The Ichthyothians grew accustomed to the extreme climate, so that any temperature above freezing felt warm to their skin. From lack of sunlight, their skin became pale. They developed their own variation of the Nurian tongue. Driven by the will to survive against incredible odds, Ichthyosis became a land of extraordinarily-brilliant technophiles and scientists—even more so than their Nurian counterparts. These ice-farers were no longer displaced Nurians, but a people of their own right.

Separated by three-thousand miles and three major bodies of water—the Septentrion Sea, the Briny Ocean and the Fervor Sea—lived the Children of the Fire in the South Conflagrablaze Captive, a tiny desert island just above the equator. The Conflagrians possessed the ability to manipulate the visible portion of the electromagnetic spectrum with their bodies and minds. As a result, these 'mages' had no need for technology or industry, for they were capable of miracles by their own hands. They were feared by all, even the haughty Nurians and the brilliant Ichthyothians. Conflagria served as the 'Authority Nation' of the Second Earth Order.

But, power steadily corrupted Conflagria, as the mages believed themselves a superior race. Conflagria sometimes disobeyed the Isolationist Laws itself, claiming it had the right to 'help the magicless.' Around the time Ichthyosis gained membership in the Order, all of Second Earth had grown to despise their mage leaders.

At first, the Conflagrian Order Chairmen thought nothing of the petty ice-nation they recently admitted. They pitied the struggling population of uprooted Nurians who actually had to depend on so many external devices to survive. Incredible power was innate for the Conflagrians, so the machine-reliant, pale-faced Ichthyothians on their seismically-unstable, ice-island seemed pathetic to their eyes. At first.

But, alas, in a couple eras, this little ice-land managed to become one of the most developed nations on the map. So, instead of considering technology a laughable substitute for magic, the mages slowly began to fear Ichthyosis's endless possibilities for advancement. Conflagria grew paranoid their authority would ultimately be threatened.

It didn't take long for Conflagria to realize what made Ichthyosis so strong: its special trade license with Nuria. They realized, without Nuria, the Ichthyothians would not have bread on their tables each day, let alone snow-gliders or flying crafts. Immediately, the Conflagrians sought to revoke that license, claiming it was a 'blatant violation of the theory of isolationism, and an invitation to repeat all the mistakes of First Earth.' Conflagria also sought to modify the Isolationist Laws to permanently secure their leadership, increasing taxes while decreasing rations, giving themselves voting veto-power, and creating legal 'safety' limitations for all scientific endeavors worldwide.

Within months, the whole world rose up in revolt against Conflagria—not with fleets and weapons, but by collectively withholding their exports to the Island of Fire. Breaking the Isolationist Laws themselves, six-hundred-ninety-nine nations temporarily bound together into a strong tapestry of resistance against the mages. The leader of this coup was none other than North Ichthyosis. Although the Conflagrians were powerful, they knew they couldn't single-handedly defy the entire planet. And, so, on May twenty-fourth of the twenty-fourth age of the third era, the Order Chairman was usurped and Conflagria was expelled—or, 'blacklisted'—from the Second Earth Order. The reign of the mages had ceased.

Conflagria did not take its defeat sitting down. It was determined to leave with a mighty bang that would resound through all of Second Earth for eras to come. As Conflagria was charged for breaking twenty-four of the seventy original Isolationist Laws, the governing entity of the Fire Island, known as 'the System,' manipulated their spectral web to make a day appear to its habitants to be only twenty-four hours. Conflagria therefore became the most isolated nation in the isolated world. Their time-keeping discrepancies, blacklisting, and peculiar powers completely disjoined the Island of Fire from the planet it once proudly led.

North Ichthyosis, now loved by all, was immediately voted into the leadership of the Order in place of the mages. For three eras thereafter, Ichthyosis maintained its lofty position and successfully led the earth into a state of quiet perfection. Conflagrian crisis over, each nation returned to their ignorance of all things international. The mind-your-own-business planet was back to minding its own business.

The Creator frowned upon the Children of Fire, for they had allowed their endowments to be used for evil. On the twenty-fifth day of the seventh month of the eighty-seventh age of the third era, He delivered a prophecy to His disobedient children. So, it was written: someday, a 'Multi-Source Enchant' would be born to the island, and this mage would 'take from the fallen children of Second Earth what was no longer rightfully theirs'

Interlude

And, so, the Creator waited, watching over his unruly flocks as they abused their gift of miracle-making, searching for the one upon whom He would bestow the gift of multiple, spectral power-sources. He searched endlessly for the individual suitable for the task at hand, for the servant worthy of the pain and suffering necessary to complete His noble work. He did not search among the mighty kings or great men, but among the weak and the simple peasantry. In desperation, He even turned his hunting eyes away from Conflagria, expanding his search to include the magic-less beings of the north.

He searched for four eras.

SCARLET JULY

The train screeched to a halt. Reluctantly, I left the warm confines of the engine room and stepped out into the chilly, drizzly, fifty-degree air of early spring of the ninety-second age. My work for the day was through.

I walked into the Alcove City Train Station and punched out on the clock. On my way to the exit, I eyed the station's arcade—a corner devoted to entertaining waiting travelers. Of course, the video games attracted much more than those in transit; it was a known hotspot for countless city kids and teens. I often saw the same trio of boys, about two or three ages older than me, huddling around the 'Submarine Adventure' consoles, near the arcade entrance. The objective of that game was to maneuver a virtual sub through an underwater obstacle course while shooting down colorful moving targets, crossing the finish line before your competitor. I looked now and, sure enough, the three teens were there, playing and making a whole lot of noise. I usually ignored them, but today was cold and rainy, so I wasn't exactly eager to head out. I leaned against a post and watched for a bit. The kid nearest to me had bright hazel eyes, a medium complexion, dark-blonde hair and a little, silver cross dangling from a leather strap around his neck. He held the joystick in his left hand.

"Nurtic, watch out for that reef!" cried the boy standing over his shoulder.

"Relax, Ecivon," Nurtic answered with a dimpled grin, darting around it.

Nurtic. Ecivon. My eyes widened. Were these the same kids I eavesdropped on at the National Library on my very first morning in Nuria, four—almost five, by now—ages ago? The ones who unknowingly lead me to the Link house?

"I want a try," Ecivon whined.

"You're gonna have to wait a while," said the guy playing

against Nurtic. "Don't you know champion pilot Nurtic Leavesleft never crashes?"

Nurtic Leavesleft frowned as he sat back. "But, I just did, Tnerruc," he murmured.

"Good," Ecivon grunted. "You've been at it forever. One of you, get up."

Nurtic didn't respond. His large eyes rose from the screen and landed on my face.

"Hey, do you want a turn?" he called.

I looked over my shoulder. There was no one.

"No, I meant you. We've been hogging the game. Were you waiting for a turn?"

"Oh, um, no." I brushed a strand of hair out of my eyes. "I was just watching."

His furrowed his sandy brows. "I see you at the station a lot, but I don't recognize you from school. Where do you go?"

I was taken aback. "I don't go to school." The words slipped from my mouth. "I'm a train conductor."

"You look a bit young to be a graduate!"

I didn't answer. I just shrugged and turned to leave.

"Wait, do you want to play a round or two with us?" he quickly asked, before I could step outside. "All I do is compete with *these* amateurs." He gestured to his friends, who playfully punched him in response.

I hesitated.

"You can race against Ecivon or Tnerruc first, you know, as a warm up before you take on the *professional*." He put his left hand on his chest.

I stared, stricken by their carefree attitudes. I looked at their cheerful, well-fed faces in wonder. They were normal kids living ordinary lives. Each day, they went to a high school where they attended classes, socialized with others, and ate a hot lunch. Each afternoon, they returned to warm homes with mothers and fathers and siblings, and ate yet another meal. They weren't forced to work since the age of ten, starving and shivering on the crime-filled streets. They didn't have to worry where their next morsel of food would come from, or whether or not they'd get through the night without being assaulted or raped. They had nothing to worry about but their studies. They had the privilege of attending a learning facility where information was neatly presented to them; they didn't have to break into public libraries after hours to teach themselves everything from scratch. They didn't have to count change and figure how many meals they'd have to skip this week so they could afford to spend the coldest night in a cockroach-ridden, cigarette-scented motel. They had change to spare for entertainment.

My hand was on the door. Nurtic saw, so he quickly gave his seat to Ecivon and gestured for Tnerruc to get up, too. He slipped coins into both machines.

"Here, try a race," he offered.

Reluctantly, I approached the glowing console. I felt incredibly out-of-place and foolish as I sat down and took the joystick in my small hands. Nurtic helped me choose a craft, race course and skill level.

"Let's put it on 'beginner,'" he suggested. He turned to Ecivon. "Go easy on her, okay?" he whispered.

Now, that really pissed me off. I survived attempted execution, deportation and nearly five ages on the streets. No well-fed, high-school, city-boy was going to play soft with me. Vindictively, I pushed 'back' and changed the skill level to 'advanced.'

"Hey, what're you doing?" Ecivon said.

Before he or Nurtic could stop me, I punched, 'Start.'

Colorful targets darted across turquoise waves. Because I was unfamiliar with the controls and the settings of the game, Ecivon's virtual shuttle easily took the lead—but only for the first thirty or so seconds. He tended to fumble with the joystick. It wasn't long before I guided my ship right past his and across the finish line, annihilating every target in my path.

Nurtic and Tnerruc broke into peals of laughter as they pummeled a very pink-faced Ecivon.

"You didn't just lose, you got creamed," Tnerruc howled, "by a *girl!*" He then saw the fury that must've been in my eyes. "Chill, it was just a joke," he murmured.

Nurtic looked thoughtful. "Have you ever played this before?"

I shook my head.

Ecivon slinked from his seat. "This round, you're going down." With a defying air, he handed a coin to Nurtic.

Nurtic may've seemed like a relaxed, easygoing guy, but when he was playing the game, he became very serious. His eyes narrowed as they focused on the screen, the knuckles white on the joystick.

So, I played against the 'champion'… and won.

Ecivon and Tnerruc gaped at me as though I were some mythological deity. I stood up and turned to leave.

"Oh no, you come back here! Do you know what you just did, my friend?" Nurtic grinned his dimpled grin, breaking out of his trance. "You just declared *war* against me. No one dethrones the record-holding pilot and just walks away! I'll play you two out of three."

Why not? It couldn't hurt to stay just a little while longer, especially since the rain had escalated into a thunderstorm, by now. I realized, with surprise, I was actually having fun.

Nurtic narrowly won the second round, and we tied in the third. The four of us were laughing and having a great time. At one point, Ecivon took a selfie of us with Nurtic's phone, which normally would've irritated me to no end, but right now, I was too amused to mind. For a few minutes, I forgot I was just a lowly street kid from Conflagria and they were middle-class Nurians with homes and families. For a moment, we were just four teenagers enjoying a free afternoon.

"Miss, you're still here?" a voice said.

I turned and saw my boss, standing in the doorway. As I rose from my seat and faced him, Nurtic and his friends watching, I felt that all-too-familiar, invisible wall re-form between myself and the youthful world.

"Yes, Mr. Eval?" I asked.

"Is it true you have no mailbox?"

Salaries and taxes were electronically 'wired' in Nuria and pretty much all other communications were disseminated via 'email.' It wasn't popular to send around physical sheets of paper, like in Conflagria. Why would I need a mailbox?

"No, I don't," I answered.

"Well, I believe this letter is for you."

He handed me an envelope. It was made of dark, coarse, woven parchment rather than seamless, perfect, white paper. I felt my eyelashes grow hot as I looked at the name at the top-right corner, in faded, berry ink.

Fair Gabardine.

"Th-thank you," I stuttered to Eval before racing out the door, Nurtic Leavesleft's eyes following me.

I ran behind the graffitied building and settled by my dumpster, cradling the envelope as one would a fragile dragon egg. I couldn't decide whether to read the letter right away or destroy it without opening it at all. My heart warred with my code of life. I longed to know how Fair was doing, to read the words of the friend I hadn't seen in nearly five ages. But, I wasn't supposed to be attached to anyone or anything. I wasn't supposed to hold onto any part of my past. I was supposed to be Nurian. If I read Fair's words, I could get emotionally sucked back into everything I left behind.

I lifted the envelope to my face, ready to incinerate it. But, then, my eyes lingered on the way both of our names were scribbled in Fair's familiar, squiggly cursive.

I scrunched my lids shut, folded the letter several times over and tucked it into my pocket, next to my crystal. Then, I curled up on the ground and went to sleep.

The next day—Sunday—passed without my daring to touch the letter. When my shift ended and I punched out and headed for the door, I carefully avoided looking in the direction of the arcade. I ignored Nurtic's voice calling out to me, inviting me to play again. Playing with them once was an incident. Playing with them twice was a habit. I couldn't make friends.

When I got back to my dumpster, I saw a box of cereal sitting on the ground, where I usually slept. A whole box. Sealed. Free. Hungrily, I snatched it up, tore open the cardboard and the plastic bag, and grabbed a handful. It wasn't stale or mealy, but crisp and fresh. I was halfway through my third handful before I paused to wonder how the box even got there in the first place. It wasn't near the opening of the dumpster, so it was unlikely someone tried to toss it in but missed. Who would throw away a full box, anyway? Nurians were wasteful, but not to *that* extreme. That would be criminal.

The following Sunday, I found a couple cans of soup, in the same spot. The Sunday after that, a package of beef jerky. And, then, a loaf of bread. The pattern went on, cycling through the same handful of foods. On the seventh Sunday, the week of my fifteenth birthday, while sipping cold chicken-noodle soup straight from the can, I finally drew Fair's envelope from my robe, sliced it open with a squint of my eyes and slid out the single scrap of parchment.

Dear Scarlet,

It's hard to begin. What do you tell your best friend after three ages of separation?

I blinked. It'd been five ages since my deportation, not three. It took two ages just for this letter to arrive?

I know it'll be forever until the System lets this through, so by the time you read this, who knows what I'll be up to. But, no matter where my crazy life takes me, I do know one thing will always stay the same: I love you, miss you and am grieved I never got to say good-bye.

I have a confession to make, Scarlet. On July 25, 87, the System forbade me from showing up for our regular Sunday visit, as a way of luring you outside. They used me as bait. I'm really sorry. I hope you'll find it in your heart to forgive me, one day. It hurt me, to follow that order, but, of course, I had no other choice. Sometimes, it's hard to accept the System doesn't make mistakes.

I've had quite a few, major life changes since you left, but unfortunately I can't elaborate. My training has taken me to places I never could've imagined, and I only wish you could share it all with me as you've shared my childhood. You'll always be my best friend, and I'll always remember your beautiful, rosy face.

Love,

Fair Gabardine
July 25, 90

SCARLET JULY

It was a breezy, August day. Autumn was on the horizon—I could smell it in the wind. I hated autumn because it was the teasing introduction to winter. Winter meant I had to go back to the motel. Going back to the motel meant less money for groceries—and, while I still received anonymous foodstuffs every Sunday, it wasn't nearly enough to tide me over for the whole week. What a sick, twisted cycle my life had become. So, I knew how to use my magic, by now; I'd taught myself, without the System's help. I had elastic hair, invisibility, excellent vision, an eidetic memory, the ability to heal fresh-wounds with hair-spectrum and, last but not least, the capacity to generate several different kinds of eye-fire, from water-catching to benign. I'd make an awesome warrior, I supposed. But, there was no one to fight. From my studies, I assumed either Nuria abstained from the wars of this Earth, or war only existed on First Earth, back when people were stupid and didn't know any better.

As I peered over an early-seventh-era history book at the Nurian National Library for the third time this age alone, my eyelids began to droop. What was the point of studying anymore when I already knew it all? I'd visited every library, lab and university in southeastern Nuria (I tended to stick to the warmer regions). There was nothing left for me to learn. I was the reigning expert on everything. My life was so pointless, so boring.

I closed my eyes, laid my head on the smooth pages and silently recited the paragraph beneath my cheek:

> *'Samitor Cul was arrested on July 7th of the 7th age for illegally attempting to cross the Briny Ocean and North Septentrion Sea. He was a stowaway on the first vitreous silica ship, commanded by the Diving Captain Terminus Expiri Lechatelierite of the North Ichthyosis Island...'*

The water pressure was intense! Every muscle in my body fought incredible resistance. And, it was far colder than the coldest winter I'd experienced yet. Tiny shards of ice pressed into my skintight, white suit. I held onto the sides of a metal sub, racing through the frigid sea faster than the nimblest dragon could gallop. Where was I? How did I get here? Fighting panic, I peered up, through my helmet's visor, toward the surface. My stomach knotted when I saw how far it was. There was no escape. My fingers ached from holding the handlebars so tightly. Cobalt blue stretched endlessly in every direction... except one. There was small light ahead. It flickered and twisted. No. It couldn't possibly be what I thought it was, because I was underwater.

Let go! I silently screamed, but my body refused to obey. *Let go, or you'll die!* I insisted, and, alas, my white-gloved hands finally uncurled. With the blink of an eye, scarlet fire engulfed the sub. I tumbled wildly into the tide—

I woke with a start, head snapping from the page. I panted as a shiver ran through my hair. What an incredible dream! I remembered each moment vividly, as though it were a real memory. Or, a vision. No, that'd be crazy. I wasn't old enough for visions. It was just a dream, a figment of my imagination. I should really continue studying, now.

But, I couldn't. Because this wasn't the first time something like this happened. Growing up, I sometimes saw what Fair or my siblings were actually doing at the moment in time I was asleep. I never told anyone about it, because normal mages weren't supposed to be capable of experiencing visions until their late teens or early twenties.

Then again, normal mages didn't have multiple sources.

Oh, Tincture, how I wished this wasn't a vision, but only a dream. My heart went out to the poor man on the sleek, grey warship. He was probably dead.

Warship? I sat up straighter. *War*ship? Yes, it was. What I witnessed was a glimpse of battle. Someone launched that underwater-fire with the intent to destroy the sub. War existed on Second Earth, after all. I couldn't believe it. A flicker of suspense and fear struck my eyes and curled the edges of my hair. Thanks to the Isolationist Laws, I really didn't have a clue what the rest of the world was up to. Since absolutely *none* of the books here mentioned wars, I knew Nuria wasn't involved. What other nations were there? There were seven-hundred, but I didn't know very many names. The only maps around here were of Nuria or the northwestern hemisphere. My mind raced. I looked down at the open page. So, someone named Samitor Cul once tried to stowaway to the North Ichthyosis Island. What did I know about the North Ichthyosis Island? Not much. It was arctic. It originated as a Nurian colony. It still received most of its resources from Nuria until this very day. It had a lot of technology, mostly because its habitants wouldn't survive without it. And, lastly, I knew a completely useless factoid about a long-dead sea captain of theirs named Terminus Expiri Lechatelierite, who somehow managed to excel at his job despite left-eye blindness.

Who else was in the northwestern hemisphere? There was Nuria's closest neighbor, Oriya—a democratic nation that religiously followed the Isolationist Laws. Oriya wouldn't be involved in any wars; it was the current Order Authority Nation. Its Chairman was none other than Mr. Arnold Link, an Orion who, amusingly enough, did something as anti-isolationist as marry his Nurian college-sweetheart, Noij Rehtegot, and father two of the only documented 'mixed' children in history: Nurtic's old science-fair teammate, Arrhyth, and his little sister, Linkeree.

For an hour, I sat there, pondering the little I knew about the nations whose names I'd read at one time or another. I considered the possibility of each participating in war, then usually ruled it out. The only one my thoughts kept circling back to was North Ichthyosis. I wasn't sure why, but every time I considered Ichthyosis, an alarm went off in the back of my mind. But, who would the ice-island fight and why?

Nuria was the closest country to Ichthyosis, only separated by the Septentrion Sea. Barely a thousand miles, from shore to shore. Land disputes were a common cause of conflict on First Earth. Ichthyosis revolted against Nuria in the past; maybe Ichthyosis still had a bone to pick with its mother? Perhaps. But, why wouldn't the Nurian public know about it, then? Perhaps because the war was new, or just on the horizon? Or, maybe, the public did know but I didn't? For the past five ages, I studied and studied and studied, but I made one big mistake. I didn't watch the news, or keep up with current events, or even chat with any Nurian city folk. Though I spent each day in public facilities, I kept to myself. Those twenty or so minutes I spent with Nurtic, Ecivon and Tnerruc at the arcade were the longest I ever interacted with anyone since arriving here. How could I be so *stupid?* I kept myself completely isolated from the modern world, burying my nose in some era-old references. It was possible Ichthyosis was at war with Nuria, and I was oblivious. I jumped out of my seat and slammed the book loudly, alarming a patron at the end of the table. Anger at my own stupidity made my hair shudder and my eyes flicker.

I marched out of the library and into the cool, late-summer breeze. There was war on Second Earth. War, very possibly between Ichthyosis and my adoptive homeland! I quickened my walk to a run. There would be no sleeping tonight. I was on a mission to verify all the conclusions I so wildly jumped to.

CEASE LECHATELIERITE

When I opened my eyes, all I could see was a blur of white. I couldn't move a finger. I was dimly aware of the bandage around my head, the brace around my neck, and the tug of needles in my arms.
Bandages and needles. I was in a hospital.

No. I was supposed to be in battle. My pulse quickened. I couldn't be in here when my men needed me out there. When exactly did I get knocked out and how? What happened to Inexor's task force? And, unit seven? Did crystalline shuttle seven transport the unit to the dragon ship in time? Crystalline seven…

The fire. So, it was true. The Conflagrians finally did it. They managed to bring their most powerful weapon underwater. Inexor badgered me months ago about a dream he had about the System's new 'secret weapon.' He said, his dream was as sharp and memorable as reality. He said, if Nordics could have visions like mages, this most certainly was one. He dreamt that a young, white-haired Conflagrian spectroscoper engineered fire that could burn the sea itself. Frightened and freaked out, Inexor didn't have the courage to share his thoughts with anyone but me. But, when he confided in me, I laughed at him. I brushed him off. Nordics didn't have visions, I said, we didn't have a place in the spectral web.

I underestimated my second-in-command and I underestimated the enemy.

We lost the battle and it was my fault.

It was the first battle I ever tanked. At the age of seventeen, I'd been through dozens of fights as commander and always won. Always.

I heard the creak of a door. I tried to focus my eyes on the face of the man coming in, but all I could see was a peach blob. I blinked repeatedly but the fog wouldn't clear. My incredible vision, like my perfect combat record, was gone.

"Commander Lechatelierite." I recognized the voice of Colonel Austere.

Though decades younger than my former teacher, I had authority over him, now: I was the Leader of the Ichthyothian Resistance. But, he was my elder and he taught me everything I knew; I always showed him the utmost respect.

"Sir," I replied immediately, wishing I could sit up. It felt strange and rude to address the Colonel while lying in bed.

"Dr. Calibre and Nurse Raef said, if you didn't wake up within seven days of the accident, you probably never would. It's a relief to see you conscious." His words were kind, but his voice was as cold as the Septentrion.

I could imagine the critical look in his sea-blue stare. I was used to being studied by my teachers throughout my life, especially him. But, this time was different. This time, I wasn't his star pupil. I was a negligent failure.

The Colonel didn't ask me how I was feeling. He didn't give me my medical prognosis. He cut straight to business.

"The underwater fire annihilated shuttle seven. You fell off before the crystalline went up in flames. The rest of unit seven, however, wasn't so fortunate."

He paused to let that sink in. Ten of my men died an unnatural death because I was too arrogant to take Inexor—whom I supposedly trusted more than anyone—seriously. One by one, the face of each unit seven diver flashed through my mind. I only survived because I listened to a crazy voice in my head screaming to let go of the crystalline.

"The majority of Buird's task force made it out alive," Austere went on, "but when Buird himself saw what happened to you, he dove to recover your unconscious body. He managed to get you onboard shuttle three, but, on his way back up, he was exposed and alone." He leaned forward and the beige splotch of his face filled my sight. "Commander Lechatelierite, he never came home. We have reason to believe he was also taken by the underwater fire."

All the air disappeared from my lungs. I felt as though smacked by a thousand gallons of icy seawater, without a diving suit. Inexor, my second, my right-hand man, my best friend, was dead. Because he saved my life. Building in my eyes and throat was a sensation I hadn't felt since I was six; I almost didn't recognize what it was. No. I couldn't cry. Especially not in front of the Colonel. Had to prevent it. I closed my eyes.

Austere *then* called in Dr. Calibre, who proceeded to tell me I was expected to make a full recovery within an age, upon which I would return to the battlefield. Diving suit scorched by the underwater fire, my body suffered excessive water-pressure. I also had a concussion when debris from the exploding crystalline knocked into my helmet. My paralysis, vision loss and internal organ damage were all severe but treatable. Over the course of the next age, I would undergo multiple major surgeries, laser eye surgery and intensive physical therapy. I would stay on intravenous nutrition until my digestive system recuperated enough to function on its own. And, I would wear one of those thin, silver 'visual reparation bands' across my eyes whenever possible, so my sight wouldn't eventually deteriorate into total blindness.

The doctor kept talking but, by now, I'd stopped listening. All I could think about was Inexor. Dead. I didn't deserve to regain my strength and keep my rank. I didn't deserve to lie in a warm, forty-degree hospital on the mend while Inexor was nothing but frozen ashes swirling in the sea. It was me, not the men I lead into combat unprepared, who deserved to burn at the hand of the Conflagrian enemy.

It was I who deserved to die.

SCARLET JULY

Since arriving in Nuria, I tended to keep to the southeastern cities, because they were warmer and because my train station was in Alcove City. But, this search pushed me out of my comfort zone. Over the past month, I rode trains to different towns, working my way northwest. In each city, I'd find the tallest skyscraper and use my hair to climb to the top balcony or even the roof itself. From there, I'd zoom out my eyesight as far as possible and scan the skyline, building by building. I prevented onlookers from spotting me by reaching through the spectral web into the internal mechanisms of their eyes, temporarily destroying their visual perceptions of me. Broad-range invisibility was one of my more strenuous magical abilities. But, it was worth it, in the end: on September seventh, after twenty-five days of diligent observation, I spotted a large but secluded facility that could very well be a military base. A military base on Nurian soil. It was at the northwestern shore. I memorized the way there from the place I now stood—the roof of a seven-hundred-story building.

I spent the rest of the day walking there. When I arrived, I saw a guard stationed at the tall, iron gate. Yes, just one. I laughed silently to myself. Nuria was obviously very new to the military world. I edited myself from sight and clambered over the gate. I entered the main facility at the first possible opportunity—when another guard emerged from inside to swap places with the original. I followed an attendant pushing a beverage cart to what appeared to be a conference hall. And, I slipped in moments before the door snapped shut.

A meeting was well underway; the attendant got to work refilling empty mugs and glasses. I stood nervously at the corner of the room and surveyed the men around the table, nearly falling through the floor at the sight of the President of Nuria himself, Mr. Georgen Winster Briggesh. As for the rest of the men, about half wore charcoal suits and multi-colored ties while the other half wore white, black or blue uniforms decorated with pins, bands and cords. Government officials and military personnel.

I watched in amazement as a small, pale-faced, wheelchair-bound, white-suited, very-heavily-decorated, angry man who must've been three or four decades younger than those around him spoke a strange tongue with astounding ferocity and exuberance. While he railed, a Nurian translation scrolled on the screen at the front of the room, typed by a woman sitting at the far end of the long table. But, after listening to his rapid speech for nearly twenty straight minutes, I didn't need the translation anymore; I'd adapted to the patterns and sounds of his language. Just as with Nurtic and Ecivon at the National Library five ages ago, I breathed in a foreign tongue. I could now understand most of what he was saying.

"Yes, sir, it is economically feasible for us to accelerate our export rate, supplying your nation with the resources necessary to continue your war," President Briggesh answered the small, angry officer, in Nurian. "And, indeed, we were happy to build this facility for your use. But, Nuria has only agreed to all of this as a precaution, because of our proximity to the parties involved in the conflict. You must understand, we have no reason to engage your enemy ourselves, Commander Lechatelierite. They never threatened us. So, to answer your final question, no, we will not allow our citizens to enlist in your military. Your nation was expelled from the Second Earth Order upon engaging in the forbidden act of war. If we are caught forging an alliance with a blacklisted nation, we will meet the same tragic fate."

Oh, Tincture, there was so much I could draw from his words. Nuria wasn't involved in the actual combat. It only agreed to accelerate its export rate to the warring state—North Ichthyosis, of course, the only country Nuria was permitted to trade independently with, outside of the Second Earth Order's rationing network. But, who were the Ichthyothians fighting and why?

The small man in the wheelchair was an Ichthyothian military commander called Lechatelierite. That name was familiar. I'd read about a stowaway on a ship captained by a Terminus Lechatelierite. But, Terminus lived over half an era ago, so this young soldier obviously wasn't the same person. His grandson or great-grandson, perhaps?

Lechatelierite slammed his fist on the table, and I jumped. "Sir, if Ichthyosis loses the war and is conquered, our enemy will have you surrounded from both north and south. And, without a military of your own to protect yourself, you are a perfect, next target. Their imperialism of my nation will be the death sentence of yours, as well. Unless, of course, we join forces, immediately." Lechatelierite said in one swift breath.

I was amazed at how a boy who looked only an age or two older than me could speak with such authority among high government officials and military officers decades his senior. His tone was strikingly persuasive and piercing—almost hypnotizing, like that of a throat mage. The young commander was full of righteous anger and energy that reminded of...well, myself. But, his loud confidence didn't seem to fit his physical state. Wheelchair-bound and hooked up to IVs, he was small and thin and deathly pale.

He also had a sharp jaw, high cheekbones, thick, tousled hair and crystal-clear, penetrating, silver-grey eyes. I would've found him attractive...if it weren't for the frightening scowl permanently carved into his stern face.

"The Alliance can easily be concealed from the Order," Lechatelierite continued, voice so slick and compelling, it made me wonder why the others weren't already shaking his hand and asking where to sign. Perhaps the Nurians were immune to his hypnotic tone because they couldn't understand him and had to rely on the typed translation, instead. "Ichthyosis managed to mask the First War for ages, without a problem, enabling our nation to retain its membership. Ichthyosis was expelled only upon the onset of the Second War with the same enemy, fifteen ages ago. We've learned a lot from our mistakes in the seventy-seventh age and are better prepared to take every precaution necessary to assure complete secrecy from the Order."

Two wars? I stared at Lechatelierite's fierce face in shock. And, the second had been going on as long as I'd been alive?

Deliberations went on and on after that, until Lechatelierite finally won. Right then and there, the men edited and ratified a document the young commander had brought with him: 'The Nurro-Ichthyothian Second War Pact of the 92nd Age.' Nurian enlistments would start tomorrow, with the goal of deploying joint troops by the following summer. Things were moving remarkably fast.

To no one's knowledge but my own, I was actually present during Nuria's very first declaration of war.

I watched as everyone lined up to sign. The primary author went first; *Diving Commander Cease Lechatelierite, Leader of the Ichthyothian Resistance* was sprawled in fine, angular cursive. Cease Lechatelierite. It sounded like archaic Nurian. 'Lechatelierite.' Crystal. 'Cease.' End. End of the crystal. Crystal's end. I found it oddly beautiful. Poetic. And, strange.

The meeting adjourned and everyone began filtering out the door, passing within a foot or so of me. I stood perfectly still, tense and nervous. Several pairs of eyes blindly slid right across my body. Then came Lechatelierite's wheelchair.

He paused.

Oh, Tincture. I could hear my heart drum loudly against my ribcage. Lechatelierite turned his head, face set, eyes tracking about. And, he looked right at my face. No way. I held my breath. He couldn't see me. It was impossible!

And, then, he turned away, wheeled himself right up to President Briggesh and solemnly shook his hand. I exhaled.

"Thank you, sir; Ichthyosis won't let Nuria down," the Commander said in a sure but not over-confident voice.

He was such a master of tone. He knew how to manipulate the subtle inflections in his voice to sound convincing, pleading, authoritative, inflamed—you name it, he could do it, abruptly and effortlessly. This man was dangerous. I also noticed he was speaking Nurian, now. But, his Ichthyothian accent was so strong, I understood why he opted for the translator earlier, even if he was technically bilingual.

"With Nuria at our side," he declared, "I believe an end is now in sight, for the Second Ichthyo-Conflagrian War."

With that, my stomach disappeared.

Conflagria.

At war.

For the second time.

Before Lechatelierite's wheelchair could pass in front of me, I turned and fled the room.

SCARLET JULY

Evening fell, and I didn't have the strength to start heading back to Alcove City. But, I couldn't sleep either. I found a payphone and sacrificed a couple coins to call Eval to let him know I wasn't feeling well enough to come into work tomorrow. That much was true. I was sick. With knowledge.

I passed the night on the roof of a random office-building, staring off into the distance, the sixty-degree September wind tossing my hair and cooling my stinging eyes. The starry night blended with the glittering skyline. I was so high up, I was untouched by the city noise. The view was peaceful and serene. I wished I could say the same about my heart.

I didn't know what to do. Originally, I'd set off in search of Nurian military presence with the intent to gather whatever information needed to get involved in the war effort. I thought I'd finally found a purpose for my spectral talents. Moreover, a purpose for my life. I was prepared to devote myself to defending my adoptive homeland.

But, then, Conflagria entered the picture. Conflagria had secretly been at war for as long as I'd been alive. How come the mage population was ignorant about both the First and Second Wars? And, what could a magical, medieval, desert-land ever hope to gain from a tiny, tech-dependent, arctic island?

Lechatelierite spoke of imperialism. Of course, what else could a totalitarian government want but more land and people to control? And, what better target was there than a country so geographically isolated, small and fragile? A country with a carrying capacity of nearly zero, on its own? Who lacked membership in the Order and thus had no known support-system? Ichthyosis was ripe for the taking. The System probably figured Ichthyosis would likely lose if the war just dragged on long enough, simply because it'd run out of resources.

Conflagria wasn't exactly fertile, but it was a wonderland compared to Ichthyosis. Perhaps a superpower like Nuria could sustain a conflict for some time without the Order's rations, but Ichthyosis surely couldn't.

President Briggesh initially objected to an alliance because of the risk of blacklisting. By forging a secret pact, Nuria was now engaged in an international conspiracy. The System knew it was unlikely Ichthyosis would gain support because of the Isolationist Laws. No one in their right mind would risk being cut off from the global trade network. But, then, Lechatelierite entered the picture. Lechatelierite, with his brilliance and remarkable powers of persuasion. With the compelling voice of a throat mage and the authoritative presence of one who'd been in command far longer than was possible, considering he looked like a teenager. He did what the System couldn't possibly anticipate; he single-handedly persuaded a formidable nation to risk everything for his people.

If Conflagria won the war, it'd gain jurisdiction over both northern and southern territory, making it the furthest-reaching nation on the map. Nuria and Oriya would be completely surrounded. Obviously, Conflagria's ultimate goal was to swallow the entire northwesternhemisphere.

Conflagria was the bad guy, here. The offender. All Ichthyosis was doing was defending itself from imperialism.

No, that wasn't right. The Conflagrians *themselves* didn't choose this war. My mouth tasted bitter. They were ignorant. They didn't know the reason for the shortages of fire, food and magic. They didn't know the war was to blame for the depression they were suffering. The depression that harried the 'termination' of 'Useless' lives. It was the System, not Conflagria, who wanted to conquer Ichthyosis. The Conflagrians were innocent. How could I join a war against a land of innocent people? *My* people?

But, on the other hand, how could I just sit back and let my magic go to waste when an evil, power-hungry dictatorship was marauding around the northwestern hemisphere, seeking to oppress more lives? My spectrum and my inside knowledge of Conflagria could provide the Nurro-Ichthyothian Alliance with an invaluable advantage. I could be a great asset and source of intel. And, there was always the possibility that, in the process of helping the Nordics, I could make them understand the distinction between the innocent, ignorant, Conflagrian people and the evil, malicious System. I could teach them that what Conflagria needed wasn't annihilation, but liberation.

***

I attempted to run my fingers through my wiry hair. Today, I was going to enlist. Overnight, the war effort became public knowledge. Ichthyosis had prepared a seven-month training program—October through May—for the Nurian recruits, to be held at none other than the base I'd snuck into. In May, the recruits would deploy overseas to join their Ichthyothian counterparts, where they would train until August, before entering the war.

The Nurro-Ichthyothian Military was trilateral. Applicants didn't get to decide which branch to enter; that was determined by a battery of physical and mental aptitude tests. The possibilities included the Air Force, Ground Troops and Diving Fleet.

New technology was on the horizon for the Diving Fleet. New, smaller 'vitreous silica' ships were designed to fly both in the air and underwater. Until now, vitreous silicas were built either as subs or planes. The revolutionary, convertible ships were being introduced into the fleet now, requiring quite a range of skill from their pilots. Not to mention, divers had to be expert swimmers and skilled at hand-to-hand combat, both underwater and on foot. The Diving Fleet was the smallest and most elite branch of the military—the core of the Ichthyothian Resistance.

I wanted to be a diver, but not just because they were the best of the best. I wanted to serve under Commander Cease Lechatelierite. Specifically. I was impressed by what I saw of him at the meeting. I wanted to learn from him. Moreover, there was something about him I was drawn to, something I trusted. I sensed that, of all the authorities in the military, he'd be the one willing to hear me out and come to understand the distinction between the System and the Conflagrian people. And, when the time was right, I wanted him to be the first person I'd reveal my magehood to. With his brilliance, I believed he'd figure how to best use my unique talents. With my magic and inside knowledge of mage culture and society, I could be a powerful weapon for Ichthyosis. And, I believed I could make the greatest impact on this war if Lechatelierite was the one wielding that weapon.

I stood in line now, in the cafeteria of Bay River Secondary—the massive, public high school that serviced most of Alcove City. All too soon, my turn came. A middle-aged Ichthyothian man in white, military dress began speaking and gathering paperwork without actually looking at me.

"…And, general information for sections 'A' through 'C,'" he was spewing. "'D' and 'E' are security questions; be sure to initial each box by the—" When he lifted his head to hand me the forms, his voice went dead. He scrunched his grey-speckled eyebrows.

"Only graduating seniors may apply," he said, flatly. Nuria's age-round school system put graduation in the middle of September. Next week. Colleges around here got started the first week of October, with winter break in February. The military academies were supposed to start up October seventh.

"I am," I lied.

He blinked. "You don't look like a senior."

It was true. I didn't even look *my* age. What grade would I've been anyway, if I attended public school? Ninth? Tenth? I stared solemnly back at him.

He folded his arms. "There are certain physical requirements, as well. The military is hardly the place for a little girl."

Little girl! My eyes grew hot. I closed them and took a deep breath. Must. Not. Roast. Recruitment. Officer.

He picked up a bright pink sheet from a small stack at the corner of the table.

"If you're interested in assisting the war effort by other means, we're starting a fundraising club. Just fill this out and—"

"I want to serve," I interrupted, coolly. The edges of my hair curled.

He blinked. "Forms '62A' through '70C,' then. The first aptitude test will be administered today, after school, at twenty-five o'clock, at the National Resource Center. Bring the completed paperwork for admittance. And, may God be with you," he added with heavy sarcasm.

I snatched the pages from his hands and stalked away, forgetting to thank him.

* * *

Diver. I couldn't believe it. I stared at the results in my shaking hands. I was in the ninety-ninth percentile of all the mental aptitude, reflex and eye-hand coordination exams. No surprises there. My top swimming scores, however, did shock me. When tasked with completing an obstacle course in a forty-degree pool, I honestly thought I'd die. In seconds, my whole body prickled as though pressed into the scales of a Conflagrian pine dragon. It was nothing like swimming in the Fervor River when I was a kid. I raced through, performance sloppier than I would've liked, just so I could get out before freezing to death. My speed must've impressed the examiners. They didn't know just why I was in such a hurry.

Did that mean I was placed wrongly? Swimming in cold water would obviously be a pretty big part of life as a diver. I folded the acceptance letter and stuck it in the pocket of my robe, alongside my crystal and Fair's note. I remembered my vision of the Ichthyothian sliding off the grey submarine. The thought alone turned my bones to ice. Didn't that indicate I was unfit to be a diver myself?

Well, I didn't get to choose where I was placed. I couldn't appeal their decision. And, I shouldn't want to, anyway. I wanted to serve under Lechatelierite. I needed to talk to him. I had to.

* * *

October seventh, seven o'clock.

My nerves jittered as I surveyed myself in the bathroom mirror, fifteen minutes before the start of my first class at the Nurian Diving Academy. White was not a color seen very often in Conflagria or southeastern Nuria. But, suddenly, I found myself in a world where everything was white—the walls, furniture, metal floors, uniforms, everything. The whiteness of my surroundings accentuated the fiery redness of my hair and skin. On my way to class, people stared openly at me. I clutched my books to my chest and tried my best to ignore them. A large group now emerged from an adjoining corridor, chattering loudly as they passed in front of me. One of the boys was very tall and had dark-blonde hair, bright hazel eyes and a steel cross dangling from a leather strap around his neck.

"Leavesleft," I said aloud. "Nurtic Leavesleft, from the arcade."

Not just from the arcade, but from the National Library, five ages ago. Not that I'd ever tell him about that day.

He turned, eyes wide. Then, he gave me a smile so broad, you'd think we were long-lost best friends or something.

"Hey, you're that train conductor!" He paused and a twinge of pink touched his tan cheeks. "I'm sorry, but I don't remember your name."

He didn't remember because I never told him, in the first place.

"Scarlet July," I responded as he shook my hand—a Nordic greeting habit I found silly; we Conflagrians preferred bowing. I noticed how very tiny my hand was in his. "So, where are your friends, Ecivon and Tnerruc?"

He seemed surprised by my recollection of his friends' names. Then, his grin disappeared.

"They didn't make it in," he answered, sadly. "But, they promised to test again, as soon as possible. And, my pals from the swim team are here: Arrhyth and Dither."

Arrhyth? As in, Arrhyth *Link*? I was flabbergasted. His father's job was to keep the seven-hundred nations of Second Earth isolated. And, Arrhyth was participating in an international conspiracy that could get Nuria blacklisted from the Order. Wasn't Arrhyth a huge security risk?

Nurtic noticed the look on my face. "Don't worry, Mr. Arnold Link is totally cool with it. I know him and the whole Link family, really well. They won't tell the Order anything. In fact, Mr. Link is in a position to help cover for the alliance."

I froze. What? Oh, Tincture, was I dying to know the story behind all *that*.

"So, you enjoyed piloting virtual subs so much, you decided to try the real thing?" I asked.

Nurtic nodded, laughing. "I was born to be a pilot," he said with that wistful, the-future-is-calling look on his dimpled face. "I'm also really fascinated by Ichthyothian technology." He leaned in and spoke in a whisper, as though relaying juicy gossip: "I heard that, in a couple ages, there's going to be this device called 'PAVLAK'—no idea what the acronym stands for, yet—which will, among so many things, provide pilots with live-action, three-dimensional, holographic displays of the battle *in* the cockpit *during* the fighting. They've been working on it for nearly a decade!"

"Wow," I said, though I didn't share his enthusiasm. My eyes easily picked up most things normal people relied on radars for.

"I can't wait to fly with one of those. Well, I can't wait to fly a military craft, period. I flew Cessnas, back home. I took lessons at the Alcove City Flight School and even did some amateur air shows. Loved every minute. I was born to be a pilot," he repeated.

"And, yet, they made you a diver."

"Yeah, but there's still plenty of opportunities to pilot in the Diving Fleet. I heard the new, mini vitreous silicas are convertible. They used to be built for either air or sea, but the new, smaller ships can do both. Two in one, plane and sub! I can't wait to get my hands on one of those."

I cocked an eyebrow. "So, were you hoping to be placed in the Air Force instead?"

"While that'd probably be a more natural fit for me, I actually wanted to be in the Diving Fleet."

"Why?"

"So I could serve under Commander Cease Lechatelierite," he answered, to my great surprise. That made two of us. "In high school, I wrote a paper on him. My twelfth-grade civics teacher was an Ichthyothian fugitive who hated the Isolationist Laws. He eventually got arrested and deported back home for it—it's long story; I promise I'll tell you sometime. But, anyway, Arrhyth, Dither and I—we all figured, if we're going to do something as crazy as participate in an international conspiracy to defend our country, we might as well do it under the best military leader in the history of Second Earth. Right?"

"Fair enough," I said.

"So, what made *you* decide to join the military?"

Well, you see, Nurtic, I was a deported Conflagrian convict who wanted revenge and to free my people from an evil dictatorship.

I shrugged. "It's better than being a train conductor. My life actually has direction, now."

His eyes traveled up and down my delicate frame, in awe. Normally, I would've found that gesture really creepy, but it seemed innocent, coming from Nurtic.

"You must be the *only girl* here," he mused. Then, he looked away. "What did your family think of your decision to join up?"

I shrugged again.

"You don't have a family, do you?"

I couldn't breathe.

"I know you lived on the streets, Scarlet," he said, quietly. "I figured it out, that day in the arcade. You said you didn't go to school—and I know you must be younger than me—and you told your employer you didn't have a mailbox, and I always saw you in the same clothes…" His gaze dropped to the floor. "I saw you behind the dumpster, sometimes. You'd make a little fire in a garbage can and huddle by it, shivering…"

Fear rippled through me. Did he ever see just *how* I made those fires?

Wait a minute—

"It was you, wasn't it," I breathed. "You're the one who left food for me, on Sundays."

Nurtic didn't answer. Which gave me his answer.

I was silent. My insides squirmed. Since the age of ten, my world consisted of cold isolation. It was incredibly unnerving to be the recipient of such generosity from a virtual stranger. I continued walking, books to my chest, staring straight ahead into the white oblivion of my surroundings. If it weren't for Nurtic, I probably would've starved to death, by now. Though I was grateful, I really didn't like feeling so indebted to anyone. Not that Nurtic expected anything in return. He probably thought, when he left Alcove City for the military, he'd never see me again.

"Well, I'm glad you're here," Nurtic plodded on, breaking the tension. "They'll be expecting a lot from all of us, you know. You're no exception, no matter how tiny you are." He paused for a moment and added, "Just like Lechatelierite." He gave me a quizzical look. "You sort of remind me of him. Or, what I know about him, anyway. He's physically little. Barely over five feet, which may sound tall to *you*, but, believe me, that's small for a seventeen-age-old guy!" he exclaimed, being comfortably over six feet himself. Tincture, Nurtic was comparing me to the Commander? He just didn't stop alarming me. "Did you have a branch preference?" He sure was chatty. And, nosy. I was starting to seriously regret bringing this conversation upon myself, in first place.

"No."

"Really? None, at all? No particular draw to swimming or flying or anything? Nothing you were aiming for, when you took the tests?"

What could I say? Well, Nurtic, I also wanted to serve under Lechatelierite, but only because I liked what I saw of him when I used my eye spectrum to illegally eavesdrop on a top-secret meeting here at this very facility, just last month.

"Well, I do love swimming," I said. It was true, though certainly not the main reason I wanted to be a diver. "Growing up, my favorite hobby was to swim in..." heh, I surely couldn't say the Fervor River, "in the Briny Ocean."

"Cool," Nurtic breathed. "I like swimming, too, but it wasn't my favorite thing, growing up. I was more into basketball and lacrosse. I only joined the swim-team in my last year of high school."

Then, Nurtic suddenly realized he forgot his calculus book and had to double back to the lockers to get it. I was relieved to finally be left alone.

My first period of the day was a calculus-oriented strategy class, taught by Colonel Autoero Austere. Colonel Austere was quite a sensation among my peers. On our way to the lecture hall, after Nurtic left, I overhead many of them chattering about what a legend he was. "The great Commander Lechatelierite was his protégé," they said.

I perked at the sound of the Commander's name. I just arrived at the academy, and I'd already heard so much about him. He was the only one my comrades talked about more than Austere. They were most awed by the fact he was made commander at fifteen. I was really confused by this. At what age did Ichthyosis allow people to enlist? The recruitment officer at Bay River Secondary seemed pretty emphatic about the necessity of my graduating high school first. How did Lechatelierite join up so young? And, why would his parents let him?

There was also a lot of talk about his near-perfect record. Near-perfect. No one seemed to know too much about his one and only loss. Neither did I, but there was a lot I could infer from the way he looked when I saw him. But, the others didn't seem to have a clue about his injuries. As far as they were concerned, he'd escaped from that battle unscathed and was still active in combat until today.

I was among the first to enter the lecture hall. I sat in the seventh row and began to absorb the incredible sight before me. Three colossal, digital boards covered in calculations dominated the front wall. The leftward wall bore a digital map delineating all seven-hundred nations of Second Earth. This was the first time I'd seen a complete world map. To my right, there was a blown-up map of the northwestern hemisphere. I eyed Conflagria and could easily locate the Fire Pit, the System Mage Castle, Fair's place, Crimson and Ambrek's cabin, and my old house. At the sight of my childhood home, my heart pounded against my ribcage and a lump involuntarily rose to my throat. I was surprised by the intensity of my reaction. After spending the last five ages trying to forget about Conflagria, my past came rushing back in a second. I was frustrated with myself; I should've anticipated something like this upon entering an academy where I'd be taught to fight mages!

Austere was watching me from the front of the room. I quickly looked away from the map. I couldn't be caught staring at my homeland with any sort of revealing expression on my face. No one could know about my heritage, at least not yet. I couldn't say anything until I graduated into the fleet. Even then, I had to be careful about how and when to tell Lechatelierite. First, I needed to earn his trust and respect, through excellence.

Students filled the room and settled down, glancing at Conflagria with, at most, an expression of mild interest. They all seemed much more fascinated by the world map—those were hard to come by. How could I be so stupid as to stare at Conflagria that intently?

Nurtic was the very last to arrive to class. He darted in a moment before the bell rang, and, of course, just *had* to push all the way to the seventh row to sit next to me. I didn't meet his eye.

"Welcome to the Nurian Diving Academy," Colonel Austere spoke Nurian with a mild Ichthyothian accent. "I am Colonel Autoero Austere, your calculus-strategy teacher," he said, as if we didn't already know all about him and his star pupil. He pushed a button on his podium and arrows began sliding across the map of the northwestern hemisphere, showing what I presumed to be troop movements from a battle. "My job is to teach you how *this*," he gestured, "is derived from *this*." Calculations now hovered above the vectors and dots. My mind immediately started correlating the two, but then Austere shut off the screen. "The state of the war is becoming desperate for Ichthyosis, which is why all courses at this academy have been condensed to get as many of you as possible into the North Septentrion Sea for final testing in seven months. No, I don't expect everyone to make it. Far from it." He paused. "From my experience, the only ones who do are those who want to." He looked at each of us in turn as he spoke. "I define 'want' here as more than just a simple desire. It's a hunger of mind, body and soul. An unwavering confidence in the belief that serving your country is not just the purpose of the next few months or ages of your life, but the very reason you were born. So, soldiers, ask yourselves right now why you're here. Are you willing to possibly endure a fate worse than death, to protect the Nurro-Ichthyothian Alliance?"

At this, some of my peers gave each other subtle, confused looks. No doubt, they wondered what could possibly be worse than death.

I had a few ideas.

"Before you can learn to destroy the enemy, you must destroy every doubt in your mind regarding your purpose in this war. If you don't kill this doubt, it will kill you." The Colonel's eyes rested on mine. "Do I make myself clear?" he barked.

"Sir, yes, sir!" we responded in unison.

I felt like my every doubt was written on my forehead for all to see; particularly my unease about my physical littleness and whether or not I'd really be able to kill a mage, when push came to shove.

Austere made no further preamble. He plunged directly into the day's three-hour lesson. Even I was struggling to stay focused, through it all. I was familiar with calculus already, but I knew little of battle tactics or military strategies; First Earth history books didn't go into that much detail. Nurtic was having far more difficulty than I. Often, he leaned over to whisper questions.

Calculus was followed by a three-hour lecture on Second Earth military history, which was followed by a seminar designed to teach us the Ichthyothian language in seven months, which was followed by a pilotry lesson. After a measly fifteen-minute break for a very late lunch, we hit the showers for 'Diving 101.' Austere wasn't kidding when he said all the classes here were accelerated. I was exhausted by the time I finished strapping on my white diving-suit and flippers.

All seventy of us stood at attention in a line around the many-mile-deep, saltwater pool. I looked down and saw my rosy-faced refection in the turquoise surface. Compared to my tall, broad-shouldered comrades, I looked laughably fragile.

The instructor, General Irri, stood on a diving board nearly half a mile high. He tumbled off the narrow plank, spun gracefully through the air and entered the water without a trace of a splash. While submerged, he moved so swiftly and invisibly, we were surprised when his head broke the surface a few feet from the sidelines. With no other introduction, he climbed out of the water and began breaking us into smaller groups. He appointed me the leader of a group of seven. A single second after the orders left his lips, I felt seven pairs of eyes size me up. I tried my best to keep my face blank as my stomach knotted. I didn't expect this much personal pressure, the very first diving class.

Time passed slowly. Irri demonstrated a handful of basic diving techniques, assigned each team a different task, then cut us loose to accomplish our objectives.

Or, *attempt* to accomplish them, anyway. I really did have decent ideas for my group. I delivered orders as clearly as possible. I was open to others' suggestions and was sure to incorporate them into my master plan. But, somehow, things just wouldn't work out. I could practically feel the resentment radiate from my peers like auras, whenever I opened my mouth. It wasn't long before the entire strategy fell apart. The only one who listened to me religiously was Nurtic Leavesleft. I clearly didn't have the respect or trust of the rest. And, they sure weren't helping me learn to trust them. I left class in the mood to set something on fire.

My next period was devoted to studying the culture and life of the Conflagrians.

"Know your friends well," General Privil echoed the cliché, "but know your enemies better."

I shifted in my seat. I most certainly knew my enemies much better, and being careless with that knowledge wouldn't just be the end of my military career, but the end of my life. It was way too early for anyone to know the truth.

General Privil began with a very basic overview: the South Conflagrablaze Captive was a spectral, medieval, totalitarian state governed by an all-powerful entity called 'the System.' Tincture, was this class going to be easy.

"The System dictates every aspect of the lives of the Conflagrian people," he said, "from where they live, to what they learn, to what trade they adopt, to whom they marry. The System even gives each newborn child their name, based off of their colorful appearances and prospective powers. For example, the third System Principal was named 'Patrician Courier' after his purple electromagnetic field and his ability to run at speeds greater than a snow-semivowel can glide."

My classmates exchanged confused glances and whispers. They didn't understand the concept of colored electromagnetic fields—or, auras. One guy raised his hand and asked, how could a person look any color besides varying shades of peach or brown? I understood their confusion; it was hard to depict the concept with words. How could one who'd never seen a mage comprehend the majestic way we radiated the essences of our colors? My sister Amytal's presence wasn't simply blue to the human eye. She had an intangible, innate, beautiful blue glow that shone through every aspect of her being.

Before entering the academy, I was sure to practice concealing my red aura. Even so, I feared my teachers would recognize me for what I was. But, as my first day wore on, this fear ebbed away. If I could fool Colonel Austere, I could fool anyone.

After the class spent a considerable amount of time tripping over the principle of colored auras, they began to digest the latter half of Privil's example: Courier could run faster than a semivowel. Semivowels were the primary mode of transportation for civilian Ichthyothians. They were flivvers, but with skis instead of wheels. They could glide at hundreds of miles per hour.

The shock in the air was thick. My peers were impressed and freaked out. Oh Tincture, if they only knew the extent of my magic…

The screen at the front of the hall flicked on.

"We've created a database of every magical power we've managed to discover. But, we know there are probably hundreds—maybe thousands—more out there that haven't been documented. So, it's important never to underestimate Conflagria. They may not have running water or electricity, but the absence of tech doesn't mean they aren't a formidable enemy. Their magic could always surprise us. When fighting against them, we must remain vigilant and prepared to improvise."

Privil began scrolling through the alphabetical database. "As you can see, a mage's spectrum originates from a specific body part. They call this, a 'source.' For example, legs were Principal Courier's magic-'source,' enabling him to run at superhuman speeds. Examples of common magical sources include hair, arms, hands, feet and legs. Examples of less common sources of magic include ears, wrists, throats, backs, internal organs and skin. Curiously, in all of Conflagrian history, there has never been an eye-mage.

"While there have been a couple recorded cases of *partial* multi-source mages—mages with one full source and a hint of unusable spectrum in a second—no mage has ever been known to possess more than one fully-functional source. However, the Conflagrians believe that, someday, one will be born among them who'll possess a vast number of magical capabilities from two or more sources. This is the myth of the 'Multi-Source Enchant.' Our biological and genetic studies have determined this is improbable."

I slid slightly in my chair. The Conflagrian 'myth' had come true right before the System's eyes, and rather than training me and harnessing my power for themselves, they cast me aside and gave me plenty of reasons to hate them.

Fools. They handed a weapon to the enemy.

* * *

So, this was the Diving Academy. Hours of classes each day. Immunization clinics for every disease imaginable. Intensive training and endless exercise in sub-zero temperatures. For the first time since my deportation, I faced true mental and physical challenges and met people as intelligent as myself. Even with my eidetic memory and lighting-quick analytical skills, I faced trials I—almost—couldn't handle.

My size made things interesting, to say the least. On the plus side, it made me comparatively light and speedy. I could be easily lifted and handled by my comrades as we practiced underwater maneuvers and formations. I could slip into tight spaces and hide where others couldn't. But, there were also several drawbacks to being tiny. There were many tasks a big, strong man could complete with half the effort. There were places I couldn't reach, equipment I couldn't carry, and people I couldn't support in formation. My physical littleness—not to mention the fact that I was the *only female*—also didn't encourage others to respect or trust me. It impacted the degree to which people were willing to listen to me. Day after day, I found it difficult to be taken seriously.

I wondered how Cease Lechatelierite did it. Being smaller and younger than his comrades didn't seem to undermine his authority or success. I couldn't wait to see him in action and learn his secret.

CEASE LECHATELIERITE

May twenty-fourth of the ninety-third age.

Nine months had passed since that battle. Nine months of surgery, physical therapy and optometry. Nine months in a wheelchair or on crutches, hooked to IVs, watching the world through a visual reparation band. Nine months unable to dive in the sea with my men. I'd failed myself, my fleet, my nation, and most of all, my friend.

The Trilateral Committee was trying its best to hush it all up. That battle was a black mark on my otherwise spotless record. Aside from the TC, only a few of my unit leaders and the Nurian and Ichthyothian heads of state knew all the gory details about my injuries. Everyone else believed I was now away on some top-secret mission.

Physical therapy. Some mission.

Today, however, I was leaving Icicle's hospital wing to head to the northwestern shore of Nuria, where I'd evaluate the recruits and select the best for my fleet. They would complete a series of challenges in the North Septentrion Sea while I watched from a vitreous silica. Then, tomorrow morning, I would meet my chosen face-to-face and bring them back to Icicle.

* * *

Strapping on my visual band, I could see a line of two-hundred men treading water, awaiting my arrival. Each wore a numbered vest atop their diving suits which relayed to me some vitals and stats, like heartrate, pulse and blood pressure. I took notes as they performed underwater maneuvers, target practices, multi-man formations and shuttle-pilotry.

Number six was strong. He could handle large pieces of equipment and support entire chains of men. But, he was awkward and incapable of subtlety. His big, blundering limbs made strong waves and big splashes. He wouldn't be good for any clandestine tasks.

Number one-ninety-four was a skilled marksman. He shot every target in his path. But, he finished all allotted tasks outside the time limit. The ability to perform quickly under pressure was crucial in battle.

Number thirty-two had decent diving technique but poor judgment. When given the opportunity to make a critical strike *here* or a life-saving swerve *there*, he often missed it. He wouldn't be considered for the fleet.

Number eighty-six had the quirkiest flying style I'd ever seen. His flight-path was about as predictable as a horsefly. I recognized his particular brand of dizzying loops, sharp turns and lightning-quick spirals from a video I saw eight months ago—this must've been the same man. Last September, his branch-placement tests caused quite a stir; the examiners couldn't decide whether to send him to the Diving Academy or the Air Force Academy. His remarkable pilotry would've immediately landed him in the Air Force… if only he didn't do so well on the swimming tests, too. His swimming scores made the cutoff, to be a diver. So, the examiners brought the matter to the administrators of the two academies, who bickered until the dispute escalated all the way up to Air Force Commander Rai Zephyr and me. I looked at his scores and watched a few of his videos and said something along the lines of: 'well, if the man can dive, let him; I need good pilots, too, after all.' And, that was that.

There was one soldier whose skill quickly caught my attention: number eighty-seven. Ironically, the first thing I noticed about him was that he wasn't easily noticed. He was far smaller than the others, so it seemed like he needed to swim two strokes for every one stroke of his comrades… but, that didn't slow him down. On the contrary: he completed the same tasks as everyone else, in a fraction of the time. He was light, speedy, precise, subtle in maneuver and incredibly graceful. He didn't swim, he danced in the water. I marked him as a strong candidate, perhaps even for an officer position.

After four hours of observation and three hours of private contemplation, I'd chosen my seventy divers. The other one-hundred-thirty would return to the Nurian Academy for additional training, until they were drafted as needed.

I gave my list to Colonel Austere. Tomorrow morning, they'd line up in the gym of the vitreous silica at seven o'clock to meet their new commander.

SCARLET JULY

We emerged from the lengthy test, exhausted and nerve-wracked. Commander Cease Lechatelierite *himself* watched and scrutinized our every move from behind the windshield of a nearby vitreous silica. He would spend the night on the ship, deciding who he wanted in his fleet.

We were also aboard the manta ray—what we called the VS, since did indeed look like one—for the night. Those whom the Commander rejected would head back to the Nurian Academy, tomorrow morning. The rest of us would travel with Lechatelierite to Icicle Base, located in Aventurine City on the southern shore of Ichthyosis, where we'd train for three more months before entering the war.

To use a funny Nurian expression, I was a 'hot mess,' right now. We all were. We laughed and talked to pass the suspenseful evening, congratulating each other on surviving the practical final. My comrades bantered along with me. It took every day of the last seven months to win their respect, but I finally had it—I think. I earned it though excellence. As time went on and I proved myself, it got harder and harder for them to ignore me just because I was small and female. Shunning an asset like me would be stupid. And, you didn't get this far if you were stupid. Of the two-hundred-eighty-seven who entered the academy, only two-hundred made it to testing. Eighty dropped out. Seven got seriously injured.

But, even now, as my comrades sat with me, I could tell from the way they stiffened ever-so-slightly when they touched my hand or patted me on the back that they were still somewhat resentful an eighty-pound girl could give them a run for their money. The only person who consistently treated me with complete kindness since day one was Nurtic.

In the barracks, Nurtic slept in the bunk above me. At night, when insomnia liked to visit me, Nurtic never missed an opportunity to try to strike up conversation. He was really attentive to me. He knew I enjoyed drawing, and actually remembered an offhand comment I made one night about how I missed using real wood-and-graphite pencils—all we had in the military were mechanicals and ballpoint pens, which weren't great for shading. And, then, a couple days later, without explanation, Nurtic conjured up a real pencil. Number two, HB. Exactly the kind I said I liked. He gave it to me with a mysterious, dimpled smile.

Nurtic was a good kid, but also a bit of a troublemaker. The academy had a strict rule against keeping non-military-issue personal possessions, but somehow—and he adamantly refused to tell me how—he managed to bring his viola with him, from Alcove City. No joke. He kept the case stowed at the back of his locker and occasionally played for us in the barracks, after hours, away from our superiors' eyes and ears. Aside from the obnoxious trumpet-blare each morning, followed by the monotonous Ichthyothian national anthem on trumpet and drums, the military world was devoid of music or art. So, everyone, even those who never cared for classical music before, appreciated Nurtic's serenades.

And, now, here we all sat, the two-hundred diver-wannabees who went through hell the last seven months just for the chance to serve in Lechatelierite's elite fleet, awaiting the moment of truth, coming in the morning. The evening passed slowly, full of mindless chatter and anxious whining.

"I need to make it in, I must," Arrhyth Link breathed in a melodramatic tone, twisting a curl from the abundant, swirly mop on his head. "I can't go back to Alcove City. Dad'll send me off to Oriya for an Order internship with my geek cousin, Kaew. I hate politics. I'm not like Kaew, or my sister, Linkeree. For goodness' sakes, Ree writes poli-sci research papers for *fun*; she's sixteen and already has stuff published in research journals! Ugh. I was born to the wrong family. I prefer to shoot things and blow stuff up."

"If you don't make it in the fleet, you won't be sent home," Dither Maine reminded him, looking a little annoyed. "Ichthyosis didn't just give you an exorbitantly-expensive, top-notch military education just to ship you back to Alcove City. If the Commander doesn't pick you tomorrow, you'll just have to stay at the academy longer. Then, eventually, you'll be drafted into the fleet, anyway, to take the place of someone who got killed."

"Uh, thanks, man," Arrhyth said, face slightly greenish. "Was that supposed to make me feel better?"

Dither snorted. "Seriously, who complains about having such a prestigious fallback, anyway? People kill for Order internships. I think isolationism is stupid, of course, but I'm not gonna feel sorry for someone whose backup plan pays better than most people's far-fetched dreams."

I listened to their conversation, curiosity piqued. The Nurro-Ichthyothian Alliance, by definition, was anti-isolationist, so the military obviously attracted those who disagreed with the philosophy of political isolationism. In my seven months serving alongside Arrhyth, I never got the chance to hear his story—the story of how the son of the Second Earth Order Chairman came to participate in an international conspiracy that'd get Nuria blacklisted, if the Order ever found out. Back in October, Nurtic reassured me Mr. Arnold Link was 'totally cool' with his son's military service and wouldn't tattle on Nuria to the Order. I couldn't understand how that was possible, but apparently it was true: eight months passed since the forging of the alliance and the Order was still ignorant—Nuria's membership was intact.

Well, if I was ever going to find out what the deal was with the Link family, it was now or never; it was possible Arrhyth and I would be separated starting tomorrow, if only one of us got chosen for the fleet. This conversation here was the perfect opportunity to get nosy—Arrhyth usually tended not to talk about his father's line of work, as no one here was really a fan of it.

"So, I'm guessing your dad wasn't too thrilled with your career choice?" I asked Arrhyth, delicately.

He shrugged. "Well, he always pushed Linkeree and me toward politics. But, he didn't object when I said I wanted to be a diver and Ree said she wanted to be a missionary."

I felt my eyebrows creep up to my hairline. A soldier and a missionary? That was as un-isolationistic as it got. Talk about rebellious children.

"He 'didn't object,' Arrhyth?" I found myself saying. "Seriously? I can't imagine the leader of the isolationist world approving his daughter's country-hopping, much less his son's participation in an anti-isolationist, international scandal."

Arrhyth gave me a sideways smile. "Who said he's an isolationist?"

I froze, staring. Arrhyth then promptly turned away and joined a nearby group conversation about a science-fiction, time-traveling television series I never saw.

My hair twitched on my shoulder. The Chairman of the Order, not an isolationist? How was that possible? All along, I thought self-preservation was the reason Mr. Arnold Link wasn't tattling to the Order about Nuria's involvement in the war: he and his wife and children all lived in Alcove City, so it made sense he wouldn't want Nuria to get blacklisted because that'd jeopardize the wellbeing of his family and country of residence. But, I still assumed Mr. Link was an isolationist. An isolationist who'd want to lock up his son for expressing an interest in the illegal war.

Lock up. Oh, Tincture. I left my helmet on the floor in front of my locker instead of putting it away, after the practical exam.

I got up and left the barracks, wandering the dark corridors of the unfamiliar ship in search of the locker-room. I wondered how I'd managed to walk from there to the barracks after the test without watching where I was going. Apparently, I followed the herd mindlessly, distracted by nerves and fatigue. Eidetic memory was no use if I didn't actually pay attention to what needed to be remembered in the first place.

I soon discovered most doors were locked at this late hour. So, I had to use my hair-magic—wrapping ringlets around knobs—to open them up. I tried the one to my left. It was a janitors' closet. The next led to the water-heating system. I hooked a right down the hall and tried the first door there.

And, when I pushed it open, my heart stopped.

There sat Cease Lechatelierite on his bed, laptop on his knees. He was wearing only his boxers, so I could see way too much of his thin, deathly-pale, horribly-twisted body. He had IVs in his right arm, a brace around his neck and a shiny strip bound across his eyes.

Lechatelierite quickly drew a sheet over his body, snatched the visual band from his face and glared at me with his dangerous, silvery eyes. His injuries were no surprise to me. But, he didn't know that.

Flinching, I stepped back. "S-sir, I'm s-so sorry—"

He slammed a fist against his nightstand and said in a low, threatening tone, "Breathe *one word* about this and you'll *never* see the outside of this ship again. Got it, Nurian?" He spoke Nurian with a heavy Ichthyothian accent. Nevertheless, his throat-mage-like tone struck me to the root of my being. I wished I could evaporate on the spot.

"O-of c-course, sir—"

"Never!" His voice sliced through the frozen air.

If Cease Lechatelierite were an eye mage, I'd be dead ten times over. He obviously didn't remove his band to see me better; he took it off to intimidate me with those iron eyes. I could tell from his dilated pupils that his sight was unfocused. But, tomorrow morning, he'd still obviously figure out the only girl in the lineup was the intruder.

"Return to your bunk, *now*, soldier!" he barked.

"Yes, sir!"

I shut the door and practically flew down the hall, forgetting all about my helmet. I wasn't going to need it anyway; my hopes of being picked for the Diving Fleet were dashed. Cease Lechatelierite would never be able to trust me, now.

CEASE LECHATELIERITE

May twenty-fifth, six-fifty-five.

"Commander, they're ready for you," Colonel Austere's voice came on the intercom in my quarters.

"Thank you, sir."

Last night, the Trilateral Committee sent me a rather curtly-worded email reminding me that my new soldiers weren't allowed to see my wheelchair, crutches, IVs or visual band. I had to be free of all physical aides whenever I appeared before my men. So, this morning, I dressed in layers, removed the band and the needles, and stood on unsteady feet. I could walk now, but not like a battle-ready soldier. Nurse Raef told me Dr. Calibre believed I'd make a full recovery by July. It was hard to believe.

That meant I had to train the Nurians without actually joining them in the water for over a month. I would act like a station-commander, giving orders via intercom, while my veterans worked with them in the sea. The academy told everyone this was a special, hands-off training method designed to cultivate their courage and independence. Right. Sure.

As I stretched my aching limbs, I wondered if all this effort to conceal my injuries was futile; one of the Nurians barged in on me while I was undressed in my quarters, last night.

I entered the gymnasium, where all two-hundred rookies were in full diving-suit and helmet, lined up according to number, standing at attention with their arms at their sides. I marched down the line, hands clasped behind my back. It took a lot of effort just to place one foot in front of the other without wobbling.

"Tomorrow morning, one-hundred-thirty of you will be on your way back to the academy," I said in Nurian. Even I could hear how heavy my accent was. It stuck around no matter how much I practiced this stupid language. "And, seventy of you will come with me to Icicle. But, making it into the fleet isn't your end goal. Beating the Conflagrians, defending the alliance from imperialism—*those* are your real objectives. For those whom I've selected, I have a warning for you: what you've faced in the last seven months is nothing. If you think you've seen a challenge yet, you're sorely mistaken. I'm going to push you beyond the limits of your imagination. Because the Conflagrians sure as hell will.

"Once you're part of my fleet, the concept of the self is dead. It's not about you, or your rank, or your personal problems. Drop your baggage at the front door, divers. It's all about *them*, the Conflagrians. It's about what you can do to further *us*, the Nurro-Ichthyothian Diving Fleet. In my fleet, we always keep our eyes on the bigger picture. So, if you don't think you're up to it, you're commanded to leave the room, now." I stopped pacing at the center of the line, and no one dared to breathe. "If I call your number, please step forward, remaining at attention."

I proceeded to recite seventy numbers. Each soldier I called took one, crisp step in my direction, showing neither excitement nor relief. As the list wore on, those who believed they wouldn't get picked began to slump with disappointment. Which was proof enough they didn't have what it took to serve in my fleet. My veterans could stand at attention through a snowstorm without so much as a shuffle, if so instructed. Once the list was complete, I dismissed the rejects to the barracks. Then, my chosen men moved closer together, forming a shorter line.

"Remove your helmets," I said. "I want to look at the faces of my new comrades-in-arms."

Seventy helmets swept off seventy heads in perfect unison.

"Congratulations," I said firmly, walking up the line. "Welcome to the Diving Fleet, Nurians. You've proven yourselves worthy of the pain ahead of you." I met each man's eye, in turn. "You'll need to have each other's complete trust and respect. I guarantee, your life will be in the hands of someone standing here at one time or another, in the months and ages to come. Judging from your performances, I trust this won't be a problem." With that, I could already feel their allegiance and motivation stirring.

The last soldier in line was the small one, number eighty-seven.

He was a she. The first female diver in Ichthyothian military history. I looked at the girl's delicate features, wild hair, blotchy skin and shocking eyes. She looked not a day older than fifteen. I recognized her as the one who walked into my quarters, last night—though all I could see at the time was a red and white blur. But, that wasn't why I was staring. There was something else about her that set off alarms in my mind.

"Name, soldier?"

I was small, but she was smaller; I could tower over her. She stared unblinkingly back, though I could tell she was afraid.

"Scarlet July, sir."

That's when it clicked.

"You're one of them," I whispered, face inches from hers. In a flash, I had my weapon drawn and pressed against her red neck. Her laser-green eyes went wide. The tension in the air was thick.

I'd fought and killed too many mages in my lifetime not to be able to recognize one when it stared me in the face. I could see her unnaturally bright features. I could see her small muscles that wouldn't be able to stand military life without magical fortification. Oh yes, she hid her aura well, but her concealment wasn't absolute; I could feel a radical photon or two hover in the air around her. My doctors and comrades believed I had a sensitivity to the spectral web that was unusual for a Nordic. I didn't understand why or how that was possible, but at times like these, I was glad for it.

"You may've tricked the others," I spat, "but you're a fool if you thought you could get past *me*."

The Nurians began to break discipline a little now, staring and gaping. Their confused faces told me they didn't see what I saw; Scarlet July looked like a normal girl to them. That didn't exactly surprise me. None of them had ever seen a mage before her. They didn't know what to look for. Sensing a concealed aura wasn't really something that could be learned in a classroom.

I was in no condition to fight with anyone, but I didn't have to. I had seventy trained soldiers with me in the room.

"Number seven, number twenty-five," I called at random, "take her to the diffusion cell, now."

In a flash, two of the men who'd been her trusting comrades-in-arms for the greater part of the age had her restrained with deadline and out the door. She didn't use her magic against them or even say a word. She let them take her.

She'd managed to dupe the recruiters, her comrades and all her teachers. If she was clever enough to trick Colonel Austere for seven months, she could very possibly dupe anyone who interrogated her. Except me.

I dismissed everyone and returned to my quarters. After strapping on my visual band, sitting down in my wheelchair and re-attaching my IVs, I began to make my way to Scarlet July's cell.

I was halfway down the hall when a white glove reached out and caught a handlebar.

"And, where do you think you're going, looking like *that?*" came the voice of the Colonel.

I sighed through gritted teeth. I may've been the Leader of the Ichthyothian Resistance, but I supposed, in Austere's eyes, I'd always be one of his little students.

"I have a prisoner in a diffusion cell," I answered, coolly. "I think one of the Nurian recruits may be a spy."

Austere raised an eyebrow. "And, you're facing him like this?"

I just told him we'd been infiltrated, and *that* what he was concerned about? This could very well be the biggest security leak in Ichthyothian military history.

"I'd see her face much better with the band on." Analyzing facial expressions—especially subtle eye movements—was critical in determining truthfulness.

Austere paused for a moment. "Her," he breathed, suddenly stricken. "Not July?"

"Were there any other women in your class?" I retorted.

"But… she's the best student I've ever seen. After you, of course. Could answer any question. Remembered everything. Top scores on all assignments and exams."

"She's a mage," I spat. "And, after I extract all possible intel from her, I'm going to kill her."

Austere, blue eyes wide, only nodded.

I rolled away.

"Commander!"

I halted. "Yes, sir?" I spoke through tight lips.

"You can keep your band on, but at least forgo the bags."

I concentrated much better when hooked to the IV pain medications. I couldn't afford to let anything detract from my focus, when interrogating the mage. There was a lot at stake here. I needed to be on my A-game. Besides…

"Sir, she already knows," I said, quietly.

There was a tense pause. "Excuse me?"

"She already knows about my… condition."

"Do you mean to say she has some sort of mind-reading magic?"

It was my turn to get impatient; he was wasting time.

"No, she walked in on me while I was in my quarters, last night."

"You didn't lock your door?"

"I did."

More silence.

"Exactly. I don't know what her source is or what her powers are, but I assure you, I will find out, and exactly how she's used them against us," I said.

Austere began another question, but I cut him off. "I'm sorry, sir, but I have an urgent duty to attend. Dismissed."

The Colonel looked slapped. I'd never dismissed him like that before. He saluted stiffly and disappeared down the hall.

Scarlet July was bound, hand and foot, in a diffusion cell. Diffusion cells scrambled the electromagnetic frequencies of anyone inside, essentially rendering mages magicless. It was cutting-edge spectroscopy.

When I walked in, I saw no sign of a struggle. Scarlet July didn't even glare back at me in hatred like so many of the POWs I'd dealt with before her. She kept her enormous green eyes on the table between us, face resigned.

So, this fire-savage was an actress.

"Scarlet July," I snapped. She still didn't lift her gaze.

I'd brought her enlistment forms, and her test results from both her branch placement last fall and her written finals from this past week. Of the two-hundred candidates, I was most impressed with number eighty-seven's performance in the sea yesterday and wasn't too surprised to discover that the class's top, written-exam scores belonged to the same individual. It'd been a long time since I'd gotten this excited about a subordinate. I was eager to meet this soldier face-to-face. I couldn't wait to see what I could do with 'him.'

I never imagined our first meeting would be like this.

I pulled out 'General Information 71D' and placed it on the table before Scarlet.

"This says you were born in Alcove City," I said in Nurian, studying her face. "Is this true?"

"No, sir," she responded, in Ichthyothian.

POWs tended to call me a variety of names during an interrogation, but 'sir' usually wasn't one of them. She was showing respect, as though I were still her commander. And, she was speaking Ichthyothian. She could tell from my accent I had difficulty with Nurian, so she was… trying to make it easier for me to question her…?

"Are you from the South Conflagrablaze Captive?" I barked in Nurian, refusing to submit to her lingual shift. Switching would be an admission I needed her help.

She hesitated.

"Yes or no?"

"Yes, sir, I was born in Conflagria," she worded carefully, still in Ichthyothian.

"You lied on your enlistment forms," I pressed.

"Yes, sir."

She was offering no resistance. This was too easy.

"You lied on your enlistment forms with the goal of infiltrating the Nurro-Ichthyothian Diving Fleet to convey intel to the System."

"No, sir!" she burst—in Nurian this time—as her face grew even redder. Her eyes shifted frantically across the table.

"Are you in contact with any other mages?"

"No, sir! I'm not a spy, Commander Lechatelierite. I'm not passing information to the enemy!" she piped, switching back to Ichthyothian.

She called Conflagria 'the enemy.' Interesting.

"Respond to me in Nurian. We aren't playing language games," I ordered, coldly. "Why are you here?"

"The same reason you are, sir. I want to fight the System." She still wouldn't look at me. "I have no loyalty to my homeland. None, whatsoever, to anybody there. I swear."

I detached my IVs, emerged from my chair, removed my band and leaned over the table. I gripped her chin and tilted her head up, so her gaze would meet mine. Her jaw trembled in my hand. I fixed my eyes on hers for quite some time. She didn't blink once. It was the longest I'd touched the bare skin of a mage without killing or destroying. I searched and searched, but couldn't find a trace of malice in her large, glassy stare.

"Did you use magic at the academy?"

"Yes, sir," she said, quietly. "But, never to hurt anyone, and never in a way that could benefit the System. I used it to help me study and perform. I have no special gift of communication or anything that'd allow me to contact anyone in Conflagria."

"What is your source?"

"My hair," she said, which didn't surprise me, considering how thick and wiry it looked, "and my eyes."

I froze. Was it possible the Multi-Source Enchant was sitting before me? Moreover, she wanted to offer her talents to my nation? Did the most powerful mage in history actually turn against her own people and hand herself to me? No. That'd be too good to be true.

The general Conflagrian population wasn't aware of the war. Only the System and their military knew.

"How did you find out about the war?"

"I was deported to Nuria when I was ten. I lived there five ages before coming to the academy. I learned about the war last fall, like everyone else." Her face burned; I could feel the heat on my fingertips.

There was something really fishy about that story. "You were deported?"

"Yes, sir, because of my eyes. The System didn't know how to train me. The shortages came, and I was declared Useless—a waste of island resources."

How very nice of her to define what a 'Useless' was, as if I wouldn't already know. Moreover, the System didn't deport Uselesses when times got rough. They killed them.

Scarlet answered my unvoiced question: "They tried to execute me, but couldn't. I was the first one they couldn't kill when they wanted to. So, they murdered my family and shipped me off to Nuria." Her voice quivered.

It all became clear.

"The military is no place to seek revenge," I said, pitch low. I released her chin. "*My* fleet will not be used for your personal vendettas."

"That's not my intention, sir."

"Then, what *is* your intention?" I growled.

"I came here because I want to fight the System. The System, not Conflagria. They're separate entities, sir. The Conflagrians are innocent; the System isn't. My goal isn't merely revenge, but to destroy the oppressors of my homeland to liberate my people. I didn't think any of the other officers would understand, but I was hoping… I was hoping…"

"You were hoping I'd be the one to understand," I finished, quietly.

She nodded.

I thought back to the emotional turmoil I suffered when I was six, when I first leaned about Conflagria's dictatorship. I'd long since been aware of the distinction between the System and its constituency. I already saw what Scarlet wanted me to see. And, as she predicted, no one else in the Nurro-Ichthyothian military world really did. Even

Colonel Austere shut me down when I tried to talk to him about it, eleven ages ago. Scarlet was right to try to seek me out.

"You were the one I wanted to reveal my magehood to, sir," she continued. "Ever since I learned about you, Commander Lechatelierite, I knew I had to find you, talk to you. That's why I wanted to be a diver. So, I could be a part of your fleet, not the Air Force or the Ground Troops. Because I believed that, of anyone in your military, you could be trusted with this information and you'd know how to use me best. I wanted to come to you with the truth as soon as was feasible. But, then, *this* happened before I had the chance."

There was a pause. I didn't speak.

"Sir," Scarlet breathed, "my magic could be a great asset to you. I know things about the spectrum and about Conflagrian society that could benefit the alliance. I'm the only chance you've got, to fight fire with fire."

I turned away, unwilling to meet her earnest eyes any longer. I simply didn't know what to do. She seemed sincere and full of good intentions, but I couldn't help but still feel uneasy about her. She very emphatically declared her allegiance not only to Ichthyosis but to me in particular, yet she still called the Conflagrians 'my people.' I knew, no matter what, she'd never be one of us. The Nurians were our brothers, but magicfolk might as well be a different species, altogether. In the end, she'd always be a person of the fire and we'd always be people of the ice.

"I'm sorry, Scarlet, but I don't think we can trust you," I said, back still turned.

"Is it your fleet who can't trust me, or just you?" she growled. "Because I've seen the legendary Commander Cease Lechatelierite crippled and half-blind?"

I was definitely taken aback. She just told me, moments ago, how she wanted to be a diver just so she could work with me—how she believed, out of anyone in the alliance, I'd be the one to listen to her, understand where she was coming from, and make optimal use of her talents—and, now, she was turning around and attacking me personally.

"If I were afraid of revealing my weaknesses to you, would I've come in here like *this*?"

I threw my visual reparation band at her face. It hit her cheek, leaving a bloody scar—a scar she could've healed instantly with hair magic, if we weren't in a diffusion cell. I leaned over the table so our faces were an inch apart.

"This war isn't about you or me," I said, voice barely above a whisper. "And, if you can't see that, you don't belong in my fleet, after all."

"Sir, I promise I belong in your fleet more than anywhere else on Second Earth," she responded after a long, heavy pause. "And, I can be a great source of inside information for the Nurro-Ichthyothian Alliance… if you don't stop me, Lechatelierite."

"That's *Commander* Lechatelierite to you, soldier."

SCARLET JULY

For the rest of the day and well into the night, I stayed bound to the cold, metal chair, harassed by several, obnoxious interrogators from the Ichthyothian Intelligence Agency. After Lechatelierite, everyone else seemed lame. One particularly amusing way they attempted to intimidate me was by placing a bright light above my head. How did they expect to frighten a Conflagrian like that? Ichthyothians were the ones who couldn't stand a little heat and light. Their idea of a scalding day would be forty-five degrees and only partly cloudy.

None of their silly tactics could rattle me. The only thing that left me shaking in my shackles was Lechatelierite's silver-grey stare. His eyes were like crystals. Clear. Faceted. Sharp. And, he had the jawline to match. His face was severe—when he looked at me, it took all my courage not to flinch or turn away. During the interrogation, I couldn't even bring myself to meet his eye on my own accord; he had to force me to. Even in his crippled state, his every movement seemed to convey his power and authority. As did his voice. His voice was like a scalpel. Cutting. Compelling. Convicting. Even when he spoke his accented Nurian. His tone could capture, control. Hypnotize, almost. Like a throat mage. Like a throat mage who'd trained diligently at the System Mage Castle for ages.

And, yet, as intimidating as he was, there was something about him that made me volunteer a sliver of something I'd kept under lock and key for nearly six ages, now—the story of July twenty-fifth. I thought I'd take that story to the grave, but Lechatelierite drew it from me by doing nothing but simply being himself.

When I showed up at breakfast this morning, no one questioned me. I assumed that was on Lechatelierite's orders. I figured there was no way he'd let it spill I was a 'trustworthy mage'—that'd be far too large a pill for anyone here to swallow. I figured he told them his accusation was incorrect and I was Nurian, after all. With his reputation, it'd take a lot to admit to being wrong about anything. But, he took the bullet for my sake. He lied to prevent my comrades from rejecting me. The Nurian Academy instilled such a strong hatred of all things magical in the minds of its students, Lechatelierite didn't want to risk the coherence of his fleet by revealing the truth. The Nurians surely weren't capable of recognizing a mage on their own, so it made sense they'd accept I was Nurian simply because Lechatelierite said so. Whatever he said, went. That was the way things worked around here.

Though, I could already tell Lechatelierite wasn't an oppressive leader. He had control, but he wasn't like the System. The System made the magical masses believe they couldn't survive without herding. The System governed by instilling fear and a sense of one's own weakness and helplessness. Lechatelierite's command, on the other hand, was one born of trust and respect. He made you believe you were needed. That you were capable. That you couldn't dare but give anything less than one-hundred-percent because that's simply what it took to achieve collective success. He made you want to be excellent. He made you hunger for his approval. I never wanted to let him down.

I could also tell that, while Lechatelierite strove to put out an impression of perfect confidence and self-control, deep down, he actually struggled with both. I caught a glimpse behind the mask of the 'perfect commander' during my interrogation; when I accused him of distrusting me because I'd seen him in his all his crippled splendor, he threw his visual band at me with more force than an arm mage could toss a taro. It was like he couldn't stand the possibility of anyone, even his potential enemy, thinking anything but the best about him. He cared too much for image and reputation. This wasn't necessarily his fault—after losing that battle last age, he probably toiled daily under the pressure of having to redeem his name. He had big boots to fill. His own.

***

The manta ray finished its trek across the Briny Ocean and the Septentrion Sea by mid-day on the twenty-sixth of May. At sixteen o'clock, the vitreous silica rose to the surface of the frigid water and emitted the seventy new divers of Commander Cease Lechatelierite's fleet onto the southern shore of Aventurine City, Ichthyosis.

I emerged from the ship and stood on the icy land where no Conflagrian could possibly belong. Although I learned all about Ichthyosis at the academy, nothing could've really prepared me for the sight

I beheld now. The white sky seemed to melt into the unblemished, white land, making the horizon difficult to discern, even to my eyes. I found Ichthyosis's blaring monochrome disorienting. Even the buildings around here were either white or a pale silver that reminded me of the Commander's eyes.

Wind howled in our ears and blew snow into our faces. After mere minutes of standing outside, we were soaked. We weren't wearing diving suits, just our regular uniforms, so it took a lot of discipline—and spectrum—not to shiver openly. I could hardly stand the way the cold fabric clung to my skin. I was wearing both my mage robes overtop my uniform, cloaked by eye-magic. Just as I did at the academy, I was planning on storing them in the back of my locker on base, winding a strand of my impenetrable, magical hair around the handlebar.

Lechatelierite exited the ship after us, satisfaction in his eyes. "Nice day," he commented. I stared. "Light snowfall was originally predicted for this afternoon—only about two or three feet—but, lucky for all of you, the latest reports now state it's just going to keep flurrying like this, instead."

Light snowfall of *only* about two or three feet? I peered at the buildings nearby and realized what initially looked to me like the top story was really snow accumulation. Most of my comrades originated from Nuria's northern regions; they looked slightly less disconcerted by their surroundings than the handful of us from the central and southern regions—Nurtiç Leavesleft, Arrhyth Link, Dither Maine, Apha Edenta and I. (It made sense that northern Nurians were more likely to become divers, considering the frigid underwater obstacle course we were given last September. I imagine *that* test weeded out a lot of candidates, particularly southerners). Lechatelierite was the only one who looked completely at ease. He was on the ice, in his element.

The Nurians and I watched in silent awe as a band of white suits emerged from the invisible horizon in perfect unison, motions as fluid as mercury.

Lechatelierite addressed them in Ichthyothian: "Veterans, these are your new comrades-in-arms, from Nuria." He turned to us, gestured to his fantastic fleet, and spoke in his accented Nurian, "Nurians, meet the veterans."

The Ichthyothians stood before us with their shoulders and backs straight. They wore the same uniforms as us, but cobalt blue or silver bands, which I assumed represented rank, streaked a few of their arms. Lechatelierite himself had three blue bands on each arm.

Standing in front of these men, I felt rather second-rate, clumsy and weak. The Nurians beside me undoubtedly shared my thoughts. We thought we were so strong and powerful. We were proud to be Lechatelierite's chosen. What a joke. These divers before us were his *real* fleet. We were just an afterthought. Especially me. How could a sub-five-foot, eighty-pound, Conflagrian mage ever expect to become one of these ice-faring, fluid-moving, steel-boned soldiers?

"For the next three months, all of you will train together," Lechatelierite said, voice all the more convicting and captivating in his native tongue. "There'll be less time in the pools or with anchored articles, Nurians. I want you to learn to navigate the sea, making optimal use of the natural terrain. Let the veterans be your examples. I won't join you in the water until July. Until then, I'll watch and provide instruction from a vitreous silica. I'm doing this because it's important for each of you learn to think for yourself and, should the need arise, take charge. We're only as strong as our weakest link, and the weakest link in *my* fleet is expected to know how to lead beautifully under pressure. Let this be a challenge to all of you."

Oh Tincture, was he lying. Sure, it was a good idea to rotate command during training so the fleet wouldn't go under if Lechatelierite got killed or captured during a real battle. But, I knew the *real* reason for his absence and it had nothing to do with preparing us for the worst.

"You must learn to trust each other and function seamlessly, like a single organism with many limbs," he continued. "From this moment on, there's no such thing as Nurians or Ichthyothians. We're united by a single cause: to eliminate the Conflagrian threat to the northwestern hemisphere." He stood in the center, crystal eyes sweeping over us. "All one-hundred-ten of you, we're the one, the Nurro-Ichthyothian Diving Fleet."

At that moment, I realized what it meant for there to only be forty Ichthyothians here. There were supposed to be seventy. I felt as though I'd swallowed a large chunk of ice. Lechatelierite's lost battle cost him thirty divers? I stared at him in horrified amazement. He had thirty lives, fresh on his conscious. At seventeen ages old.

***

Lechatelierite ordered us to change into our diving suits and flippers. He had us Nurians strap on our numbered vests overtop our suits. I looked down at the large, blue '87' on my chest and felt a prickle of nervous fear. I assumed the vests weren't only for visual identification, but digital tracking as well. Who knew what sort of information Lechatelierite got from them. Ichthyothian technology never ceased to surprise me.

For today's practice, I was placed in a temporary unit of fifteen soldiers—ten Nurians and five Ichthyothians. The one in charge of our group was a burly guy named Amok Kempt, Lechatelierite's second-in-command. As we set off and Amok began rattling off instructions, I could immediately tell why Lechatelierite prized him. He was clever in a sort of malicious way. He came up with unusual answers to usual problems and had plenty of wild tricks up his sleeve.

He was also really obnoxious. At least three times during his dispatch orders, he managed to throw in what apparently was his tagline, 'A soldier is never unprepared!' followed by a handful of obscene Ichthyothian words the academy obviously never taught us.

And, when he first laid eyes on me, he laughed openly. "A little girl, just what the fleet needs! Come to use those big, bad muscles of yours to scare the fire-savages, Miss Bloodclot?"

My eyes grew hot, and not just because he called my people by that derogatory name. It was stupidest thing a leader could do—break group unity by putting down the one who could very well be the most brilliant. The Nurians knew and respected me well enough, by now. They knew what I was capable of and could mostly see past my size and gender. But, we were still making our first impressions on the veterans. How could the vets ever learn to trust me with their lives in battle if I was immediately made into a mascot? Was Lechatelierite unaware of his second's attitude? Maybe. Lechatelierite had been out-of-commission for the majority of an age, after all.

My unit was now surface-riding on the outside of crystalline shuttle three, piloted by Amok.

"Unit one, you're too nose-heavy," Lechatelierite's voice sounded in our helmets. He watched us from the vitreous silica above. "I need at least four of you to move toward the tail."

Unsure and afraid, no one budged.

"Come on, you heard the despot," Amok growled privately to our unit. "Move it!"

Despot. So, Amok despised Lechatelierite. I wouldn't dare speak so disrespectfully of my commander, especially one so excellent. Especially if I were his second. What did Amok gain from doing that? All it did was create divisiveness. With a single word, he relayed to every new recruit there was an instability in the chain-of-command. A power struggle, perhaps.

As I moved from rung to rung, heading toward the tail, it was hard not to be at least a little afraid of falling off. Which, of course, made me think about last summer's vision of the poor surface-rider whose crystalline, though underwater, got swallowed by fire. He was probably one of the thirty Lechatelierite lost. I saw through that man's eyes and experienced his terror. I remembered exactly how it felt to twist into the tide, colliding with shuttle debris—

No, the vision didn't continue that long. I woke up right after letting go of the rungs. But, alas, now, I couldn't stop the series of new images from cascading through my mind. Flames scorching a white suit. A scrap of crystalline, hurtling at hundreds of miles per hour, crashing into a helmet. Unbearable water pressure. Guilt, horrible guilt, for leaving the fleet behind and for failing Ichthyosis. And, the pale, anguished face of—

Lechatelierite! The truth hit me as forcefully as the swing of a hobnail-dragon's tail. *That* was how he got injured! Hyperventilating now, my hands grew prickly, which made holding on even harder than it already was.

But, how could I have a vision of Lechatelierite—or any infrared Nordic, for that matter—in the first place? We mages could only envision those we're spectrally twined to. How could my wavelength twine to someone who didn't even have a colored thread in the spectral web, at all? And, even if Lechatelierite did have one, why would my wavelength attach to it? I knew all *about* him, but it's not like we had much of a personal relationship. Our few face-to-face encounters—when I burst into his quarters after the practical final and when he accused me at gunpoint of being a spy then interrogated me in a diffusion cell—weren't exactly the bonding kind.

"Jump in forty-five seconds!" Amok's voice rang in my helmet, snapping me from my thoughts. It was hard not to keep thinking about Lechatelierite. I gnawed my mouthpiece. I couldn't afford to be distracted at a time like this.

"Five seconds after I start the barrel-roll, kick off," Amok instructed. "Keep your body erect and your arms up, behind your head. Ten seconds after launching, either shuttle one, two, four, or five will pass in front of you. Grab hold where you can. Ready? Go!"

I strung my body out and pushed off the hull. Sure enough, in exactly ten seconds, a blur of grey—my target shuttle—swooped in and I latched onto it.

It was madness! Adrenaline coursed through my veins. Three of my comrades grabbed on at the same time as me. The fourth, however, wasn't so lucky.

Apha Edenta held the crystalline's tail with one hand, his heavy, panicked breathing echoing in our helmets. He was several feet from the nearest handlebar, legs flailing. My heartrate quickened. I wasn't exactly close, but I was the closest diver here to him.

I hooked my feet on the rungs and arched my back with the curvature of the shuttle, hands high above my head. My hair extended, slithering like a snake beneath the liquid fabric of my diving suit to wrap around my arms, so I could better support a two-hundred-pound man. Apha caught my hands. I bent my elbows and knees, pulling him in, within reach of a handlebar. He grabbed it. I exhaled.

"Spin two in thirty seconds! Same drill. You know what to do," Amok announced. I closed my eyes. It was going to be a long day.

* * *

The Ichthyothians emerged from training, unscathed. Many of them even looked bored. We Nurians, on the other hand, came back limping and out-of-breath. But, with the exception of Apha's slip-up, I thought today went well.

Apparently, Lechatelierite had different standards.

"Well, that freak-show was entertaining," he greeted us crossly as we entered Icicle, tracking saltwater all over the polished, white floor. "I'm not sure what you all spent the last seven months doing."

Before we even got to change out of our suits, he ushered us into a lecture hall and launched into a seventy-minute critique, complete with playback footage. His analysis was shrewd and his awareness was sharp; he noticed things that even evaded my eyes and drew correlations that escaped my mind. Exhausted as I was, I listened attentively, absorbing his words like a sand dune in a rare Conflagrian rain, in awe yet again of his brilliance.

But, all the while, it was hard to watch his face and not think about that battle from last summer.

When the lesson finally ended, we trudged to the locker room. My whole body ached. I collapsed onto a bench and put my head in my hands, too tired to change.

"Hey, bloodclot!" came Amok's voice, from behind. "The despot wants to see you, now."

I lifted my head and looked at him, wearily.

"Hey, if you're late, *I'll* get in trouble. Move!"

I got to my unsteady feet and headed out into the hall. No one else had orders to see the Commander. Just me. My nerves jangled. I didn't need this after the most intense day of exercise in my life. I just wanted to go to sleep.

I stood in front of Lechatelierite's door, forced my back straight and pressed the intercom.

"Uh, Commander, sir," I breathed in Ichthyothian. "This is July. Kempt sent for me."

"Enter."

My stomach knotted at the sound of his cold voice.

His door wouldn't budge. "Sir, your door. It's, um, locked."

"Didn't stop you before, did it?" he snapped. "I said, enter."

He *wanted* me to magically break in? Very well, then. I guessed he was testing my obedience to his orders, however strange. I wound a lock of hair around the knob and pushed.

"Soldier, I commend your performance today," he said in his accented Nurian.

My heart leapt as I closed the door behind me. As I turned toward him, I fought hard to keep the excitement from my face. Cease Lechatelierite was complementing me! He thought highly of my performance! But, then—

"The way you handled Apha Edenta's slip was worthy of even an Ichthyothian diver."

Worthy of *even* an Ichthyothian diver? This was the *Ichthyothian* Diving Fleet—who else was I supposed to perform like? A flicker of anxiety and anger coursed through my hair as I realized what those words meant: he expected less from us newbies. From me. What I did today was nothing special for a real diver.

"Thank you, sir," I answered in Ichthyothian, hoping he couldn't see how his words really made me feel. Lechatelierite took me from exhilarated to irritated in about three seconds flat.

He didn't take his dangerous, silver-grey eyes off my face. There was a long pause in which neither of us blinked. I was becoming too tired to draw breath. I just wanted to hit the barracks and pass out.

"Am I dismissed, sir?" I asked in a small voice.

"How many times did you use magic, today?" he asked, suddenly.

I felt slapped. He didn't think I could dive decently without spectral help?

"Only once, sir." It felt weird to explain this to someone. To my Nordic Commander, of all people. "I used my hair to strengthen my hold on Edenta as I pulled him to safety."

Lechatelierite nodded. "Could you've done so without it?"

"I think so, sir." I finally resigned to speaking Nurian, too tired to think of the Ichthyothian words anymore. "I only used it for reinforcement, as an extra precaution."

"Sit," he ordered stiffly, gesturing to his desk chair.

There was only one seat in the room. So, I would sit in it and he would... what, stand over me? Talk down to me? His penetrating eyes already made me feel small enough, like an amoeba under a microscope. Moreover, it felt disrespectful to address my commander while sitting.

Well, it's not like I had a choice. Orders were orders. I sat.

"We need to discuss your powers and how we can make optimal use of them without exposing your heritage to our comrades or to the enemy."

He watched me expectantly, folding his arms across his chest and raising his eyebrows slightly. It was like an enormous spotlight turned on above my head. What to say? Where to begin? I fixed my eyes on the triangular emblem on his chest, unable to endure his drilling stare any longer.

"Speak," he demanded. "I'm not that frightening, am I?" He tried to sound lighthearted, but it came out all wrong. For once, he didn't have complete control over his tone.

I lifted my chin and forced myself to look at his face. The face of the man who didn't know I'd witnessed the greatest failure and pain of his life. Through the spectral web, I invaded his privacy, feeing his guilt and hearing his dying thoughts as if they were my own. For some reason, this made me feel like a traitor. Like I stole from him. Violated him. I didn't want to have his secrets in my head. Not ones he didn't volunteer himself. Not that he'd ever willingly confide in me...

And, I still didn't know what to say. I was paralyzed by exhaustion, not to mention the anxiety of being put on the spot by the man whose opinion I valued most in the world.

Lechatelierite sat on the edge of his bed, clasped his hands and leaned forward. Trying to get down to my level and come across as more approachable, perhaps? I wished it was working, but my nerves weren't exactly cooled by his coming closer. He was barely two feet from me, now.

"You're the first eye mage, correct?" he asked, sharply.

"Yes, sir."

"And, that's why your people exiled you?"

"Yes, sir."

"How exactly did that play out?"

I looked at him in tired disbelief. Was he really going to make me relive the worst day of my life, *now*?

"Sir, I already shared the important parts, during my interrogation."

Oh, Tincture, did I really just say that? Fatigue was making me snappy.

"It came out too fast and scrambled. I need details."

This was a conversation I didn't want to have. Especially with him. Talking about the day I was orphaned and deported would sound like I was inviting pity. I didn't want him to feel sorry for the poor, little girl. I wanted him to respect me. To think highly of me. To believe I was just as strong and capable as all the other big men in his fleet.

"I understand this may be difficult to talk about." His words were kind but his voice was hard. "But, I need to know. I care to know."

Oh, he *cared*, did he? Now, I was really getting angry. We could easily discuss the extent of my powers without speaking a single word about July twenty-fifth. He didn't *need* to know anything more about that day besides what I already shared during my interrogation. He only *wanted* to know, and certainly not because he cared, but so he could psycho-analyze me and figure out if my baggage would impede his use of me in battle. I was a tool for him to manipulate, nothing more. It would've been better if he owned up to that rather than feigning concern.

"Come on, Scarlet, talk to me," he said, all prior awkwardness in his voice now masterfully replaced with that dangerous, hypnotic, convicting persuasiveness I couldn't resist.

I also noticed he called me by my first name. He usually addressed his subordinates by our last names, or as 'soldier,' or even by our numbers. But, to him, I was Scarlet.

"This is all off the record," he went on, authoritative and magnetic tone overtaking me, though his face was still completely deadpan. "I'm not writing anything down or adding to your file or reporting a word to anyone; I just want to learn about you. Because you're unique and talented. I don't praise often, so listen up: your test scores and performance caught my eye from the start. You're someone I could potentially see myself and this fleet depending on, in the months and ages to come. But, we can't get to that point until I gain a better understanding of who you are, where you've been. So, Scarlet, either talk to me now, or handicap this fleet."

I could hardly breathe. Was it true? He saw potential in me from the get-go? He thought I was talented? Someone he could rely on? Trust his men with?

Or, was this all just more manipulation to get me to reveal my vulnerabilities so he could cast me aside?

He watched with fierce alertness as I found myself spilling my entire, tragic life story—everything from my Christening Ceremony when I was an infant; to my Circle Trial at six; to the day my family died and I was deported at ten; to how I survived on the streets of Alcove City for five ages, counting coins, eating out of dumpsters and studying day and night; to when I enlisted in the military, hoping to be picked for the Diving Academy so I could ultimately meet him…

I left out the part about my vision of his battle loss and my secret presence at the Nurro-Ichthyothian Alliance Conference.

When I was finished, a long pause ensued. Cease's severe face hadn't changed the entire time I spoke. He managed to absorb every word without revealing a single thought or emotion.

Oddly enough, I now felt *more* comfortable in his presence. I normally would've hated being so exposed. But, to my surprise, I didn't mind Cease broke my guard down. He was the first person I'd opened up to, since Fair. As frightening as it was, there was something refreshing about finally being real with someone.

"I've studied the files of all the Nurians," Cease finally spoke up, "and, from what I gather, none of them have seen a real fight before. Not like you. Not a fight for their lives. An experience like that really gives you a sense of your own mortality."

"You'd know a little about that yourself, wouldn't you, sir?" I said, to my own disbelief.

"Yes, I would," he said, voice suddenly hard.

Did I cross a line? I just spilled my guts to him, and he was offended by that? It wasn't even a real question. He was the Leader of the Ichthyothian Resistance, for Tincture's sake; of course he'd know what it's like to fight for his life! It didn't take a military genius to figure that.

"The others will have to learn the hard way," Cease continued. "Their first time *really* feeling unsafe—knowing someone is out for your blood—will be in battle."

"Did you know what it's like, sir?" I spurted, against my better judgment. "Before becoming a diver, I mean. Did you ever have to fight for your life when you were a civilian?" Now, I knew I was pushing the envelope. I kicked myself, internally.

Cease blinked. "I was never a civilian."

It figured he'd say something like that; Colonel Austere always emphasized the importance of letting go of the past and considering our military service as the only life we should focus on, from here on out. Even so, Cease's evasiveness frustrated me. We just spent the last hour or so discussing the past, so clearly, we were ignoring the taboo against 'dwelling,' for the time being. I told him absolutely everything about mine, yet he wouldn't answer one 'yes' or 'no' question about his? Ugh, for Tincture's sake!

"Is something the matter?" Cease asked, sharply.

What? How could he tell? I thought I was keeping my face straight. Then again, Cease was clearly above-average at picking up on subtleties.

"No, sir, not at all."

"Yes, there is," he insisted, and my pulse quickened. "Do you have a problem with the way my country trains its soldiers?"

What in the world was he talking about? "No, sir, of course not."

"Does it bother you I was never a civilian?"

Wait, what? I stared, flabbergasted.

Now, it was Cease's turn to look surprised; I saw a slight shift in his eyes.

"So, you don't know," he said, quietly.

"Don't know what, sir?" I piped, voice barely above a whisper.

I was already beginning to figure it out, but I didn't want to admit it. I couldn't. I refused to believe something so horrible was possible. Ichthyosis was supposed to be the pinnacle of the 'civilized' world. Abducting infants into the military sounded like something that'd happen in Conflagria, where the System reined. Not here.

"About the Childhood Program."

All the air disappeared from my lungs. So, it was true. His answer wasn't evasive, it was literal.

"I've always been a soldier, Scarlet," he said, spreading his arms. "This has always been my home. My comrades always been my family." What exactly would the word 'family' even mean to him? "And, this," he touched the emblem on his right chest pocket, "has always been my life's direction. That's how things work, around here. When a son is born, the military decides if they want him, and the ones they choose grow up on a base."

I thought back to Cease's last, fleeting moments of consciousness during his lost battle. I heard what he believed were his dying thoughts. He felt guilty, more than anything else, for failing to see the war through. Nothing else—no loving images of *real* family, no desperate prayers or silent good-byes—flashed through his mind before he passed out. He thought of only his duty.

"No," I breathed. "Sir, I thought I was leaving tyranny behind when I was deported from Conflagria. How could you—you Ichthyothians—do something so *terrible* as to abduct newborns and transform them into—" And, my voice abruptly died in my throat.

"What?" Cease demanded loudly, silver-grey eyes flashing. "Turn them into what?"

I couldn't hold it in any longer: "Into you! They turn you into fighting machines with no emotion, no personality, no diversity of thought or ambition! Even on First Earth, civilized western nations waited until men were adults before throwing them in the line of fire! Ichthyosis is committing an awful crime—a crime worthy of the System—by taking entire generations and depriving them of lives and childhoods and turning them into angry, unfeeling, factory-produced soldiers like *you!*"

Cease's face was expressionless. I'd just committed the greatest act of disrespect imaginable: I attacked my commander personally and insulted his nation. The nation I was supposedly willing to die for. And, what was Cease's reaction? Nothing. Come to think of it, I'd never seen Cease exhibit any emotion besides anger. I'd assumed, since I met him, he was hiding his *real* personality behind a tough exterior shell, to stay strong for his fleet. I had no idea he didn't have a shell at all, but was hardened throughout. Maybe there once was a real Cease Lechatelierite, but the Childhood Program killed him.

He still hadn't responded to me. His face was set, eyes staring off in that paradoxically intense yet unfocused gaze. My words, even if they were true, were cruel and unwarranted. I felt guilty and ashamed. And, I desperately wanted a reaction from him. A reaction besides rage. Something to prove me wrong, to prove my harsh judgment wasn't right. Come on, Cease, I thought. Act hurt from what I said. Show me a softer side. Prove to me you're human, after all.

"Cease?" I whispered.

At the sound of his name, his eyes shot through mine like bullets.

"I wasn't aware we were on a first-name basis, soldier." His voice chilled the already-frigid air. "Attention!"

I popped out of his seat.

"This conversation is over. Get the hell out of my quarters, now!" he ordered, tone loaded with unadulterated fury.

My worst fears were confirmed; all the humanity was beaten out of Lechatelierite long before I'd ever met him.

I saluted and ran from his room.

CEASE LECHATELIERITE

I threw my door shut, sat on the edge of my bed and put my head in my hands, wondering what in the world to make of the conversation I just had with Scarlet July, already the most peculiar and intriguing comrade I ever had. In one sitting, she went from being scared silent, to pouring out every detail of her crazy life, to brazenly insulting me and the program that made me who I was today. And, as I listened to her speak her myriad of thoughts, I was startled to find myself interested, not just because I wanted to learn how to best exploit her talents, but because…well, because I was interested. In her. In who she was. In how and why she came to be the way she was. In how her crazy past cultivated such an eclectic assortment of gifts and personality traits. Not just so I could use her, but for her sake. I was fascinated by her person. And, that frightened me. I didn't usually feel that way about anyone. I wasn't supposed to. I only remembered being genuinely interested in a person once before, when I first befriended Inexor. But, my draw to Inexor never got as intense as my draw to Scarlet was now, for two main reasons. Firstly, there was the obvious fact that Inexor was a guy and Scarlet was a very attractive woman. Secondly, Scarlet's story was simply more captivating than Inexor's. Upon first meetings, there was simply less to learn about Inexor than there was to learn about Scarlet. Less to hold my attention. Having grown up on base, Inexor's past could never really surprise me—there wasn't much he experienced that I hadn't. And, as the ages went on, our conversations grew more and more impersonal. Our friendship mostly revolved around work. It started off focused on work, too: when I was seven and he was eleven, we were lab partners in physics class. And, when he discovered how horrible I was doing in Nurian, he offered to tutor me. I learned later he didn't do it out of the goodness of his heart, either. I already had a prestigious reputation and he figured it'd be a smart career move to get close to me while we were still students. He set out to befriend me for self-advancement. And, he wound up getting what he was wanted, in the end; he ultimately became my second-in-command.

Presently, I had the admiration, respect and fear of everyone in my fleet, but not friendship. Nor did I want it. I learned my lesson, after losing Inexor. The Trilateral Committee was right to create the Laws of Emotional Protection, and I was going to obey them from now on. The emotions friendship entailed weakened militancy. I couldn't have that. I couldn't afford to carry the baggage of 'attachment' to anyone, ever again. Everyone I worked with here was a soldier, which meant their lives were expendable. Who'd be so foolish as to attach to an expendable resource? Inexor disobeyed orders and abandoned his task force to save my life, not because it was the smart or logical thing to do, but because he was attached to me. Because he wanted to save his friend. And, look where that got him.

Inexor was the only one in the fleet to ever call me by my first name. It distinguished our relationship. Since Inexor got reduced to a handful of frozen ashes in the sea, I hadn't heard my first name alone issue from anyone's lips. Until Scarlet came along. She called me Cease, asked personal questions and seemed to care too much about the way the Childhood Program 'damaged' me. So, I had to consider the possibility she was also feeling tempted to blur boundaries.

My draw to Scarlet threatened my way of life. It threatened my ability to function rationally and do my job as I was raised to do. And, if the attraction was at all mutual, which I had some reason to suspect, it was twice as dangerous. I had to nip it in the bud. I couldn't talk with Scarlet alone like that again, unless absolutely necessary. I needed to avoid any further interpersonal communication until I was positive I could do it without being plagued by that dangerous sense of intrigue.

Muscles stiff and tense, I forced myself to lie down on my bed. Scarlet July was a fool to think I could be just 'Cease' with her, or anyone, ever again.

SCARLET JULY

The weeks wore on and spring dissolved into summer. Today was July seventh, my sixteenth birthday and the warmest day I experienced in Ichthyosis, thus far. It was thirty-two degrees.

We were scheduled for 'ice-surface' practice, all morning. In the afternoon, we would train with Lechatelierite underwater, for the first time. He finally made a full recovery.

Of course, Lechatelierite's return to the sea was reason enough for us Nurians to get jittery and for the Ichthyothians to scoff at us. The Ichthyothians were so cold, so calculating. Their scrutiny and callousness reminded of the System mages. But, they were still able to banter and chat with us, on occasion. The only one who didn't was Lechatelierite. I'd never seen him crack a smile.

Lechatelierite. He and I hadn't spoken in six weeks, not since our talk that went horribly wrong. I endured six solid weeks of being completely ignored by the person whose opinion I valued most on Second Earth. He didn't even look at me. It was weird. When we stood at attention and he paced up and down our line, his gaze always slid right over my head and to the face of the next man. Whenever we passed in the corridors and I saluted him with a solemn, "Commander, sir," he responded with a curt nod, eyes elsewhere. It was agonizing, to face him day after day, knowing we both knew secrets about each other but had no relationship whatsoever. As weeks passed, my fear of him only grew. These days, I was surprised I ever felt comfortable enough around him to let my guard down, even for a moment. A week from today, he would choose the best Nurians to join the ranks of the Ichthyothian unit leaders. The night he called me to his quarters, he said he could see himself leaning on me someday, putting his fleet in my hands. Not anymore, I'd bet. I had no hope of being promoted, now.

I was supposed to be the secret weapon of the Diving Fleet. The Conflagrian Multi-Source Enchant came all the way to Ichthyosis to become a diver just so Lechatelierite, of all people, could figure out how to wield that weapon best, for the benefit of the alliance. But, by ceasing all interaction, we were letting that asset go to waste. It was infuriating. It was stupid. It was too stupid a move for either of us to make. And, yet, we both continued to make it, every day we let pass. Why? It made more sense for *me* to be intimidated into silence, since he was the one with the power here and I was the one who stepped out of bounds. But, why would *he* avoid *me*? Moreover, for this long? Because of one rude outburst? I understood if that'd make him blow me off for a day or two. For a week, even. But, surely not a month and a half. The punishment didn't seem to fit the crime.

"Hey, Miss Bloodclot!" Amok's obnoxious voice drew me from my thoughts.

I looked up at his smug face and the band of men behind him. They were wearing short-sleeved, tight, white shirts stamped with a blue triangle. Yes, *short-sleeved.* We were all issued such 'summer trainers,' but I didn't think it ever got warm enough to actually wear them. Thirty-two degrees wasn't exactly what I had in mind when I thought about t-shirt weather.

Amok clutched his shoulders and faked an exaggerated shiver. "Are you cold, bloodclot?"

I was wearing my diving suit, minus the flippers. I knew we were staying on land today, but I decided to wear my arrhythmic suit and boots because there was a limit to the amount of magic I could continually use to keep myself warm enough not to lose circulation to my extremities. Even the diving suits were only heated to about forty degrees. I found that the crystal the System guard gave me on July twenty-fifth made me feel warmer and stronger, when kept close to my body. I didn't understand why, but I welcomed any help I could get. Nowadays, I kept it in the utility belt of my diving suit.

"Change into your summer trainer," Amok ordered.

I stared.

"You heard me, little girl," he barked, adding a handful profane, Ichthyothian words to that address. "That's an order from the Second-in-Command. Now, move it!"

Embarrassed in front of my comrades and infuriated by Amok's stupid orders, I hastened back to the locker-room. I emerged a minute later in my white shirt and pants. Already, I felt goosebumps rise on my pink arms.

This morning's practice entailed a mock skirmish against unit two. The Ichthyothians were quick and alert, as usual. The Nurians were slower and more reserved. But, no one suffered as much as the one whose heart pumped Conflagrian blood. Fumbling with my electro-shock gun, my extremities prickled and my face flushed.

"South wing's spotted us; get down!" Amok hissed, and fifteen bodies went flat as salmon patties against the ice.

Something was wrong. Despite the numbing cold, my mind continued to race, piecing together a puzzle, making sense of a subtle nuance my eyes picked up, just moments ago. I turned my head and zoomed out my sight seven miles, scouring the invisible skyline. My suspicions were confirmed.

"Face front and be ready for the slide, bloodclot!" Amok hissed.

"Sir, they're coming around, from the north," I spurted.

"What?" He squinted at the blinding horizon. "I don't see a thing. And, Edenta's heat-sensor only detected the presence of—"

"They divided into three groups and sent the biggest one north. Now, they're deploying via left shift slide, coming in fast," I interrupted.

Fifteen pairs of eyes looked at me in surprise.

Amok snapped his head forward. "Four way split!" he ordered, actually listening to me. "Circle back. Right slide into the shoots at twenty-five, forty-five, seventy-five and one-oh-five degrees. Quickly, now, move it!"

I wasn't sure everyone really believed me, but they followed Amok's orders. And, sure enough, all four of our sub-groups emerged from the ice-tunnels right where the majority of unit two was gathered. We had them completely surrounded and quite thoroughly surprised. They didn't last very long after that.

They would've been the ones surprising *us* if it weren't for me.

After practice, we returned to the locker-room. I gratefully wrapped myself—soaked summer trainer and all—in a towel. Amok swaggered over to me, flanked by his favorites, a Nurian named Apha Edenta and an Ichthyothian named Illia Frappe. As Amok approached, I dropped the towel and rose to my feet. He looked pissed. I guessed he didn't come to commend me for making the observation that saved our unit.

"How did you see unit two from seven miles away?" he demanded. "You didn't have any tech on you."

Uh oh. "I just… noticed some movement in that direction and figured it was probably them."

"Don't lie to me. You knew the details of their groupings and methods of approach. How?"

I was silent.

Amok folded his bulky arms. "Stealing intel from the real enemy in battle is great, but that's a hell of a lot more difficult than nicking info from the unit two soldiers who bunk with you. Cheating like that now isn't going to help you later when you're out there, facing the Conflagrians. I have half a mind to send you to the despot, so he can kick your lying, red ass." And, with that, he stocked away, Apha and Illia following suit.

I sat down very suddenly on the bench. How stupid of me. Stupid! I risked exposing my magehood to my comrades. And, for what? A stupid drill. I couldn't get caught using magic again. Sure, Amok only believed I was spying on my bunkmates, but sooner or later, if he kept noticing more strange 'incidents' like this, he'd figure out the truth. Either that or he'd report me to Lechatelierite who already *knew* the truth and would get angry at me for being sloppy. Then, I'd really be in trouble.

But, what was I supposed to do? My magic could very well save lives and make a difference in battle. Was I supposed to withhold my assets and hamper the fleet's effectivity just because I didn't want to get in trouble with the officers?

My mind was swimming. Lechatelierite had offered to help me with this. Six weeks ago, he called me into his quarters to talk about this very issue. But, what did I do instead of seizing the opportunity? I insulted him and pushed him away. Now, he didn't want anything to do with me.

"We're meeting the despot in ten minutes!" Amok shouted. "Diving suits, now!"

***

We were used to being supervised by Lechatelierite during our daily practices. But, he was always at a distance, watching from the manta ray. It was easier to forget to be nervous when you couldn't actually see him. Now, it would all be different. Now, he was going to join us in the water, like it really would be in battle.

This afternoon's lesson entailed learning a 'tricky water fighting technique' called the 'spin-toss maneuver.' The name sounded silly to me, but of course I kept that thought to myself. We lined up by the shore in eleven columns of ten. I was at the center of the first column, right behind Amok. Snow began to fall.

Lechatelierite emerged, wearing a diving suit identical to ours, except for the three, cobalt-blue, upside-down-V bands on his upper arms. Amok had two such bands on each arm, as second-in-command. The rest of the Ichthyothian unit leaders had one blue bar per sleeve and the sub-leaders had one silver bar per sleeve.

Lechatelierite walked with a steady and confident gait. He had made a full recovery, at last. In the natural light, his skin seemed almost the same color as his suit. That kind of pallor would make anyone else look weak or anemic. But, the Commander pulled it off; his white face seemed all the more threatening and dangerous in contrast to his thick, unruly, dark hair.

Without a word, we followed him into a convertible vitreous silica which rocketed forth as soon as we boarded, ascending until we were about half a mile above the raging sea. When the manta ray began circling, Lechatelierite yanked open the floor-shaft and stood dangerously near the opening. Air whistled through, tossing fat flakes onto the visors of our helmets. We backed away, leaving the Commander alone at the edge, looking down into the dense snowfall and the distant, tumultuous waves. It was all a rather intense sight, to our Nurian eyes.

He turned and faced us, stretched his arms into a point high above his head, bent his knees and simply said, "Follow me, soldiers."

He tipped backward into the opening, tumbling gracefully through the air, disappearing into the storm. It was hard to believe this was the same man who'd spent a good part of the past age in a wheelchair.

My pulse shot through the roof as we prepared to follow him down. From the corner of my eye, I saw Amok smirk at me. That sent a flash of heat through my hair. Before thinking twice or contemplating the appropriate steps or maneuvers, I defiantly strode forward and hurled myself off the edge. Dumb move. Instead of dropping in a straight line, the wind threw my body to the left, creating a chasm between myself and the rest of the tumbling divers. While I sloppily somersaulted, the white blur of the snowstorm made it impossible to tell which way was up. Fighting panic now, I strained my eyes to see *between* the flakes, focusing on the approaching sea. I was getting close, now. I thrust my arms above my head, forced my spine straight, kicked my legs back and pushed a button with my tongue on my helmet's mouthpiece to seal the vents and activate the oxygen beads. And, cold striking my body, I broke the surface.

Once underwater, I looked around for my comrades. Not too many got blown this far off-course, like me. Furious with myself, I swam toward the cluster, as quickly as possible. I hoped to slip into the crowd unnoticed, but I should've known better. From behind his visor, Lechatelierite's critical eyes followed me. I screamed in my head. It was our first drill with the Commander present, and I blew it. He was choosing his officers in less than a week, and I allowed my anger against that heap of dragon dung, Amok, to ruin my concentration and wreck my performance.

Lechatelierite didn't leave me with much time to lament my mistake, though. He set us hard at work learning the spin-toss, a funny-looking but apparently effective maneuver. It required three soldiers: a tosser, catcher and flyer—though, when needed, the flyer's trajectory could be altered so one person could play both tosser and catcher. First, the tosser and flyer would launch in unison from the hull of a submerged ship. Then, upon breaking the surface, the tosser would, well, *toss* the flyer into the air, sending him on a wild, tumbling arch during which he'd shoot while being a tough target to hit. Finally, the catcher, stationed several feet away, would, well, *catch* the flyer and bring him safely below the surface.

Lechatelierite ordered everyone to triplet-off. I was about to join up with Nurtic Leavesleft and Tose Acci when the Commander suddenly materialized beside me and declared, "July, you're my flyer. Acci, tosser."

That left him as the catcher. My stomach knotted. I absolutely couldn't mess up. Of all one-hundred-ten in this fleet, Lechatelierite would work closest with me.

We all spread out, scattering across a square mile of sea. My group wound up much further southwest than the rest. My nerves twisted as I followed Tose twenty feet below the surface and prepared to boost off the hull of crystalline one. I stood with my back just a few inches in front of him.

"Ready?" he asked. "Three… two… one!"

We took off in unison. So far, so good.

The moment we broke the surface, Tose launched me on a wild, disorienting tangent through the air. As I spun, I tucked my knees, tensed my muscles and kept my spine and neck erect. I had no control over my own landing. It was terrifying, to feel so helpless and uncertain.

Without warning, my body hit Lechatelierite, hard. Or, rather, that's how it *felt* to me; in truth, he just caught me from behind, arms locking securely around my ribcage. He pulled me underwater. Several seconds passed but my dizziness didn't relent; I hoped he wouldn't let go, quite yet. There was no way I'd be able to swim on my own like this.

Lechatelierite didn't let go. It took me a moment to realize we were heading back toward the crystalline. His hold on me was so tight, my breathing was restricted.

"I have to toss you again, Scarlet," his urgent voice sounded in my helmet, but the words didn't register. "Kick off with me once we reach the hull. I won't let go of you until we break the surface. I'm going to throw you straight up this time, but you'll still be spinning. Fire your weapon, but only when facing southwest. Don't shoot the whole time—you could hit our comrades or blow our cover. I'll catch you. Ready?"

"W-what?"

"I spotted a Conflagrian scout ship, to our southwest," he spoke very quickly. "We're the only ones within firing range, so we're going to have to take it down ourselves, before they see us and call for backup. We've got one chance, Scarlet. One toss. Ready?"

"Commander?"

Lechatelierite shouted through his intercom to the entire fleet, "Attention! There's a Conflagrian scout patrolling to our southwest. All of you are out of firing range. Don't approach or engage. Halt all practice until the threat is eliminated. Stay still and below the surface. July and I are going to take it out, before it calls for reinforcements."

My feet came in contact with the crystalline. Lechatelierite's arms were tense, around me. "Ready?"

No. "Yes, sir."

"Now!"

Lechatelierite supporting my weight, we rocketed up insanely fast. In a matter of seconds, we broke the surface and he launched me at least three times higher than Tose did. Spinning, I closed my eyes, pictured my body's trajectory in my mind and fired only when appropriate.

Lechatelierite caught me the moment I heard an explosion in the distance.

"You got it," he declared.

Relief swept over me like a warm ray of Conflagrian sunlight. He pulled me back underwater.

"Reoriented?"

Wait, which way was up? "Yes, sir." I didn't want to tarnish this triumphant moment by asking him to baby me.

He let go, and, immediately, I began to tilt. I was so dizzy, I didn't even realize I was tumbling headfirst until a hand roughly caught my collar.

"Liar!" Lechatelierite barked, in Nurian. He wound an arm around my waist, swam to crystalline one and grabbed a rung.

"Sir, I'm... sorry." I fought the urge to bang my head against the hull. I shot down a real enemy ship, for Tincture's sake, and I spoiled the victory like this?

"All divers to the shore!" Lechatelierite called, universally. "We took out the Conflagrian scout, but we have a critical matter to discuss."

Everyone was further north than Lechatelierite and I. Which meant the entire fleet was already assembled by the time we arrived, watching the incredibly embarrassing sight of Lechatelierite dragging my limp form through the water and helping me onto land.

Face burning, I felt dozens of pairs of eyes follow me to my place in line. I felt like a little girl. Next week, when deciding who to promote, would Lechatelierite remember the Conflagrian ship I destroyed and the soldier I saved during our first surface-riding practice? Or, would he just remember how he had to pull my flaccid form to safety after our first tossing drill? And, the lie I told him about reorienting? And, our dreadful conversation from six weeks ago?

"Attention!" Lechatelierite called in Ichthyothian and all eyes thankfully turned from me to him. "We took care of the enemy craft. However, we must note, this is the first time Conflagrian presence has been spotted this far north in the Septentrion Sea. Which means all of you need to be ready, at any moment, to switch from training to real combat." Lechatelierite began pacing, hands clasped behind his back, as usual. "We can't afford to let another week pass before officer appointments. We need our units organized by the end of tomorrow."

A single day. I gulped. I had just one day to undo every one of my million mistakes.

Lechatelierite determined it would be best to lie low for the remainder of the afternoon. So, instead of heading back out, we sat in a lecture hall, on base, listening to him critique our ice-surface practice videos from this morning.

"These videos will be replaced by three-dimensional holograms, once the PAVLAK is up and running," Nurtic whispered excitedly from his place beside me. "We'll have hand-held devices that can project—"

"Attention, Leavesleft!" Lechatelierite snapped. "As I was saying," he continued, testily, "unit two, you need to sharpen your awareness." He played a bird's-eye-view video of my unit encircling them and taking them apart. "Nice ambush, unit one. I commend you for anticipating your opponents' actions so well," said the Commander—the man who rarely issued praise.

At this, Amok shot me a wicked glance that silently screamed 'cheater!' Lechatelierite noticed, but went right on speaking. It didn't matter; he was only too smart to understand what Amok's glare meant. A knot formed in the pit of my stomach.

"Now, we'll proceed to the pool, so we can go over the spin-toss, one more time," he declared, after he finished lecturing straight through dinner. We'd already missed lunch today. Did Lechatelierite ever get hungry? "We won't practice in it now, as it's getting late. But, I need to give you a more thorough demonstration of the move before we return to it tomorrow."

One-hundred-ten tired, famished divers followed him to the pool and stood in a line at the edge.

"A few key things," he began. "Tossers, the whole performance depends on the takeoff. Poor throwing technique can easily destroy in-flight coordination and extend post-flight disorientation. Flyers, don't relax your muscles while in the air. Keep your head, neck and body erect. If you loosen up while airborne, you could easily pull or dislocate something. But, don't go the opposite extreme either and hyper-extend or lock any of your joints. Catchers, you must be ready for the flyer's momentum or you'll be thrown on your backs. Redirect their velocity downward, bringing both of you neatly below the surface of the water. Don't allow them to swim on their own until they're oriented. With practice, the flyers will learn to reorient faster, so you shouldn't have to hold on for too long."

Lechatelierite strapped his helmet on and dove into the pool.

"Monitors on." His voice activated the enormous, water-proof screens on the far wall, playing a live, underwater feed. "I'm going to play the roles of both tosser and catcher." Lechatelierite's penetrating eyes found me in the crowd. "July, you're up."

He wanted *me* for a demonstration? Why didn't he get an Ichthyothian to do it? I was still learning, like all the other Nurians. How could I be the example?

My comrades watched intently as I made my way to the front. I stood at the edge of the pool and fumbled with the four fastenings on the back of my helmet. Lechatelierite waved impatiently, and I hastily dove in before securing the fourth latch.

Everything went smoothly until we emerged from the surface and my helmet went rocketing off my head while I spun. It soared across the room and collided with one of the screens, shattering it spectacularly. My face burned as Lechatelierite caught me. All eyes fixed on me like crosshairs as I hoisted myself from the pool and made the long, embarrassing trek to retrieve my helmet. I looked down at the floor as I walked.

Lechatelierite insisted on executing the move again.

This time, we pulled it off perfectly, and I managed to keep my suit intact. For once, I didn't humiliate myself. And, I did it all without using a photon of spectrum.

Lechatelierite played the video of our second performance over and over in slow motion, explaining every move, twist and turn. Finally, two hours after our usual lights-out time, we were dismissed.

Trudging back to the barracks, it wasn't long before I realized the Nurians were hanging back, keeping their distance. When I glanced at them, faces went deadpan and mumbles quieted. I closed my eyes and quickened my pace, suddenly upset.

They weren't laughing at me or making fun of me for messing up, as I expected. They were…jealous? Of what?

Of course. I took down a Conflagrian vessel. I played a role in the real war while we were all still in training. I mastered the spin-toss and demoed it with the Commander himself, while they were still struggling to learn the motions it involved. Oh, Tincture. After all my hard work these past eight-and-a-half months to become one of the guys, I was alienated, again!

"Well, *someone's* getting promoted tomorrow," I heard Apha mutter from behind.

I never disagreed more. None of them knew how weird things really were between Lechatelierite and me. They had no clue how many times he caught me doing something stupid or insubordinate. Or, that he knew all my secrets and weaknesses. Or, that I once walked in on him in his crippled state. Or, that I insulted him and the country we were all risking our lives to defend.

I shed my diving suit in the locker-room, wrapped a towel around my body and waited until the coast was clear before heading for the showers—I was shy about lathering up around dozens of older guys. On the way, I dropped my washcloth, but before I could pick it up and tuck it back into my bath bag, Amok dove for it. I was surprised to see him; I thought everyone was already gone. It wasn't easy to sneak up on an eye mage. But, I supposed, thinking about Lechatelierite was one way to get me really distracted and absent-minded…

"Why, here you go, Miss Bloodclot," Amok said, as obnoxious and smarmy as ever.

I snatched it from him and kept walking.

"What, aren't you going to thank the gentleman?" He tailed me.

"Buzz off, Kempt."

"That's Officer Kempt, *sir*, to you!" He jumped in front of me, bulk blocking my path. "Even if the despot gives you a unit, I'll still be a rank above you, so you better show me some respect."

"Get out of my way," I said, calmly.

Amok grabbed me by the towel. "You gonna fight me, bloodclot?" He threw out a few, choice words. "Out of the water, you're nothing but a little *girl*. A pathetic, Nurian cheater who manages to stay sunburnt even though there ain't no sun in Ichthyosis."

"Get out of my way," I repeated, firmly.

"Listen here." He drew me close. "I've got just as much power over you as the despot. But, unlike him, I don't like you one bit. There's only one thing stopping me from icing you and sending you back to Nuria on your bony, red ass. And, if you don't give me what I want, that's exactly what I'm gonna do."

What? "What are you talking ab—"

He ripped the towel from my body and slammed me into the lockers, pressing his lips roughly against mine. His hands probed my bare stomach and chest. My hair flickered, sending flames onto Amok's sleeve. Screaming, he jumped back. It took a lot of self-control to only ignite his sleeve and not unleash a literal firestorm. If I was the same person I was when first deported, that's exactly what I would've done, without question. But, after five ages in Nuria and eight-and-a-half months in the military, I was finally learning some discipline.

Amok scrambled beneath the shower-spouts and turned the water on, full blast.

"How did you—how did that—?"

"I've got a lighter in my shower bag," I quickly lied, snatching my towel from the floor and covering back up. "A soldier is never unprepared," I threw his own words at him. Then, I grabbed my nightgown from my locker and fled the bathroom, abandoning my sack and washcloth on the floor.

Was Lechatelierite unaware of what a terrible person his second was? If this was the type of man the Commander saw as promotable, I really didn't stand a chance of becoming an officer.

I ran down the dark corridors and slammed right into Nurtic Leavesleft, lurking in the shadows. The impact literally knocked me off my feet.

"Sorry," I murmured.

Nurtic took my hands and pulled me up. "Oh no, I was too late!" he breathed, eyes like hazel stoplights. "Are you okay, Scarlet?"

No, I definitely wasn't, but that was none of his business.

"Too late for what?"

"When I got up to go to the bathroom, I noticed Amok Kempt's door was open and his quarters were empty. I know you wait to shower after everybody else, so you always get to bed pretty late, but when I saw Kempt was also gone, I decided to go looking for you." He swallowed and grit his teeth, fury in his usually soft gaze. "Did he hurt you? I'll kill him." Nurtic was always so mellow; this was the angriest I'd ever seen him.

"I can fight my own battles, Nurtic," I retorted. I knew I should've been grateful for his concern, but, for some reason, it irritated me. "I'm a soldier like anybody else here. I don't need your help."

And, with that, I pushed past him and headed for the barracks where I threw on my gown and lay down in my cold bed, trembling as I reflected on all the craziness of the last thirty-six hours. I didn't hear Nurtic return to the bunk above me until well after midnight.

That was one hell of a sixteenth birthday.

SCARLET JULY

It'd been so long since I felt it, I almost didn't recognize it for what it was. Heat. I was hot. I didn't need to actively raise my body temperature with spectrum; I could finally relax and feel comfortable in my own skin. But, the warmth wasn't the only reason I felt so good, now. I just made a discovery I couldn't wait to tell my superiors. I smiled broadly, air actually moist enough for my lips not to crack in the process. I felt a thrill of excitement ripple through my hair, from root to tip, as I looked up into the orange, Conflagrian sky. This changed everything, absolutely everything!

I rolled over in my bunk, entangled in cold, white sheets, and opened my eyes to the sight of a white, metal wall. What did I just discover? What was the good news? I wasn't used to forgetting things. Did I have a vision? I shivered as I hugged my thin pillow to my chest. I dreamt I was in Conflagria. Who in Conflagria could I possibly be twined to? I had no roots there anymore. No relationships.

I stretched my stiff muscles and got up, though the trumpet hadn't sounded, yet. I missed my shower last night, thanks to Amok, and yesterday's sea salt was making my skin crawl.

Amok. I dreaded having to look at his smarmy face in the mess hall.

But, he never showed up at breakfast. Neither did Lechatelierite. I assumed the two were conferencing about the promotions that'd be announced, later today. If Amok hadn't told Lechatelierite about my 'cheating' yet, I was sure he would now, dashing what small chance at leadership I may've had.

Nurtic arrived in the cafeteria with a black eye.

At practice, instead of working in our usual units, Lechatelierite rotated the Nurians into different groups every two hours, to observe how we interacted with various people. All day, I didn't even have to see Amok's beady eyes or hear his obnoxious voice.

That evening, after Lechatelierite spent an hour alone, finalizing his decisions, we lined up in the gym.

"From now on, the fleet will be organized into eleven units of ten," he began. "Each unit will be led by one officer and one sub-leader. If I call your name, please step forward to receive your bands." Lechatelierite paused as the entire room held its breath. "The sub-leader of unit eleven is Arrhyth Link."

Barely containing his excitement, Arrhyth bounded forward, grabbed his silver bands, and boisterously shook the Commander's hand. His curly hair bounced with his every motion. His closest friends, Nurtic and Dither, beamed.

"The sub-leader of unit ten is Dither Maine," Lechatelierite continued.

All too soon, he finished calling all the sub-leaders and began listing the principal officers. As the ceremony wore on and on, the few butterflies of hope in my stomach began to die.

"And, finally, the principal officer of unit two is Nurtic Leavesleft."

The last of the new officers stepped forward, grinning his dimpled grin, eyes bright despite the black ring around the left one.

"Congratulations, all of you," Lechatelierite said as the room broke into applause.

Of course, I wasn't chosen for anything. Who could possibly look at an eighty-pound girl and see a strong and capable military leader? I'd probably get placed in unit one, under the original principal officer. I swallowed as I thought about having to serve right under my molester's nose, every day. I could've reported him for what he did, but I had a feeling we were expected to clean up our own messes, around here. The last thing I wanted to do was come crawling to the Commander or to Colonel Austere for help.

"In the barracks, I've posted a list of who belongs in which unit, and where each unit will bunk," Lechatelierite continued, but I wasn't listening anymore. "But, first, before you go, there's one more position I have to appoint."

Some 'secret weapon' I was turning out to be. I had no rank, no authority, no idea how to use my magic for the benefit of the fleet without screwing everything up and, worst of all, no trust or respect from the man I came all the way here to give that weapon to. I didn't even have a semblance of a working relationship with Lechatelierite. My disappointment in myself piled on top of my anger toward Amok. I just wanted to get out of here as fast as possible and bury myself under the covers.

"He's facing a court-martial due to an incident one of you notified me about, last night," Lechatelierite was saying. "So, I've chosen a new second-in-command and principal officer of unit one: Scarlet July."

The gears in my mind jammed. Wait, what did he just say? I lifted my head in disbelief, brain piecing his words together, very slowly. Amok was in trouble. He wasn't here anymore. Someone told Lechatelierite what happened. Nurtic, no doubt. I looked at Lechatelierite's pale face in disbelief. Second-in-command? *Me?*

"Scarlet July, please step forward."

Numb with shock, I floated to the front of the room. Lechatelierite handed me four, cobalt-blue, V-shaped bands, two for each sleeve. Then, he took my hot, sweaty hand in his icy grasp and shook it firmly.

"Congratulations, soldier."

CEASE LECHATELIERITE

Upon dismissal, everyone stormed out the door in a frenzy to get to the barracks, where the unit assignments were posted. You'd think they were six-age-old Childhood Program trainees about to take their first surface-ride, not adult military geniuses preparing for battle in a matter of weeks or days. It was ridiculous.

Then again, maybe I shouldn't have been surprised. Sometimes, the most brilliant soldiers turned out to be disappointments. I never expected someone with so much to lose like Amok Kempt to wind up actually losing it all, for nothing. Sure, he didn't have the best personality around—he had a tendency toward obnoxious arrogance, but only because he truly had something to be arrogant about. He was a no-nonsense leader who always had ears for the craziest suggestions from his subordinates, and he was skilled at piloting even the oldest and most cumbersome vitreous silicas. He was an even better pilot than Nurtic Leavesleft, who flew as though born with a joystick in his left hand. When faced with the decision of replacing Inexor last age, I thought of Amok, right away.

It'd been a rough age for him. During my recovery, he was forced to assume command. My job wasn't easy. Amok often called to me through his intercom during combat, in need of guidance. I helped him out as best as I could from bed, but the truth was, Amok was the one in charge. As months passed, I could tell he was bending. But, with Inexor out of the picture, I couldn't think of anyone better than him to fill my boots.

Despite it all, he kept winning battles. His track record became second only to mine. And, then, the Nurians arrived and my fleet was pulled out of the war to train with them. The pressure of near-daily combat was instantly lifted from Amok's shoulders. Apparently, after six weeks away from the battlefield, Amok must've started to forget how much he used to struggle. His command became less of a burden and more of a power-trip.

Then, July rolled around and I returned to my post, stripping Amok of command. He had to step back into my shadow and, unsurprisingly, he didn't like it. Until Nurtic Leavesleft reported him last night, I wasn't aware Amok's power-hunger had begun to manifest itself in bullying. I didn't know, when I assigned Scarlet to his unit, I'd given him exactly the kind of target he was looking for: he assumed the eighty-pound girl would be easy to push around. No doubt it didn't take Amok long to discover Scarlet was actually just as capable a fighter as him, and with a creative streak that rivaled his own. As the promotions drew near, he probably realized her excellence threatened his position. So, he found a way to break her down, to mark his territory, to dominate her, once and for all. He decided to rape her.

Late last night—after running into Scarlet, fleeing the scene in a towel—Leavesleft confronted Amok in the locker-room. They got into a fight that ended with Leavesleft restraining Amok with a length of deadline and literally dragging him to my quarters. One could imagine my surprise when Leavesleft banged on my door in the middle of the night—not bothering with the intercom—hollering for me in Nurian at the top of his lungs, Amok cursing with equal volume in Ichthyothian. Of all people to get in a brawl with a comrade, I thought Leavesleft the least likely. But, pieces fell into place when I learned what exactly Amok did to provoke him. When I asked Amok how his uniform got scorched, he told me Scarlet used a lighter she kept in her shower bag. Right. Sure.

As grateful as I was to Leavesleft for bringing the incident to my attention, the way he went about it grated against me... because it was exactly how I would've reacted, in his position. In other words, he seemed rather *personally* invested in Scarlet's wellbeing. The magnitude of his uncharacteristic violence and fury made me wonder if he was motivated by more than just the normal, dutiful desire to look out for a fellow comrade. Leavesleft could've quietly reported Amok and justice would've been served all the same; he didn't have to actively avenge Scarlet's virtue with his own two hands like he was some First Earth knight. My chest ached a little as I allowed myself to briefly entertain the possibility there was something going on between Leavesleft and Scarlet—something more than the awkward, one-sided, mildly-illegal friendship I initially perceived them to have.

I hated how jealous the thought made me.

Anyway, now, Amok's story would go down in Ichthyothian military history as an example of what could happen when power, fear and stress intermingled in the mind of a disturbed, traumatized, messed up twenty-three-age-old. Amok was facing court-martial for assault and attempted rape. And, his rank was occupied by none other than his victim.

I was aware what a flight-risk Scarlet was. I was confident in her abilities, yet I knew there were also many dangers to promoting her. Last night, after seeing Amok off, I created a list of potential pros and cons and ultimately decided she was worth the risk.

For one, Scarlet could think like a Conflagrian—cunning, creative, resourceful, adaptive—because she was Conflagrian. Her insight into the mage mind was an asset no one else in the history of the Diving Fleet could offer. The fact that she was a mage—the Multi-Source Enchant, at that—was a huge advantage over her comrades in another way, too: even when stripped of her utility belt, her body was an unparalleled weapon. Her magic overcompensated for her small stature.

But, spectrum aside, she still impressed me. The foremost 'pro' on my list was that she was an out-of-box thinker. She had ideas so wild, most officers would dismiss them immediately, in favor of what was known and comfortable. Her ideas typically worked, and in ways that surprised anyone she was up against. So, the logical conclusion was, Scarlet needed freedom from any authority too narrow-minded not to give her wild ideas a chance. Which meant she couldn't afford to be underneath anyone at all. Except me.

Another pro was that, though she wasn't a war veteran like the Ichthyothians, she was no stranger to facing and defying death against all odds. She'd managed to defend herself from the System in hand-to-hand combat when she was only ten, though outnumbered and untrained.

Scarlet also had great foresight. At sea, she could glance at any situation and almost instantly figure out what was likely to occur next and how it should be handled. She was always several steps ahead of her comrades. She could keep track of a dozen things at once; she saw everything and remembered everything. She moved through the water nimbly and gracefully, her body a white blur that evaded every crosshair. She had Amok's dexterity, Inexor's dependability and the awareness and aim of...well, an eye-mage, I supposed. All in all, Scarlet was simply the most brilliant and capable subordinate I'd ever had. I was excited about working more closely with her. And, I was far from easy to impress.

But, the risks of promoting Scarlet were also many. For one, her authority would be hard for the others to swallow, despite her obvious brilliance. Scarlet was younger and smaller than everyone else, and a woman. And, to everyone's knowledge, Nurian. I knew the Ichthyothians would be uncomfortable with having to answer to any Nurian, much less a petite Nurian woman. I was well aware of the chasm that persisted between the two nationalities, despite six long weeks of joint training. I knew the only thing that could begin to close that gap was the harrowing life-and-death experience of real battle, which we were yet to experience together.

Scarlet was also a risky choice for personal reasons: my bizarre draw to her hadn't abated, despite my best efforts. It was going to be tough to work so closely with her without that feeling intensifying. For six weeks, I ignored my best soldier, hoping that strange interest would fade. For six weeks, I didn't make optimal use of the incredible asset she could be. And, for what? Nothing. I hadn't made any progress with stamping out my dangerous fascination with her. Instead, I was just frustrating myself every day, knowing I was willfully wasting her incredible talents. I couldn't do that anymore. It was stupid. The fleet needed her. Ichthyosis needed her. I needed her, working with me, in position of influence, where her brilliance wouldn't be hampered. As for my draw to her, I was just going to have to suck it up and have some discipline, because Ichthyosis needed me to and my job was to do whatever was best for my country, no matter my personal struggles. Having Scarlet as my second-in-command was the best choice for this fleet, and I was just going to have to deal with whatever challenges that tossed in my path. Just because I was attracted to her—intellectually and physically—didn't mean I had to be a fool and act on it. I figured I, of all people, would have the self-control to maintain a professional relationship with her. I had the willpower to interact with her without things escalading into a violation of the Laws of Emotional Protection.

Not that she'd necessarily want it to escalade, anyway. Whatever spark I'd perceived between us during our talk in May was now long gone, at least on her end; these days, she only ever regarded me with a distant, fearful gaze.

As my divers headed for the barracks, I caught Scarlet's eye and motioned for her to come speak with me.

"Call everyone to attention," I told her. "I have one last announcement to make."

I stepped back a few paces, giving Scarlet plenty of room, waiting to see how she'd handle this.

Wide-eyed, she turned and called, "Attention!"

And, for the first time in the history of my command, my men didn't respond to a call of attention.

"The Commander has another announcement!" Her face reddened all the more. "Hey, everyone!"

Those nearest to us turned and watched with some amusement on their faces. The ones closer to the door just kept walking. Scarlet was rapidly failing her first test. I took three strides forward.

"Atten-HUT!" I erupted.

The room went silent as every man halted and whirled around, snapping their boots together.

"I believe my second called you to attention, soldiers! I don't care if the System dropped an incendiary in here; there's never an excuse to break discipline in *my* fleet! Understood?"

One-hundred-nine hands saluted in unison, to the sound of, "Sir, yes, sir!"

I could practically feel the heat of Scarlet's cheeks burning, beside me. She looked down at her boots.

I went on with my original announcement: "I'm holding an officers' meeting in the lecture hall, promptly at thirty-four o'clock. Be late, and that'll show me just what kind of leader you're going to be. Now, go check your unit assignments. Dismissed."

They filtered out into the corridor. Scarlet hesitated, looking at me.

"Go," I ordered, rather sharply. "I'll see you at the meeting."

And, she fled, like she couldn't wait to get away from me.

Fifteen minutes later, my twenty-two officers entered the hall. They were exactly on time. I knew Scarlet arrived at least five minutes ago—I saw her small boots pacing, below the door-crack—but she waited for the others to catch up and walk in with her. She was that afraid to be alone in a room with me?

I went over what I expected from them, as leaders and sub-leaders, then opened the floor to tactical discussion. They took notes, asked questions and addressed one another with confidence and respect. The Nurians—who usually tended to be wordy, beating around the bush with tiresome 'pleasantries' whenever they needed to say anything—made a special effort to be direct and concise, as they spoke with the Ichthyothians. The only one who didn't make a peep the entire meeting was Scarlet. She had the most brilliant, creative mind of anyone at the table, and she didn't make a *single comment.* I was seeing red.

At thirty-six o'clock, I dismissed them. Scarlet was the first one out of her seat.

"Miss July, a word," I ordered, in Nurian.

She turned with that disorienting, astonished expression on her face as the last of the officers disappeared down the corridor. We were alone.

"Close the door." I didn't make further preamble, or suggest she sit down, or anything of the sort. I was pissed off. "Let's get one thing straight, right now," I advanced on her, pitch low and intense. She actually took a step back, lower lip trembling, ever so slightly. "I don't care if you've got more magic than the entire Tincture administration." I grabbed her roughly by the collar. "If you're going to be my second, you're going to cooperate with me. Period. That involves opening your damn mouth in a strategy session. We're re-entering this war in a matter of weeks—maybe even days—so you better drop the wide-eyed-shy-little-girl act or I'm demoting you to the pit of hell. Got it?"

The surface-rider-in-the-shuttle-lights look didn't leave her face, but she saluted me solemnly.

"Yes, sir," she breathed, in Ichthyothian.

Suddenly, the door opened. Colonel Austere, a laptop and binder in his arms, stopped dead when he caught sight of us. His eyes slowly traveled from my angry scowl, to my hand on Scarlet's collar, to her saucer-stare.

"Is there a problem, Commander?" Austere asked, faintly.

I let go of Scarlet and she backed away from me about three yards.

"No, sir," I answered. Austere always had a way of making me feel like a schoolkid.

He blinked. "Should I come back later?"

"No, sir. We've just finished."

I waved for Scarlet to go and she practically flew out of the room. I gave Austere one last glance before following suit.

His eyes were confused and suspicious.

"If you ever have trouble disciplining your soldiers, Commander, you can always come straight to me," he called when I was halfway down the hall.

"Thank you, sir, but that won't be necessary," I retorted over my shoulder.

Scarlet was already about a hundred feet ahead of me. She had a lot of weight on her small shoulders, now. No one in this fleet would carry the brunt of the war like the two of us. As I watched her tiny body flee, I wondered if I made the right decision, after all.

SCARLET JULY

What was wrong with me? I tore down the hall like System warriors were on my tail. What was I so afraid of? I skidded to a stop, unbuttoned my collar and inhaled the frigid air, still feeling the aftereffect of the Commander's grasp. So, I was a good flyer and a quick strategist. So, what? That just made me a better diver. That didn't mean I could lead. My head spun. Since I laid eyes on Lechatelierite, there was nothing on Second Earth I wanted more than for him to think highly of me so he could use my gifts against the System. All I could think about since setting foot on base was how badly I wanted him to promote me so I could finally work closely enough with him to make a real difference. I would've been comfortable with becoming a sub-leader, perhaps. But, second-in-command of the entire fleet? I'd never really led a group in my life. Most of my existence was spent in some degree of solitude. And, now, I was supposed to be the right hand of the Leader of the Nurro-Ichthyothian Resistance.

Something small and white passed silently to my left, in the darkness. It was Lechatelierite, making his way back to his quarters. His last words to me tonight were a threat of demotion. I'd been his second for all of two hours, and already he was considering taking it away.

I forced myself to continue down the hall, creeping quietly past Lechatelierite's quarters. *Right next door* was Amok's old room. Mine, now. So, I wasn't going to hear Nurtic's viola serenades in the barracks, anymore. I'd miss them.

I entered the unfamiliar space. It was small, with a bed, desk and laptop. I sat down on the edge of the bed, put my burning face in my hands and wondered what would happen, now. It'd be irresponsible not to do my best with what Lechatelierite gave me. I may not have felt ready to take on this position, but he apparently thought I was, which meant I was obligated to give it everything I had. Sure, I had plenty of ideas. But, knowing what to do with the fleet wasn't the problem. It was getting the others to listen to an eighty-pound, sixteen-age-old, 'Nurian' girl with secret Conflagrian origins—*that* was the real problem. Despite his age and physical littleness, Lechatelierite's authority came forth from him like breath. He managed to keep everyone under his thumb, but while still giving us enough freedom to contribute our individuality. But, what was I supposed to do, imitate him? I pictured myself pacing, hands clasped behind my back, mimicking his glower and bellowing at guys twice my size with, 'There's never an excuse to break discipline in my fleet! Understood?' What a joke. Of course, I couldn't imitate him. I had to find my own leadership style. What I *could* borrow from Lechatelierite was some of his confidence.

I pulled off my uniform and lay down for a while, listening to the furious clicking of Lechatelierite's computer keys, next door. I got up, dug through Amok's—my—drawers until I found a supply kit with a needle and thread. Then, I collected the rank bands I haphazardly tossed onto my desk and got to work, sewing them on my sleeves.

In the kit, I also found a coil of coated wire and steel clippers. I cut a length of the wire, wrapped one end a few times around my crystal, and created a loop with the rest, wide enough to fit over my head. Now, I'd always carry the stone against my skin; I had continual access to the inexplicable warmth and strength it provided.

Though I was way too tense for sleep, I made myself lie back down. I was determined to be the best officer Lechatelierite ever had. I was going to give him my all. The alliance possibly depended on it. And, I couldn't let my commander reenter the war with a shred of doubt in his mind.

SCARLET JULY

I woke up late, this morning. I slept right through the trumpet call. I didn't know it was possible to stay unconscious through that blaring alarm. I was so wound-up last night, I lay awake until almost three o'clock, listening to Lechatelierite's keys pitter-patter like a sleet-storm on a metal roof. I guessed he also had trouble with insomnia.

I entered the mess hall after most of my comrades had already gotten their meals. Every head near the door turned to look at me as I walked in. Face burning, my eyes dropped to my white boots. *Confidence*, I reminded myself. I lifted my head and marched to the serving line. I pulled a tray off the rack and looked unappetizingly at today's offering. As a former street urchin, enough food was a godsend to me. But, nonetheless, I doubted I'd ever adapt to the strange things military Ichthyothians ate. Everything was bland, tasteless and cold. This morning's breakfast was unsweetened frozen yogurt and chilled green melon. Yesterday, lunch was cold, plain chunks of tofu with half-cooked rice and dinner was partially-defrosted salmon paste on crackers. Salmon was one of Ichthyosis's few edible natural resources, so one would think the Ichthyothians would've become creative at preparing it, by now. Wrong. Everyday, we ate the same, disgusting goop made from boiled salmon that tasted like it'd been frozen for months. Living in Ichthyosis made you frigid both inside and out. I took a cup of plain yogurt and left the line.

I scanned the mess hall for a place to sit. My unit was on the far right. But, I didn't want to sit with them; they needed at least one part of the day without their officer's eyes on them. So, I looked to the left and saw Lechatelierite speaking with Illia Frappe over a tray of untouched melon. I didn't want to sit anywhere near the Commander, either. I settled in the center of the room, by Nurtic—who gave me a big, dimpled grin as I approached—and Tose Acci, the most un-Ichthyothian Ichthyothian I'd ever met. Unlike the other veterans, Tose was moderately approachable and actually capable of holding friendly conversations with Nurians without inevitably finding some way to offend or condescend. When he didn't understand the endless media references the Nurians tended to spout, he didn't do as most vets did and stalk away while making biting remarks about wasting time and mental energy. He'd listen attentively and try to remember things. He was one of very few Ichthyothians with the humility to learn from Nurians, whether the topic was pop culture or pilotry. When we Nurians arrived at Icicle, Tose took an immediate interest in Nurtic, because of his flying skills. Nurtic was currently giving Arrhyth Link after-hours piloting lessons, and I had a hunch it wouldn't be long before Nurtic would take on a second student.

After about five minutes of trying to force down some yogurt—whose sour taste and rubbery texture reminded me of unwashed socks—while listening to Nurtic and Tose chatter about how to avoid weathervaning while navigating vitreous silicas through snowstorms, I felt a shiver run down my spine that had nothing to do with the cold food. I turned around. Lechatelierite towered over my shoulder.

"We're not training until seventeen o'clock today," he said in his accented Nurian, without so much as a good morning. "After breakfast, we're going to the lecture hall for tactical review with Colonel Austere."

To keep my nerves in check, I avoided his eyes. He didn't call me to attention and he wasn't giving orders; this was supposed to be casual, mealtime talk. I had to act cool.

"I didn't see a notice posted this morning, sir. How will everyone know?" It was like some sort of game between us; he always spoke to me in Nurian—though he was well aware it wasn't my native language—and I always spoke to him in Ichthyothian.

"You're going to tell them," he answered brusquely as I thrust an overfilled spoon into my mouth.

And, with that, he marched back to his table. I glanced at the clock, cheeks packed with yogurt I didn't really want to swallow. There were only seven minutes of breakfast left. I hastened out of my seat, slime slithering down my throat.

"Attention!" I called.

The room buzzed on. I could practically feel the Commander's critical, knifelike stare.

"I said, ATTEN-HUT!" I snapped in a more Lechatelierite-like manner.

The hum gradually died down. My face heated as dozens of pairs of cold eyes surveyed me with amusement.

"Immediately after breakfast, go to Colonel Austere's classroom for tactical review until seventeen o'clock. Thank you."

I sat down. Some of the soldiers bit their lips, like they were withholding laughter. What was so funny? The little girl playing leader?

"It's 'lecture hall,' not 'classroom,'" Lechatelierite's voice was in my ear.

It took all the discipline I had not to jump out of my seat. Wasn't he sitting at the far-left corner of the mess hall? How did he get over here so quickly? Sneaking up on an eye mage was quite a feat. He turned in his tray and left breakfast early. I scowled at his retreating back. So, what if I said 'classroom' instead of 'lecture hall'? Did he enjoy putting me down so much, he had to point out such a minor error? I dropped my spoon and got to my feet. When I turned in my tray, I saw Lechatelierite hadn't eaten very much of his breakfast, either.

The lesson was nine and a half hours of intense boredom. I couldn't believe the administrators of Icicle Academy actually thought we needed to review such basic concepts. I glanced around the room, struggling to keep my eyes open. I could see just fine through closed lids, but I had to at least give the impression of paying attention. The Ichthyothians looked as bored as I. They shuffled and stretched and yawned, momentarily forgetting their military discipline, while the Nurians strained forward and hung onto Austere's every word. Nurtic, who was sitting next to me and diligently writing everything down in his sloppy lefty handwriting, often leaned over to whisper questions to me. Lechatelierite was in the very last row, pen in hand, stern eyes not on Austere, but all of us. So, he was observing and analyzing us. Everything we did meant something. Apha and Nurtic, paying attention and doing their work. Me, sitting there like a rock, spiral notebook untouched. Knowing how much Lechatelierite would love to catch me doing something else wrong, I quickly grabbed my mechanical pencil and opened my notebook. But, my mind groaned at the prospect of taking notes on pre-calculus. Pre-calculus! We were up to multi-variable calculus by the time we were brought to Ichthyosis.

So, instead of doing math, I began scribbling down random battle plans and crazy solutions to nonexistent problems. Sometimes, I drew up ideas I knew would never work simply because they were too wild and stupid. Often, my diagrams were more like artwork—sketches of divers tumbling from vitreous silicas into the raging sea, surface-riders streamlining between crystallines, and foot-soldiers leaping over vast, icy fjords, weapons in hand. I never spent more than half an hour on a sketch before yanking it out and starting another. I was dreaming up a thought process on paper. I was so caught up, I didn't even realize when class was coming to a close. I was in the middle of a realistic depiction of Lechatelierite and me, performing the spin-toss with my helmet flying off, when a shadow fell across the page.

"What are you doing?"

For the second time that day, I almost jumped out of my seat. Lechatelierite loomed over my desk. I quickly covered up my drawings with my knapsack.

"Nothing." My voice shook. Now, he'd know I hadn't been paying attention. It was yet another mark against me in his mental dossier. I was furious with myself. He always, *always* caught me doing something stupid!

"Let me see those." He held out his hand. I couldn't defy a direct order. Reluctantly, I removed my bag from the desk, revealing the stack.

He leafed through them, an indiscernible expression on his angular face. "You did all of these today, in class?" His voice sounded far-off.

My stomach twisted. "Yes, sir."

He looked closely at a crazy battle-plan that involved deploying from the Fervor Gulf of Nuria. The map was drawn to scale, individual ships and units labeled.

"I'd like to hold onto these for a while," he said, eyes still on the same image.

My stomach knotted. "Of course, sir."

He nodded and drifted toward the door, my drawings in his pale right hand.

CEASE LECHATELIERITE

I looked at each of Scarlet's drawings. At first, I didn't know how to react. Never before had I seen sketches whose primary purpose was to entertain. The Childhood Program made sure of that. Until the Nurians came along, I always thought art had to have a distinct, functional purpose. A battle diagram, for example. So, when I caught Scarlet doodling in class, I was torn between reprimanding her for not paying attention and praising her for her astounding gift.

The piece at the top of the stack was an unfinished depiction of us performing the spin-toss, her helmet flying away. The body positions were accurate and proportionate. The surface of the water was realistically rippled. Subtle lines and shadows conveyed the surprise on her face as her hair flew in all directions. I noticed, with an odd feeling in my chest, how accurately she depicted the scowl on mine.

The next few images were meant to be battle diagrams, but they were too beautiful. All of her ideas were unrealistic but thought-provoking. One involved deploying from the southeastern coast of Nuria and fighting in a body of water other than the Septentrion Sea or the Briny Ocean, which would risk exposing Nuria's involvement in the war to the System. Some of her plans even involved invading Conflagria *itself*, which would reveal to the mage population their state was at war. As ridiculous as her concepts were, I couldn't force myself to cast them off. Wasn't her wild creativity the foremost reason I promoted her?

I put the stack in my desk drawer and headed out to practice.

SCARLET JULY

I tightened my white-gloved hands around the joystick of crystalline one. Today, I was piloting while my comrades surface-rode. Instead of launching from a shuttle's hull at exactly the right moment and snagging onto the handlebars of another racing by, I was maneuvering a crystalline alongside the ten other unit leaders, catching streamlining divers and giving orders. I was no longer responsible for just my own survival, but that of dozens. If I was late or early, or a few degrees off, or inaccurate with my calculations or commands, my men could wind up hurling aimlessly through the sea.

So, yes, I was feeling the pressure.

"Units two and three," I addressed those clinging to my right and left sides. "Twenty-five degree descent in eighty-seven seconds."

I bit down on my mouthpiece, changing my intercom's transmission so I could speak privately with Lechatelierite. "Commander, permission to revise your launch orders to a jackknife? I'll be rendezvousing with shuttle two and four in a minute."

"Permission granted," his voice sounded in my helmet.

I bit my mouthpiece again. "Alright units, jackknife in seven seconds. Catch onto shuttles two and four. Hitch hold. Three...two..one... go!"

I accelerated as soon as units two and three kicked off, diving sharply to catch one and four. I saw a flash of their white-suited bodies then heard the loud *smacks* of their landings. Tincture, you'd think I were hauling elephants, not people. Sometimes, I wondered if the shuttles could really take the beating, day after day. I could just picture my hull caving, water rushing in, carrying my comrades' limp bodies—

I shoved the unpleasant images from my mind. I was being dumb. These shuttles were shielded. They were designed for surface-riding. The only thing I should be worrying about now was the well-being of the men I was carrying.

WHAM!

The louder-than-usual thump was followed by a sharp screech; it resonated from the right side, where my unit just landed. Oh, Tincture. Someone was sliding across. The texture and volume of the scratches and kicks helped me imagine what position he was in and how far he was from the handlebars and the others. In a flash, I sketched the scene in my mind.

"Lie on your back and straddle the fin with your legs," I broadcasted to the entire unit since I wasn't sure which man was in trouble. "Hold it with both hands, too. I'm ascending as quickly as possible." I bit my mouthpiece. "Attention!" I called to the entire fleet. "Abort spin seven. We have an unbounded unit-one soldier on the right dorsal of crystalline one. I'm resurfacing, now." But, the surface was still quite a distance away. My heart thudded. "Unbounded, report," I said to my unit. "Have you followed my instructions? Are you holding on?" Silence. A shiver of fear ran through me. Did he fall off? Why wasn't he answering? "Anyone who can see, report the status of unbounded!"

With a crackle and a hiss, I saw a red light flash at the corner of my visor. Outgoing unit one communications were down. Of all times to have a malfunction!

There was one diver I still could hear, though.

"SHE SAID LIE BACK AND STRADDLE! DON'T SIT UP!" Lechatelierite's voice exploded in my helmet.

I heard a scrape and a swish, and it was all over. My world stood still. I turned and looked out the rear window, watching a white suit twist out of sight, into the cobalt-blue oblivion of the sea.

I finally reached the surface, but it was too late. My hands were numb. I lost a soldier. We were yet to enter the war, and a man from my unit was already dead. I was his commanding officer. He was my responsibility. A life was lost because of me.

I docked, crying and gasping, on the brink of hysteria. Sure, the academy taught us the concept of 'acceptable losses of battle.' But, we weren't in battle, yet. It wasn't an enemy who killed this man.

Maybe he wasn't dead? I scrambled out of the cockpit. Lechatelierite didn't die immediately after falling off his crystalline, during that infamous battle last summer. Inexor was able to find and rescue him. I checked the watch on my suit's left wrist. Only a few minutes had passed since the surface-rider fell. He could still be alive!

I had to find Lechatelierite and tell him what needed to be done. I scanned the crowded platform. Everyone was clambering on it, a note of chaos in the air. I ran, slammed very hard into something and fell backward.

Lechatelierite loomed over me, face contorted. The look in his silver-grey eyes could extinguish the entire Fire Pit in a split second.

"Commander!" I gasped, jumping to my feet. "We need to send out scouts and find him!"

"It's too late to save Edenta," Lechatelierite spoke with a tone that could freeze Conflagria. So, that's who I may've killed. The same man I rescued during our very first practice. Apha Edenta.

My Nurian comrades, frightened and confused, almost all turned in unison at the sound of the Commander's voice.

Blood pounded in my ears. "No," I breathed. "No, it's not! How is this any different than when you fell off a crystalline, last summer? Inexor Buird was able to find you, without a scout," I babbled. "And, look, you're fine, now! You didn't even need a full age to recover from being almost *paralyzed*—" At that moment, I realized just what was escaping my lips, in front of the entire fleet.

Lechatelierite didn't blink. "How do you know all that?"

"It—it doesn't matter, right now," I stammered. "We're wasting time we should be using to find Apha!"

The Commander, whose secret was now in the open, turned and faced his men.

"Leavesleft, Frappe, Tacit, Lee, Acirema, Austere Jr.!" he called the first seven officers. "You and your sub-leaders, to scouts two through seven! The rest of you are dismissed!" He sprinted to scout one. "Scarlet, come with me."

Half an hour later, Apha's twisted body was found, impaled on a reef. He was confirmed dead in the hospital wing within an hour of returning to base, organs ruptured and spinal cord twisted. Practice for the rest of the afternoon was cancelled. While all the Ichthyothians had seen death before, the Nurians hadn't. The air was thick with tension and shock, throughout Icicle.

That day, I understood what I always saw engraved in the Commander's eyes and etched into the lines of his young face. It was the look of someone who'd caused and embodied death—the scars of a man who carried the burden of countless lives on his shoulders, every day. I finally recognized this look, because now I could see it in the mirror.

* * *

I lay on my bed as night fell, the day's events washing over me. Breaking my military discipline in the solitude of my quarters, I did a very un-soldier-like thing. I cried.

I cried for the fleet I let down. I cried for Lechatelierite's big mistake of promoting me, in the first place. But, most of all, I cried for the life I cost. I never knew Apha Edenta very well, but it hurt all the same. Every photon in my aura cried out for the single, precious life that was lost, even before we Nurians saw a minute of combat.

There came a faint knock on my door. I had no desire to talk with anyone, right now. I just wanted to burrow under the covers and drown my mental image of Apha's twisted body in tears.

The knock came again, this time more insistent.

"Go away." My voice wobbled like a little girl. That's all I really was: a little girl trying to step into the large boots of a soldier.

The door opened. Only one man in this fleet had the authority to disobey a direct order from the Second-in-Command. It was Lechatelierite. The very last person I wanted to see at a time like this.

"I heard you through the wall," he spoke softly in Nurian.

Against my will, I pulled my trembling body from bed and stood at attention. Tears streamed openly down my face.

"No, Scarlet, it's okay," he said, holding his hands up. "You can sit down."

My knees gave way. I buried my face in my hands. "What do you want, sir?" I said through my fingers.

"Edenta's death wasn't your fault."

Lechatelierite wasn't known for subtlety. He was always very direct and blunt, even in sensitive situations.

"You don't have to try to make me feel better, Commander." My tone cracked as I rubbed my eyes. "It's not your job."

Lechatelierite ignored my rude attempt to make him go away.

"You did *your* job," he said. "You gave him directions that should've saved his life. Without seeing him, you knew exactly what to do. He died, Scarlet, not because of you, but because he didn't listen to you."

I hiccupped and sniffed. What was I supposed to say? Come to think of it, Commander, you're absolutely right! I guess I shouldn't feel sad and guilty, after all!

"Apha is dead, and not by the hand of the System," I murmured. "Whether or not it's my fault will never change that."

Cease Lechatelierite sat down beside me, mattress creaking noisily. To my great shock, he put his right arm around my shoulders and pulled me toward him, resting my head on his collarbone. That was the first time I noticed he had a scent. It was salty, like the sea. The tip of his sharp, ice-cold chin pressed against my forehead. My tears soaked into the fabric of his uniform. We sat there in silence, frozen in time for just a few moments.

"I'm sorry, sir," I whispered into his chest. When I glanced up for a second, I thought I saw his lips twitch. My gaze dropped.

"You have nothing to apologize for." His voice was thick in my ear.

He stroked my wiry hair with his cold left hand, and I couldn't breathe. A minute later, he gently pulled away, stood up and walked to the door. He looked back at me with an indiscernible expression on his pale, pointed face. For the first time, I didn't want him to go. The same man I usually feared and avoided somehow managed to comfort me during the worst thing I'd experienced since the death of my family, six ages ago.

"See you tomorrow," he said, voice regaining its usual, stern edge. I sniffled and nodded, cheeks streaked with mucus and tears. And, he was gone.

PART II

Fire vs. Ice

That iron man was born like me
And he was once an ardent boy:
He must have felt in infancy
The glory of a summer sky.

—Emily Brontë

SCARLET JULY

I entered the mess hall to the sound of tense silence. After spending another insomniac night listening to Lechatelierite's furious typing, I welcomed the dull peace. My mind was dampened by yesterday's events; every sight and sound seemed distant, as though received by a badly-tuned, First-Earth television set. My face was a rictus of death, eyes sore and half-closed. I was drained, emotionally and physically.

But, it was back to work, as usual. The war had to go on. I had to sacrifice a bit of my humanity for the sake of the Nurro-Ichthyothian Alliance. It was my duty, my privilege, my honor, my condemnation.

Breaching my usual mealtime protocol, I sat with my unit. With both Apha and I missing, the table would've looked too deserted. My men were careful not to even glance at me as I sat down and mechanically bit into a styrofoam-like rice cake.

Breaking the mundane atmosphere, Lechatelierite bounded into the mess hall with such ferocity, every head in the room turned. His skin was even paler than usual and his sharp face was fixed in a tight contortion.

"Attention!" he called, as though he didn't have it already. "Another Conflagrian scout ship was discovered in the vicinity and has probably called for reinforcements, by now. We're expecting an attack within the hour. We're on the defensive. Everyone report to the hangar, immediately. Practice is over, divers. From now on, we're at war."

The Commander's intense eyes fixed on mine, all comfort from last night forgotten. Adrenaline and spectrum coursed through my veins, forcefully pulling me from my stupor. I leapt to my feet. I couldn't believe it. We only had a single day to adapt to our new unit assignments, and we were already going to face the System. Lechatelierite was right to move up the promotions. If he didn't, we would've been horribly unprepared.

We're at war. His words rang in my head. I'd dreamt of this moment since discovering war existed on Second Earth. But, somehow, I always imagined myself going in strong and invigorated, not drained and doubtful. Losing Apha took the novelty out of combat. Toying with death just didn't appeal to me as much anymore.

But, it was my duty. It was what I was born for. To destroy my people today, to liberate them tomorrow.

Units one and two lined up on the hull of my crystalline. Units three through nine would dive from an overhead vitreous silica, piloted by Nurtic Leavesleft. Units ten and eleven were surface-riding on a crystalline piloted by Illia Frappe. The rest of the unit leaders were taking their crystallines in empty, so those deploying from above would have a place to surface-ride after entering the water.

"Hitch-hold on the rungs while we're riding out," I reminded units one and two. "Keep your bodies flat and erect against the surface of my shuttle until spin-off. Jackknife and streamline, on my mark."

And, so, we rocketed into the turbulent depths of the Septentrion Sea.

And, we patrolled for three hours without spotting a single Conflagrian vessel.

"Lookout clear, Second," Nurtic reported. He and sixty soldiers were aboard the manta ray, soaring half a mile above the sea.

"Roger, Leavesleft."

"July, do you think the scout retreated without summoning backup?" piped Arrhyth Link, the Nurro-Orion sub-leader of unit eleven. I sighed to myself. Of all Lechatelierite's appointments, Arrhyth's was the one I didn't understand. In my opinion, he was naïve and quick to jump to conclusions. He was an outstanding pilot, thanks in large part to Nurtic's off-hours instruction, but that didn't mean he had the capacity to lead.

"No, I think that's just what they want us to think."

"Ma'am, we're not picking up a single ship or soldier on our radars or spectrometers," Illia reported from shuttle two.

"The Commander said we're on the defensive," Arrhyth bellowed. "If there's no one attacking us, we should go home, especially since we aren't really through with training. If we don't have to fight, we shouldn't."

"Thank you, Link," I silenced him before he could start convincing me. Call it spite or call it pride, I decided if Lechatelierite didn't call off the battle on his own, I wouldn't suggest it.

The water was unusually tumultuous, and there was something odd about the current coming in from the south. My shuttle tended to veer off-course. How on earth were the surface-riders going to handle it?

"Scarlet, keep the surface-riders moving," Lechatelierite commanded from the vitreous silica. "You're easy targets."

"Commander, we're fighting an unusually powerful current. The surface-riders will have a difficult time making a clean run."

'Difficult time' was surely an understatement. I could already picture all of units one and two ending up like Apha.

"Do it," he ordered.

"Commander, I must insist," I responded.

"Override," he snapped.

Flustered, I bit my mouthpiece. "Lechatelierite wants the surface-riders to start shuttle-hopping," I said. "No repeating patterns. Keep it unpredictable. Sub-leaders, this is your moment. Take your units between crystallines one and two, however you like. We'll be descending eighty-seven degrees for the next seven minutes and ascending at twenty-five degrees for three. Use crosstalk to prevent in-flight collision or hull-overcrowding. Go."

Immediately, my ship was assaulted by irregular smacks and thuds. I could follow no pattern whatsoever. We were as unpredictable as unpredictable could get.

Now, free of the burden of surface-ride instruction, I returned to zooming out my eyes in every direction, searching for Conflagrian presence. I could see far beyond the range of our radars and spectrometers.

There was nothing in sight.

But, something nagged at the corner of my mind. I couldn't bring myself to write off the crazy current as just another summer storm. There was something strange about the appearance of the waves and ice-blocks themselves. They were too defined, too perfectly formed. And, too rhythmic. They were evenly spaced, like polka dots on a wrinkled sheet. My heart thudded.

"Units one and two, fire at the icebergs while maintaining your irregular motion," I ordered, suddenly. "Units ten and eleven, surface and use the spin-toss to attack the oncoming tide."

"Wait, what?" Arrhyth breathed, bewildered.

"July?" Dither asked.

"Do it!" I snapped, sounding a lot like Lechatelierite.

Heeding my own orders, I aimed my crosshair at the ice-chunk nearest to me and fired. With a thunderous rumble, the front of it turned to light. As the flash died down, a half-demolished, auburn vessel became apparent. My suspicions were confirmed: the Conflagrians were magically camouflaging their ships to make a covert advance. And, they allotted a portion of their spectrum to tampering with our radars and spectrometers, deleting their presence. It was something I might've thought of, if I were commanding the System Water Forces—except I wouldn't've kept the camouflaged vessels in a visible formation. This battle plan reminded me of when I snuck into the Alliance Conference, using my eye-magic to edit myself from sight. I could think like the mages—to assess their abilities and decipher their likely actions—because I was one myself.

Lechatelierite ordered the units riding with him to dive from the vitreous silica, opening fire as they dropped. The air was soon speckled with dozens of falling, firing bodies, fluttering into the sea like salt into a soup-bowl. Some unlucky divers wound up landing on the hidden ships; I could see them shudder upon impact. If it weren't for the arrhythmic suits, they probably would've broken their backs or necks. Explosions resounded from every angle. As the disguised Conflagrian ships burst apart, it looked like the sea itself were on fire. All the while, I called out instructions, aimed at our invisible attackers, caught surface-riders and coordinated with the other unit leaders.

"Units three through nine," Lechatelierite's voice came on the intercom, "beware of every iceberg and wave, especially if it appears to be part of a pattern. Time your dives appropriately."

Lechatelierite himself, weapon in hand, now dove from the manta ray, literally taking out one ship per second. The Conflagrians must've noticed what an extraordinary amount of havoc this one soldier was wreaking, because a lot of turrets then turned to him. Soon enough, he got nicked, and the back of his diving suit went up in flames. I held my breath as I watched his blazing figure tumble toward the water. Even as he burned, he continued firing, aim extraordinary. A second later, he slipped into the sea and the flames extinguished.

I was so distracted watching the Commander dive, I didn't notice there was a dragon ship tailing me until my engine got hit. My shuttle, luckily bearing no surface-riders at the time, began to whirl violently.

An oddly-familiar glimmer appeared in the distance, heading straight for my out-of-control craft. I'd seen that eerie glow only once before in my life, during a vision that involved Lechatelierite's limp body twisting in the tide.

"Attention!" I hollered to the entire fleet. "The Conflagrians are using the Underwater Fire!"

I ejected, upside-down, plummeting toward the seafloor. In seconds, my shuttle was consumed by a single flash, leaving nothing behind but a whirlwind of frozen ashes. I lay very still on a reef, hoping to give enemy passerby the impression I was a fallen surface-rider. After they were out of sight and spectrometer-range, I kicked off the reef and began to swim back to where the brunt of the battle was raging.

It was a long trip, during which my mind raced. No doubt the Underwater Fire required a whole lot of spectrum, which was in short supply these days. Why else would the System wait so long before unleashing it? Why else would their use of it be so reserved? They were probably waiting to see if they could handle us without it. They deployed it now, as a last resort. I also noticed that, for some reason, they refrained from using it against lone swimmers—they only shot at ships and larger clumps of divers. Was this just for the sake of conservation, or was there more to it? How could this information be used to Ichthyosis's advantage, in future battles?

When I finally made it back, I discovered most of our vessels bore at least a few singes and scorches. Repair and replacement costs would be hefty. The only craft of ours that remained totally unscathed was the airborne vitreous silica. Nurtic was putting up a formidable fight, nimbly dodging all skyward shots while simultaneously taking out his attackers. Hardly a bullet of his was wasted; his accuracy was remarkable. And, the Conflagrians couldn't use their inexorable Underwater Fire against him because he wasn't submerged.

After three more hours, Lechatelierite decided the threat was neutralized and we were clear to head home. Nurtic brought the manta ray near the surface and dropped deadline, for us to climb. Lechatelierite and I were the very last to board, as we took on the task of rounding up the injured.

If anyone doubted my ability to co-command, surely their reservations were eased by now. We wouldn't have won without my early decipherment of the enemy's plan. Though there were over a dozen injured, there were no Nurro-Ichthyothian casualties. I wondered if this could possibly redeem me in my own eyes for Apha's death. Could I forgive myself?

I wasn't so sure.

CEASE LECHATELIERITE

We won the first battle since the Nurro-Ichthyothian Alliance was forged. I couldn't say I wasn't surprised. We looked more like a raft of blind penguins than a professional diving fleet. It was the most shameful pack I'd ever lead into combat. If Scarlet hadn't deciphered the enemy plan so early on, we would've surely gotten toasted. Literally.

But, that didn't mean Scarlet was off the hook, quite yet. There were many aspects of her performance that were disappointing. First off, she sent out the crystallines in a straight line, surface-riders sitting neatly in rows. Then, she was so afraid of a little current, she objected when I told her to get the men moving. When I overrode her stupid objection, she went to the opposite extreme and allowed everyone to pretty much do whatever they wanted. I watched in horror as they nearly collided into one other while bumbling through the water, nearly missing the handlebars of the shuttles. What a fiasco. It was a miracle all her surface-riders survived stage one.

Not that my own task force performed much better. When units three through nine began diving from the vitreous silica, they didn't time their jumps to avoid landing on any of the Conflagrian ships. As a result, seventeen soldiers were fresh in the hospital wing with brakes, twists and sprains. Fifteen of them were Nurian. Shocker. We would receive a batch of replacements from the Nurian Academy in a matter of days. Just what we needed—more rookies.

Though Ichthyosis owed Nuria a lot, I couldn't help but feel as though my fleet was somewhat weakened by their presence. There was a reason only five of my twenty-two officers were Nurian: Nurtic Leavesleft, Asu Acirema and Elijah Rain, who lead units two, six and ten, respectfully; and Dither Maine and Arrhyth Link, who sub-lead units ten and eleven. The rest of the Nurians seemed hopelessly behind their Ichthyothian comrades. While we were in desperate need of numbers, quantity still could never make up for quality, especially when facing such a creative and ruthless enemy. Unlike us Nordics, Conflagrians lived in a land void of the luxuries of technology; mages had to be resourceful and inventive just to make ends meet every day, let alone wage war. These sloppy, lazy, civilian-raised Nurians were simply no match.

Scarlet had the imagination and spontaneity of a Conflagrian with the efficiency and precision of an Ichthyothian. But, she was also emotional and insecure. She lost composure when the System deployed its most dangerous weapon, screeching into the intercom and scaring the wits out of all the rookies. She should've kept her cool when disseminating the bad news. If the Second-in-Command yelped like a frightened child, how were the newbies supposed to react? She let everyone know she was afraid and had no control of the situation, inviting them to panic, too. What kind of leadership was that?

I realized my mistake in all of this. By comforting her last night and allowing her to cry in my presence, I gave her the impression it was okay to fall apart in front of others. Scarlet needed to learn she was free to act however she liked in private, but once she was in front of her men, she had to keep a level head and lead by example. My mistake was that I violated her privacy. Why? What came over me yesterday? Why did I make her pain my business? Why did I feel compelled to intervene and try to make her feel better? I didn't do that sort of thing. It was too stupid for me.

With a strange tightness in my chest, I realized why. It was obvious; I just didn't want to admit it to myself. I did it because of my inexplicable interest in her. I was intrigued by her belief in the sacredness of human life, by her ability to cry for a soldier she never really knew—that drew me to her all the more. My interest was bordering on attachment, now. It was excruciating. It was dumb. It went against everything I'd fought for since learning my lesson with Inexor. Everything the Childhood Program taught me.

I thought I had the discipline to keep my interest in Scarlet at bay. I thought I wouldn't dwell on it, much less act on it. I was furious at myself for slipping up. And, it was a big slip. I hugged her. I actually put my arms around her. I never held anyone like that before. I pulled her head to my chest. Stroked her hair. Inhaled the wood-smoke scent I didn't know she had. Worried about her pain. Wanted her to be okay. Enjoyed the feeling of her warm body against mine. Felt my own lip-muscles twitch as I wondered what it'd be like to kiss her. Had a hard time forcing myself leave her quarters.

I needed to be more careful around her from now on. I had to. Not only for my sake, but hers. Scarlet had to learn to fight her own battles without anyone's help. I had to back off and let her cope on her own. Because forging her into a fighting-machine was my first priority. Even if that meant breaking her. Even if that meant destroying the part of her I admired most.

SCARLET JULY

Two and a half weeks passed, in a flurry of battles. We won them all, but not without heavy losses. Each day, the score became closer. Each day, more divers dropped like flies buzzing near the mouth of a yawning dragon. Each day, I grew wearier and Lechatelierite grew more on edge. He and I received regular statements from the Trilateral Committee and the other two branches of the Nurro-Ichthyothian Military, each relaying dismal figures. Us divers may've been winning individual conflicts at sea, but overall, Ichthyosis was losing the war.

It was now the morning of July twenty-fifth of the ninety-third age—the sixth anniversary of my family's execution. I'd spent yet another sleepless night, listening to the incessant clicking of Lechatelierite's laptop keys. I spotted him on the far side of the mess hall now, totally ignoring Illia Frappe sitting across from him, staring intently at a packet by his untouched plate. The dark circles around his eyes made the silver glow of his penetrating stare all the more frightful. I assumed he was reading yet another depressing report, which he'd pass to me, wordlessly, once finished.

The System was still unaware of the Nurro-Ichthyothian Alliance. Respecting Nuria's rights as a 'neutral'—in other words, refraining from provoking a mighty superpower against them—Conflagria kept their naval attacks in the Septentrion Sea and the northernmost regions of the Briny Ocean, steering clear of Nurian sea-space. And, the alliance, on the defensive, rarely initiated attacks itself or tried to push further south into the Briny Ocean or the Fervor Sea. All battles were basically fought in Ichthyosis's backyard.

I was convinced *that* was the problem. I thought it was worth making the enemy a bit suspicious of our secret ally to strike further south, like from the Fervor Gulf of Nuria. That'd take the System by surprise for sure. For once, we'd be the ones thinking outside *their* box.

But, my ideas were too 'wild' for anyone to take seriously. My unit listened, but didn't care. They believed the secret of Nuria's involvement should only be risked when 'absolutely necessary.' Well, when would it be 'absolutely necessary?' Hadn't we reached that point already?

In a measly two and a half weeks, we'd lost a significant portion of our fleet to the Underwater Fire. All we had left now was one of the older, air-only vitreous silicas, two crystalline shuttles, thirty of the forty Ichthyothian veterans, twenty of the original seventy Nurians and thirty-seven even greener Nurian rookies, fresh from the Academy. There were only eight units now: seven groups of ten and one group of seven.

Eighty-seven divers were left to carry the brunt of the war on our tired, beaten shoulders.

Eighty-seven divers were left to stand against a ruthless army of magic-wielding warriors.

CEASE LECHATELIERITE

I couldn't eat. I couldn't talk to Illia. I couldn't breathe. Sweat beads broke out on my forehead and neck. With every word I read, the pH of my stomach seemed to drop.

> *To the Leader of the Ichthyothian Resistance, Diving Commander Cease Terminus Lechatelierite,*
>
> *After sixteen ages at war with the South Conflagrablaze Captive, the Trilateral Committee would like to offer its sincerest thanks for your service in the Diving Fleet and lifelong commitment to the defense of the North Ichthyosis Island.*
>
> *We regret to inform you that the Alliance Committee, Trilateral Committee and the executive offices of the Ichthyothian and Nurian governments have collectively recognized the futility of perpetuating the current international conflict. To obtain the greatest possible concessions from the South Conflagrablaze Captive, we request your immediate surrender on the behalf of the Alliance.*
>
> *Respectfully,*
>
> *Ichthyothian Prime Minister Rime Gelid Ascet*
> *Nurian President Georgen Winster Briggesh*
> *Alliance Chairman Cartel Aliquot Juncture*
> *AND Trilateral Committee Chairs:*
> *Admiral Oppre Is Sive*
> *Commodore Rettahs Krad Slous*

I stared in disbelief. White-hot rage began coursing through my veins, as though I'd swallowed venom. Hyperventilating, I squeezed the packet in my right first and pushed aside my untouched plate of crackers and salmon paste. I put my left elbow on the table and held my forehead in my palm.

Surrender.

My chest quivered.

End the war.

Forfeit to Conflagria.

No. Defending Ichthyosis was the purpose of my life. The reason I was born. The only job I had. Why I did nothing each day but kill and teach others to kill. It was the reason I was denied all the things the Nurians spoke of every day. Family. A home. Friendships. Love.

Inexor died for this war. The only person I ever had a real relationship with was nothing more than frozen ashes on the seafloor. For what gain? For surrender? To submit our country to the tyrannical rule of a primitive people?

Dizzy, I sprung up from my seat, sending my glass of ice-water to the floor. Illia jumped as it shattered. My knuckles went white as I clutched the packet.

The corner of a sheet of notebook-paper poked out from between its pages. I pulled it out. It was one of Scarlet's drawings from the review class, weeks ago. How did it get in here? I stared. It was an insane battle plan that involved dispatching from the Fervor Gulf of Nuria. I blinked, mind slowly digesting her delicate strokes. Of course. *Of course!*

"Attention!" I called, pages dropping to the floor, atop the broken glass. "Leavesleft and Frappe, take units two through four on the remaining crystallines. Units one, five, six, seven and eight are with me in the vitreous silica. Breakfast is over. Move!"

"Where to, Commander?" Arrhyth Link piped, eyes wide.

"Across the Septentrion Sea, the Briny Ocean and around the east coast of Nuria," I said, firmly. "We'll refuel at the Fervor Station."

"Sir?" Scarlet breathed.

I was defying direct orders from the Trilateral Committee and the Ichthyothian and Nurian governments. But, I was doing it to save them. I swallowed.

"We're attacking the Conflagrian Water Forces Base, in the Fervor Sea."

SCARLET JULY

Deadpan was Lechatelierite's default facial expression. Thirty Nurro-Ichthyothian casualties last week? Deadpan. Single-handedly slaughtered thirty mages yesterday with his sidearm? Deadpan. A solid hour listening to his new subordinate's tragic life story? Deadpan. Embracing his crying co-commander in her quarters in the middle of the night while stroking her hair and whispering in her ear? Deadpan.

So, one could imagine my alarm during breakfast when this same man jumped from his seat as though electrocuted, face beaded with sweat and body trembling. I knew something must've gone horribly wrong. Something big. Something concerning the greater state of the war.

We rushed from the mess hall to the locker rooms to suit up, and from what I gathered of the nervous chatter on the way, everyone was convinced the Commander had gone mad. Only my unit was aware of the origin of his crazy idea, but that didn't do much to comfort them. I was worried sick, feeling very responsible for the doom I sensed was coming.

We headed out. Nurtic and Illia were piloting the crystallines bearing units two, three and four. I was with units one, five, six and seven aboard our old, air-only vitreous silica, soaring a couple thousand feet above. Wind whistled noisily as the manta ray sliced through the sky. I peered out the windows, straining my spectrum to see through the thick snow.

It was a long, nerve-wracking trip. The forty of us onboard stayed still and silent, waiting, wondering and worrying, as Lechatelierite, hiding his anxiety with a brave face and a confident voice, ran his mouth. I considered his constant reassurance as indicative of his internal unrest. Never before did he need to actively convince us of the infallibility of a plan; it was always obvious. Until now. And, his voice was so authoritative, so assertive, it wasn't too long before he had everyone convinced. All around me, my comrades gazed at him with admiration and awe, all unease apparently forgotten.

I was unmoved. Everyone believed Lechatelierite's one lost battle was a fluke, but I alone heard his dying thoughts and knew his failure was the result of serious misjudgment. I'd seen behind the mask of the 'perfect commander' and knew, despite his stoicism and reputation, he was breakable and fallible. My stomach churned like it was trying to digest a lump of raw dragon meat. What could've possibly happened in the grand scheme of things to make him desperate enough to use one of my fantasy battle-plans?

"This ship, along with our two remaining crystallines, have been recently fortified with diffusion shield technology," Lechatelierite told us, like we didn't already know. "Completely undetectable by spectrometer."

Well, now the blindness went both ways, I supposed—none of *our* radars or spectrometers were able to function properly since our first battle. There were teams of engineers working on the mystery as we spoke. Good luck trying to make sense of magic, I thought.

We stopped to refuel at the Fervor Station, on the southern coast of Nuria. I crossed and uncrossed my legs, refraining from clutching my stomach openly. The single, stale wheat cracker I managed to choke down at breakfast with a gulp of ice water was now threatening to come up. Abdominal pain was a regular part of my life in the military, but not to such an extreme as this. Goosebumps rose on my arms beneath my diving suit as anticipation welled in my chest. Though the cabin of the manta ray was kept at about forty degrees, I began to feel hot, all over. Especially my scalp. My stomach swooped, but from what seemed to be excitement. Like I just made some big discovery. *That's it!* my mind screamed. Wait, what's it? What was happening? Did my eyes subconsciously detect something? I peered out the windows. There was nothing going on.

Another hour passed. The ship was on autopilot, trekking across the Fervor Sea. We were getting close. Lechatelierite fell silent in mid-sentence, staring out the window, face losing what little color it had. Almost in unison, forty heads turned. It's too painful for me to describe in much detail what we saw. A full Conflagrian fleet—each craft equipped with every sort of spectral enhancement imaginable—awaited us in formation, turrets pointed north, as if expecting our arrival. It made no sense. We never came this far south before. We launched at the spur of the moment, without prior preparation or discussion. With our ships cloaked by diffusion technology, they had no means to detect our advance. There was simply *no way* they could've known we were coming. At yet, here they were, ready.

In a flash, Lechatelierite dropped open the diving shaft.

"Out, now!" he ordered us.

"The enemy is still mostly out of the firing-range of our sidearms," Arrhyth piped. "I mean, the manta ray can hit them, but *we* can't individually, so I think we should fly a little further before deploying—"

"Shut up and get the hell out, NOW!"

The rear of the vitreous silica burst open in a flurry of color and sound. The ship began to spin wildly towards the bubbling-hot, Conflagrian water. Lechatelierite dove for the controls and took us off autopilot. I pulled on my helmet, stepped back from the shaft, snagged a handlebar and held on tight, allowing the others to evacuate first. The manta ray gyrated; white suits flung through the air and slammed into walls. Several men hurled through the gaping opening, unprepared, tumbling to the choppy sea. At last, there was no one left inside the half-demolished vessel besides the Commander and me.

He was still at the console, trying to direct our course. I didn't see the point. If he didn't get out now, the carrier was going to end up crashing and exploding with him on it.

I lifted my visor. "Commander, you can't salvage the ship!" I yelled through the wind and the crackling. "Leave the controls and dive!"

He literally jumped at the sound of my voice—I'd never seen him so startled before. "WHAT'RE YOU STILL DOING HERE?" he erupted.

"You have to get out!"

"GO, NOW!" he screamed.

"But, sir, you can't stay here—"

"THIS IS A DIRECT ORDER FROM YOUR COMMANDER! DIVE, SCARLET, NOW!"

I couldn't leave him behind to die! "But, sir!"

He actually abandoned his seat then, but not to save himself. He came at me, slammed my visor down and literally shoved me right off the edge. I sloppily somersaulted through the hot air, intense wind blowing my body south. I hit the water, hard, on my side, screaming inside my helmet. I resurfaced as quickly as I could and saw I was only seventy or so yards away from the shore. No wonder the Commander was so desperate for me to jump!

A deafening rumble sounded from above. I looked up and saw the massive, half-ablaze vitreous silica soaring overhead. It spun and crashed right into the headquarters of the System Water Forces Base. And, everything exploded.

A shockwave swept through the sea as debris streaked the sky. I bit my mouthpiece and ordered everyone to dive as deep as possible to avoid being crushed by the falling rubble. No one responded. I didn't know how many were still alive in this chaos.

I was responsible for the fleet, now; there was no way anyone still aboard the manta ray could've survived the crash.

I was the Commander.

Lechatelierite was dead.

"Officer two, report!" I called.

"Scarlet?"

"Nurtic!" I felt a surge of relief, forgetting, like him, to use last names as we were supposed to in battle. "Do you still have your crystalline?"

"For now, yes." His voice sounded strained. "And, Frappe still has his. But, I've got three dragon ships on my tail and four units clinging to me for dear life."

Four units? I didn't know that many could fit on a crystalline's hull.

"You and Frappe—round everyone up and retreat! We're in no condition to continue this battle."

"Yes, ma'am."

A couple minutes passed.

"Okay, Scarlet, I've shaken my pursuers. Coordinates?"

I gave them to him.

"Alright, I'm coming for you. You're farther south than everyone else. Between Frappe and I, I think we've got everyone."

There was another long pause.

"Scarlet, what was that loud noise?"

What? Didn't he see the System Water Forces Base Headquarters and our last vitreous silica literally burst into shreds?

Of course, not. Our radars weren't working properly, and he stayed too far below the surface to see anything, this whole time.

"The vitreous silica has been shot down," I said, bluntly. "It crashed into headquarters."

We didn't exactly win this battle, but we weren't at a total loss, either. Lechatelierite single-handedly transformed what would've been a terrible defeat into a decent strike.

"The ship crashed *into* the base? No way!" Nurtic sounded, for all the world, like a teenager who'd just been told his high school principal was caught making out with the cafeteria-lady in a broom closet. "There's just *no way* the Conflagrians would be stupid enough to shoot it down while it's flying right over them."

"They didn't." I swallowed. "The engine was taken out long before the ship made it above land. It took the Commander a lot of maneuvering to glide there."

There was a stunned silence.

"But, doesn't that mean Lechatelierite is—are you saying he's—?"

"I'm not sure," I answered, quietly. "But, I think so."

Nurtic had no response for that. His crystalline soon came zipping in my direction, and though nearly every square inch of his hull was already occupied, I managed to grab on.

We rode home in complete silence.

CEASE LECHATELIERITE

"THIS IS A DIRECT ORDER FROM YOUR COMMANDER!" I screamed. "DIVE, SCARLET, NOW!"

"But, sir!"

That was it. I couldn't go knowing I was taking my replacement—the best replacement I could've possibly hoped for—with me. Moreover, I refused to spend my final minutes agonizing over the imminent death of the first person I'd come to care about since Inexor. So, I lunged at her, snapping her visor shut and pushing her right through the open shaft. I breathed a sigh of relief as her tiny body tumbled into the wind.

I returned to the console and strained forward, nose nearly touching the windshield. I fixed the ship's path straight for the base's main facility. Then, I put on my helmet and sat back, not bothering with the harness.

The vitreous silica lurched and I was thrown out of my seat. This was it. I was choosing the destruction of headquarters over my life. But, I was going out with honor. Perhaps, upon dealing the enemy this blow, the Trilateral Committee would decide it wasn't yet time for surrender. Finally, I would be redeemed for Inexor's death. This was my payment, my sacrifice.

The ship was perpendicular to the ground, now; my head slammed violently into the windshield.

For you, Ichthyosis.

For you, Inexor.

Blackness engulfed my sight.

SCARLET JULY

It was past midnight before we got back to Icicle. There were two-dozen more divers entering hospital wing, but we'd all managed to make it home alive. Everyone except Lechatelierite.

I tried to understand why he did it. Why he sent us off, unprepared, on a stupid mission based on a stupid battle plan.

My battle plan.

He died because he took me seriously. Because he trusted me when no one else even wanted to hear what I had to say. If Apha died because he didn't listen to me, Lechatelierite died because he did.

Lechatelierite didn't just do dumb things for no reason at all. Something must've pushed him to abandon reason and take this step. Something must've made him loose his mind. I found the answer while pacing the empty mess hall after lights'-out. I found a soggy stack of paper on top of a crushed water glass.

It was a report from the Trilateral Committee—the first one Lechatelierite didn't immediately share with me. I read it in the dark. As usual, all the stats and projections were dismal. That alone couldn't have sent the Commander into desperation.

I flipped to the last page and found a letter addressed directly to Lechatelierite, signed by the chairmen of the Trilateral Committee and the Nurian and Ichthyothian heads of state. And, sticking to the back of the wet packet was a battle diagram sketched on lined notebook paper—one of my drawings from that boring review class, earlier this month.

I threw the stack on the table and kicked the remains of Lechatelierite's glass on the floor, suddenly furious at him. We were supposed to surrender. We'd lost the war in any case, and Lechatelierite had to go get himself killed for nothing. Destroying the headquarters of the System Water Forces Fervor Sea Base didn't win the war for Ichthyosis, it just pissed off the enemy to whom we now had to make amends. Today's battle was a waste. His death was in vain.

I sat in his seat at the table and put my burning face down on the cool, wet pages. My tears seeped into its thickness. The war was lost. The Conflagrian people would never be liberated. The System was going to take over Ichthyosis—

Cease was dead.

Oh, Tincture, Cease really was dead. I'd never see him again. I'd never hear his hypnotic, authoritative voice blare in my helmet, again. He'd never lead the fleet into battle, again. He'd never scold us, or glare at us, or pace up and down our line and critique us, again. He'd never lay his stern, silver-grey eyes on mine and tell me what to do, again. He was gone. I killed him. Me and my damn creativity.

FAIR GABARDINE

The ship the Ichthyothians called 'vitreous silica' spun wildly as it dropped, like a hobnail with its tail on fire. Dragon ship six shot its windshield and the glass shattered spectacularly, sending the pilot's limp body tumbling through the air, heading straight for me. In a flash, I caught him with a lock of hair. The Ichthyothians were retreating, but I figured we should take at least one prisoner—if he was still alive, anyway—because we needed to find out why Ichthyosis, after sixteen ages, suddenly decided to pick a fight this far south, and why Nuria would break the Isolationist Laws and allow foreign warcrafts to refuel at its ports. I used the rest of my hair to latch onto dragon ship eight, flying overhead.

I was a System soldier. Leader of Flame Team Seven of the Water Forces. I was chosen by Principal Tincture himself to join the secret war against North Ichthyosis. I received the notice six ages ago today, on July twenty-fifth of the eighty-seventh age. Though it was the best thing that ever happened to me, I remembered that day with mixed feelings. It was the day my life gained direction, but it was also the day my best friend, Scarlet Carmine July, was deported. Though I loved Scarlet like a sister, I couldn't visit her that afternoon because the System ordered me not to, and System didn't make mistakes. I didn't always understand their decisions, but it wasn't my place to question them.

Dragon ship eight began its descent, cloaked from sight, now. We were arriving at the Mage Castle on the Fervor River, which fed into the Fervor Sea. The Castle's underground floors and hangar served as our primary Water Forces base. Thankfully, the one in the Fervor Sea didn't house the majority of our men, materiel, crafts or supplies.

Cradling the Ichthyothian diver in my hair, I went inside and bound his limp form to a seat in a POW cell, took off his helmet and removed his utility belt. He was still breathing.

He also had three stripes on each arm.

Holy Tincture. I didn't just capture any old pilot, but the Leader of the Ichthyothian Resistance, himself!

"Ma'am!" I called to Crimson Cerise, who was in the corridor just outside the cell. My Commander—whose aura was so red, she nearly received the Reserved Name of 'Scarlet' when she was born, but was denied it the moment my dear, troublemaking friend came around—entered hastily, arms swaggering at her sides.

"What is it, Gabardine?" she snapped.

Crimson was always snippy to me because she knew I was once close with Scarlet. But, I could hear the winds of change begin to blow; capturing Cease Lechatelierite would surely land me a promotion. Already, I was the one responsible for predicting today's attack. I saw the Ichthyothians coming in a vision, a mere hour prior to their arrival. I had no idea how that was possible, since I had no connections to anyone who could've possibly been in the Diving Fleet. But, I sure wasn't complaining; the intel was invaluable.

"Commander, I captured an Ichthyothian diver from the vitreous silica."

"Goody for you!" she yelled. "If you haven't noticed, we have an enemy carrier sitting *inside* Fervor Headquarters! We'll question your little trophy later!"

So, the Ichthyothians damaged our oldest, most deserted base. Conflagria was still going to win the war. Today's battle hurt us but didn't exactly turn the tables.

I gestured to my prisoner. "Ma'am, it's the Diving Commander, Cease Lechatelierite."

Her burly frame froze as her gold eyes went wide. Her eyes always reminded me of her brother, Ambrek Coppertus, a two-tone, 'Iridescent' hand-mage who always had a weird thing for Scarlet, growing up.

"But, he's in critical condition," I continued. "We must hurry—we can't interrogate a dead man."

CEASE LECHATELIERITE

My body was on fire! At least, that how it felt when I opened my eyes. It was as though liquid plasma surged through my veins. My mouth was bitter with blood. I blinked several times, but the haze wouldn't clear. I couldn't make any sense of my surroundings. I assumed, from the oppressive heat and humidity, I must've been somewhere in Conflagria. I couldn't move—ropes burned around my hands and feet. Stomach twisting, I tucked my chin and vomited on my lap.

How on earth did I survive the crash?

I heard the creak of a door. Two figures, one a splotch of red and the other a splotch of brown, advanced on me. I tried to focus on the red blur.

For a fleeting moment, I allowed myself to hope.

"Scarlet?" I whispered.

"No. The System wasted that name on a Useless," a voice spat in accented Ichthyothian.

This mage remembered Scarlet? Moreover, she held onto resentments for six ages?

The woman moved close enough for me to perceive the general outline of her face. It was Commander Crimson Cerise of the System Water Forces.

My eyes shifted to the soldier beside her. It took a moment to decipher the mage's dark, brown face framed by long, white hair.

"You are dying, Cease Lechatelierite," Cerise's comrade carefully tried out my name. Her Ichthyothian was slower and more accented than her commander. "We can help you, if you agree to answer our questions."

"Agree? Gabardine, look at who he is—at *what* he is!" Cerise burst in Conflagrian, which sounded to me like nothing but a slur of long, drawn-out vowels. I would've found the language beautiful if I weren't distracted by the fact I was slowly dying in a prison cell, tied to a chair, at the mercy of my enemies. "Just give him the truth serum, right off!"

"Ma'am, the serum is very potent; it might kill him," the soldier called 'Gabardine' said in her strange tongue. It sounded like they were arguing. What a time to be arguing. "He's in critical condition."

I coughed up some blood, then; I felt something sticky, hot and bitter dribble from my lips, down my neck and collar.

"There's no point resisting, Ichthyothian," Gabardine said in my language. "Your nation is losing the war, no matter what. Your Air Force and Ground Troops have already expressed their intent to surrender. And, your divers just lost their last carrier and their only good leader. There's no way your people can fight us, now."

"Oh, yes, they will fight," I mustered, struggling to stay conscious. "They do have a good leader. A great one. And, she won't surrender."

"I told you he won't cooperate, Gabardine!" Crimson screamed in her tongue. "Administer the serum, now!"

My dulled senses picked up a stale stench. I felt a hand clamp my jaw, pry it open and thrust a nozzle into my mouth. Gabardine poured something slimy and yellow into the top of the funnel and frothy acid began eating its way down my esophagus.

"Now, tell me, Ichthyothian," Cerise barked, "why did Nuria disregard the Isolationist Laws and allow your carrier to refuel in their port?"

How did they *know* we stopped at the gulf? How did they know to prepare for our attack, at all?

I tried as hard as I could to fight the word-vomit—I pressed my lips together and bit down on my tongue—but, it was no use. My jaw muscles obediently relaxed, throat opening and lips curling: "Ichthyosis and Nuria are allies, as of last fall. Nuria is hiding its involvement in the war from the Second Earth Order to evade blacklisting."

There it was. After nearly an age of careful concealment, Ichthyosis's greatest secret was divulged to the enemy.

Cerise started talking again, but halfway through her sentence, my ears stopped working. Colored blobs and points of light swam before my eyes then turned to black.

FAIR GABARDINE

The Ichthyothian slumped in his ropes. Blood trickled from his open mouth and contributed to the grotesque puddle on his lap.

The great Commander Cease Terminus Lechatelierite. The Leader of the Ichthyothian Resistance. The legendary diver who was feared by Principal Tincture himself. The man who was responsible for the death of hundreds upon hundreds of my people.

He didn't look so mighty, now.

But, we couldn't let him die. Not yet. Not until we had all our questions answered. He had invaluable intel. He wasn't just a foot-soldier; he was privy to every secret the alliance had.

I trembled as I untied him and took him into my hair. It was easier to handle him before I knew who he was. Even while unconscious, he intimidated me. Aside from Crimson and I, had any Conflagrian ever come this close to Lechatelierite and lived to tell of it?

I sent a steady stream of spectrum from my hair into his weak frame, giving life to the man who'd kill me with without question, if given the opportunity.

Cerise dared to touch Lechatelierite's sweaty forehead with her bare hand, pushing aside his thick, dark hair. Then, she pressed her fingers against his neck. I shuddered. I couldn't imagine touching his skin willingly.

"He's hot and his pulse is weak. Move him to a rime room."

"Yes, ma'am."

Rime rooms were where we kept long-term prisoners and those in critical condition. Even healthy Ichthyothians had a low tolerance for any temperature too far above the point in which water froze. A Conflagrian child could handle cold weather far better than the strongest Ichthyothian could a little heat. We mages could moderate our body temperatures with spectrum. Ichthyothians were frail, magic-less beings who relied on external 'technology' for everything. It was their greatest weakness.

I carried Lechatelierite into a rime room, Crimson at my heels. I couldn't believe the man was still unconscious despite the amount of healing spectrum I gave him. Dread surged through me—did the serum kill him, after all? I channeled even more of my aura into his limp frame. Please wake up, I thought, feeling my promotion slip away with his life. Please stir, twitch, do *something*.

At last, I'd reached my limits; I didn't have a photon left to spare. I stumbled. It was hard to draw breath.

"Gabardine?" Crimson's voice seemed strangely faraway.

Suddenly, something tugged hard on my hair, snapping my head back. From the corner of my drooping eyes, I saw Lechatelierite spin out from my locks. Oh, Tincture! He tricked me! How was I so stupid?

He jump-kicked a very surprised Crimson in the head; I heard the sickening snap of her neck breaking as she dropped to the floor like an anvil. Her blood showered him, speckling his white suit with vivid red. Then, he rounded on me, unfocused silver-grey eyes glinting dangerously as I sank to the floor, dizzy and breathless. As he advanced, he pulled a metallic band from under his collar and snapped it across his face. Cease Lechatelierite could see me clearly, now; he could see his next victim lie helplessly at his feet.

He loomed over me, I braced myself for his blow of death to fall. But, instead…

"Where are the other prisoners?" he barked in Ichthyothian.

I opened my mouth, but only to gasp at the frigid air. He responded to my silence with a swift kick in the ribs. I cried out.

"Where are they?" he shouted.

Whimpering, my mind raced to find the Ichthyothian words to answer. The speech tumbled from my mouth. He took his utility belt from my swathe, strapped it on, turned and raced from the room, leaving me battered and bleeding on the floor beside the corpse of my commander.

CEASE LECHATELIERITE

I bolted down the corridor. The white-haired mage called Gabardine said there was only one other Ichthyothian prisoner at this facility, held in rime room two.

I banged on the door. "Whoever's in there, stand as far back as you can!" I yelled.

I drew my weapon and quite literally blew the door off its hinges. Before the smoke could clear, I dove into the icy cell. A man in a yellowing, torn diving suit turned to face me. He had olive skin, blue eyes and brown hair.

It was Inexor Buird.

"Cease!" he cried.

"You're alive!" I breathed, stupidly. "But, the Underwater Fire…?"

"UF can only catch onto large masses, like crystallines and vitreous silicas, not lone swimmers," he explained in a matter-of-fact tone.

"Well, come on!" I ushered him. "I just killed the Water Forces Commander—it won't be long before the whole army is on our tail!"

"You *killed Crimson?*" he gasped.

"Yes." Why did Inexor sounded so stricken? This was good news. "Now, move it!"

We sprinted down the hall and were confronted by a fork.

"This way!" Inexor scurried left.

But, my eye lingered on the door of rime room one.

"Wait," I said.

I ran into the cell, groping my utility belt for my weapon. But, it was gone—it must've fell off in Inexor's room. No matter. I didn't need it. I jumped over Crimson's corpse and stood over her comrade's flaccid frame. She whimpered as I grabbed her neck.

"Cease, no!" Inexor appeared in the doorway, face colorless. "Leave Fair; let's go!"

"She knows too much." I glared at Fair Gabardine, visual band slipping to the end of my nose. "I can't let her live."

"Please, Cease," he pleaded. "Don't kill her. Just drop her and come with me. Please."

What? "Why?"

"There's no time to explain, now; we've got to get out of here. Just trust me, Cease."

I trusted him. I didn't understand what was going on in his head, but if Inexor didn't want me to kill her, I wouldn't.

Yet.

"She's coming with us, then."

I bound her arms and hair with a length of deadline and, though she was far taller and larger than me, slung her over my shoulder. I followed Inexor to the hanger. We kicked in the window of a dragon ship and clambered inside.

"You know how to fly this thing?" I asked Inexor as I eyed the unfamiliar console.

"You think the mages teach their prisoners to fly their ships?" he cried.

"Well, where's the ignition?"

Inexor pointed to a knob. "Probably this thing."

I stared.

"The ship is powered by magic, Cease," Inexor said. "They don't use keys, remember?"

I snapped my fingers. The ship needed human spectral input to start up. Spectral input from an authorized System soldier. Like Fair. I wrapped a lock of Fair's long, white hair around the knob. And, sure enough, the engine whirred to life.

We flew in silence for the next few hours. I tried a couple times to make conversation with Inexor—after our long separation, I had a lot of questions for him—but, he regarded me with cold eyes and didn't speak a word. I couldn't begin to guess why, as I had no idea what his life was like for the past age. Was he in shock? Suffering from post-traumatic stress disorder? The doctors at Icicle would surely have their hands full with him.

His gaze only softened when he looked at Fair, whose gasps and cries accompanied us all the way home.

SCARLET JULY

My parents' faces flashed through my mind. Over and over, I watched them turn to ash. Amytal and Caitiff showed up, too—their blue and yellow auras dissolved into a sickening green blob, which then formed the shape of a vitreous silica, gyrating toward the headquarters of the System Fervor Sea Base. A small, helmeted figure in a white suit tumbled from the manta ray's broken windshield. The helmet exploded off the diver's head and I stared into Cease's pale face and lifeless silver-grey eyes—

I twisted in my sheets, rolled right off my bed and landed heavily on the cold, metal floor. I gasped, trying to purge the haunting images from my mind. This was no vision, just a nightmare regurgitated from the bowels of my guilty conscious. How strange it was, that the five people closest to me all died on the twenty-fifth of July, exactly six ages apart. I trembled as I hoisted myself back onto the hard mattress. I wiped my face with my nightgown, wet with cold sweat, lacking the energy to cry. Lying in a fetal position, I listened to the silence—the noticeable absence of Cease's rhythmic typing, next door—and began to think of what I had to do in the morning. It was the responsibility of the Leader of the Nurro-Ichthyothian Resistance to surrender to Conflagria on behalf of the alliance. Cease was given the order.

It was my job, now.

I joined the military last fall for the purpose of liberating my people, and now, I had to submit two free nations to the wrath of the oppressive System.

What would Cease do? I rolled over, arms wrapped tightly around my thin pillow as though trying to draw comfort from it. Cease refused to stand down. He took us back into battle. Cease wouldn't want me to surrender. He'd be ashamed I even considered it for a moment. I felt yet another surge of irrational anger toward him—how dare he get himself killed and leave me to clean up this mess!

I took a deep breath, shut my burning eyes and glanced at my digital clock through my closed lids. Two minutes to trumpet call.

The mess hall was mute, just as it was the dawn after Apha Edenta's death. We sustained several casualties since Apha, but the Commander's mandated a special silence. Just silence, no talk. No one here ever talked about the ones we lost. I was disgusted. Even in Conflagria, non-Useless deceased were publicly honored. The System itself took upon the burden of arranging funerals. But, here, we were worse than the System. Here, even the death of the greatest commander to walk North Ichthyosis was practically ignored.

At seven-twenty-five, five minutes before breakfast would end, I marched to the front of the mess hall, holding the infamous letter to Cease. I was going to be straightforward with everyone; I would tell them exactly what it said. Even if we decided to continue the war on our own, my men deserved to know the truth.

"Attention!" I called into the silence, like I didn't already have it from the moment I stood up. "Yesterday morning, the Commander received a notice from the Trilateral Committee, informing us of the current state of the war, with special orders from the Ascet and Briggesh administrations." And, I read the letter aloud, words seeming to echo off the metal walls.

I watched how my soldiers took the blow. Many forgot their discipline, pushed back their plates and put their heads in their hands.

Illia's head was still up. "The Commander got this yesterday morning? Then, what about the battle?"

His question spurred a murmur that spread like Underwater Fire through the hall.

"You mean Lechatelierite *lied* to us?" Illia continued.

The buzz grew louder.

"No!" I interjected into the hubbub. "No, he didn't *lie*, Frappe. He did what he thought was right with the information he was given. He was being strong for us—"

"Strong for us?" Illia stood up, empty water glass in hand. He was obviously thinking of when Cease knocked over his, about this time yesterday. "I was with Lechatelierite when he read the report. I didn't know what it said, but I saw his reaction, and let me tell you, it was anything *but* strong. He started shaking and he jumped out of his seat, eyes all wide and afraid. He didn't 'do what's right with the information he was given.' He acted on a crazy *impulse* and took us into a stupid, pointless battle and got himself *killed* for absolutely *nothing*!"

"That'll do, Frappe," a cold voice sounded from the far right.

Every eye turned to the entrance of the mess hall. Framed in the doorway was Commander Cease Lechatelierite in a blood-stained diving suit. All the color drained from Illia's face as he sank to his seat.

I was feeling faint, too, but in a good way. Cease was alive! I couldn't believe it. He was alive and breathing and standing *right here*, right in front of me! Before I could think the better of it, my legs carried me to him and my arms threw themselves around his tiny frame.

He immediately stiffened, recoiled and shoved me away; I hit the floor with a dull thud.

"Attention!" he called, not even looking at me.

Oh, Tincture. I just hugged my commander. In front of everyone. How unprofessional. Inappropriate. Stupid. I should be court-martialed for not only breaking the Laws of Emotional Protection, but for being a total imbecile with no dignity. I returned to my seat, horrified and embarrassed, feeling dozens of eyes on my back.

But, there were greater issues to deal with at the moment than my idiotic lapse in self-control.

"I just returned from Conflagria," Cease said. "While there, I made one rescue, one capture, and I took care of the Water Forces Commander, Crimson Cerise."

I blinked. He *took care* of the Commander? I stared at the front of his diving suit and realized not all the blood could've been his—he looked like he got splashed. And, there was no weapon in his holster, either. He killed her with, what, his hands? His boot? I turned away, the few spoonfuls of oatmeal I just ate threatening to escape from my stomach.

"We no longer have access to diffusion technology, since we lost our last vitreous silica," Cease continued, strapping on his visual band, "so, our prisoner is in a regular cell. I'm going to need the leader of each unit to assist me with the interrogation. Now."

Eight of us got to our feet. Illia obeyed without so much as a glance at the Commander's face. I was astonished Cease would trust Illia so soon after catching him badmouthing in front of the entire fleet, but I didn't question Cease's judgement. Cease led us down the corridors, silently. I looked at my boots as I marched, to avoid staring at the bloodstains all over his back.

We arrived at the cell. Cease asked five of the unit leaders to stand guard outside the door, while Illia, Nurtic and I would follow him inside.

"The prisoner doesn't speak Ichthyothian very well; I need you to translate," Cease said to me before opening the door. I nodded.

We entered behind him. I couldn't see the prisoner right away, because my view was obstructed by a big, brown-haired Ichthyothian diver I'd never met before. When he turned around, I recognized his tan face and blue eyes from a memory I'd stolen from Cease's mind. It was Inexor Buird, Cease's long-lost best friend and former second-in-command. My jaw unhinged. He'd been presumed dead since last summer.

"Step aside, Inexor," Cease instructed.

Inexor hesitated. Why?

"Dismissed," Cease barked.

Inexor's feet stayed planted. "Sir," he objected. Oh, Tincture, it took a lot of guts to defy Cease like that.

"I said, dismissed!" Cease growled. "Hospital, now. You need a medical scan."

When Inexor finally got out of the way, I could see the prisoner. I saw her mahogany face and long, lily hair. I saw her dark-orange and olive-green System uniform. I saw her oil-black eyes, glaring at me in shock and horror.

It was Fair Gabardine. My old best friend. The one who betrayed me six ages ago, yesterday. She was a System soldier. She wasn't one of the innocent Conflagrian civilians, ignorant of the war and oppressed by the totalitarian government. She was one of them. One of the oppressors. The real enemy.

"Fair?" I whispered.

"*Scarlet?*" If it was shocking for me to see her here, I could only imagine how surprised she must've been to see me in the white and blue of the Ichthyothian military. "You're an *Ichthyothian diver?*" she breathed in Conflagrian. "TRAITOR!"

I took a step forward, hot anger welling in my eyes and scalp. What right did she have to call *me* a traitor when she was the one who sold me out to the System and served in their military?

"*I'm* fighting to liberate our people from a dictatorship!" I yelled in Conflagrian. "And, in case you forgot, the System killed my family!"

"You're a traitor!" Fair screamed again. Then, she switched to Ichthyothian, for the benefit of the three Nurro-Ichthyothian divers watching us and the five listening just outside the door. And, she was sure to use my full name, as though to emphasize she knew me on sight: "Scarlet Carmine July, you're a Conflagrian mage, yourself!"

Cease, Illia and Nurtic stared at us in shock. Why did Cease look so scandalized? He knew the truth already.

He stepped forward, pulled off his visual band and glowered at me with flashing eyes.

"You know this mage?" he demanded in Nurian.

"Yes, sir," I whimpered in Ichthyothian. "She was my best friend, growing up."

"Best friend," he snorted. "You told me you had no ties left to your homeland!"

"Yes, but—" I began.

"You *lied* to me and put all of us in danger! If you're spectrally twined to her, she could have visions of you—of our entire fleet!" Cease grabbed my collar. "That's how our last battle plan leaked! There's no other way they could've known to prepare for our strike in the Fervor Sea but through YOU!"

I could feel Nurtic and Illia's wide eyes rake my face.

"I-I'm sorry, sir! I didn't s-set out to l-lie—I j-just didn't think of that p-possibility," I stammered.

Cease threw me to the floor, yanked open the door and disappeared down the hall, leaving me with one injured, shackled Conflagrian and seven Nurro-Ichthyothian divers—five of whom heard absolutely everything through the wall. They entered the cell now, weapons drawn. Nurtic and Illia already had theirs leveled at my head.

I was surrounded.

"Scarlet," Illia breathed, "you're a–a *mage?*"

"Yes," I admitted, helplessly.

"You passed intel to the enemy. You infiltrated our fleet—y-you became Lechatelierite's *second!*" he spat the last word like it tasted sour. "We trained with you, we trusted you with our lives, and all along you've been helping them!"

"No!" I cried. "No! The System killed my family! I want to fight against them! I want to save my people from *them!*"

"Your *'people'?*" Illia yelled. "Nordics are the only ones who are supposed to be your *'people,'* Scarlet!" He turned to his fellow divers and said, "Fire at her. Kill this Conflagrian spy!"

He did indeed have the authority to command everyone in the room except Nurtic, who was one rank above him. As if in slow motion, I saw seven white-gloved fingers reach for seven triggers. Though he had every right not to, even Nurtic obeyed, left hand trembling on his weapon. He was clearly the most troubled by this whole ordeal; he looked like he couldn't decide whether to vomit or cry.

In a flash, I jumped up and shot my hair out in all directions, knocking their guns from their hands. They clattered to the floor.

I heard seven shots issue from the door and every unit leader dropped, unconscious. I turned and saw Cease in the doorway, holding a stun-gun. So, that's why he left, a moment ago. He went to get a shocker because he figured the others would turn on me.

Cease recovered a real weapon from Illia's stiff hands. He pointed it directly at Fair's head.

"We may not have fancy truth serums, but if you don't answer my questions, I *will* kill you," Cease told her, brutally. "If you don't believe me, just ask your commander."

"Then kill me!" she screamed in Conflagrian. "I'd rather die than betray my country! I'm not a traitor like Scarlet!"

"Translation, Scarlet," he ordered, eyes still on Fair.

I hesitated. I was crying inside my head, torn between my best friend and my military loyalties. I felt rejected by both sides. Seven of my trusted comrades just turned their weapons on me. And, this orange-and-green-clad soldier wasn't my friend; the real Fair Gabardine was dead. The girl around whom my life once revolved was now just a tool of the evil System.

But, when I looked at her familiar features, I found it impossible to hate her, to want her to die. How could I tell Cease to kill a precious icon from my childhood?

"Scarlet, what did she say?" Cease demanded, authoritative voice overcoming me.

Tears streaming down my face, I translated for him. The words tumbled from my mouth unwillingly, falling between gasps and sobs.

* * *

Cease didn't kill Fair. No, he didn't allow her such a clean escape. The pain Cease inflicted upon her was likely far worse than any death.

For hours, he tortured her until she revealed everything she knew. He kicked her, struck her, burned her flesh with his glacier-thawing lance. He verbally abused her and played vicious mind-games with her until she committed treason. And, all the while, I stood between my commander and my ex-best friend and translated her anguished cries.

The information Cease extracted from Fair was invaluable. After the interrogation was through, Cease asked me to write a letter to the Trilateral Committee, Alliance Committee and the Ichthyothian and Nurian heads of state, relaying the highlights of what we learned and requesting permission to continue the war long enough to use this new intel against the enemy.

Though she betrayed me, my heart cried out to Fair. Cease had undoubtedly scarred her for life. It would've been kind of him to 'take care' of her after the interrogation was over. But, instead, he left her in her cell, alone. I wondered why Cease would preserve her life and if Inexor had anything to do with that.

Cease strictly forbade Inexor and me from visiting her or initiating any further communication with her, whatsoever.

"And, if either of you go behind my back and talk to her, I'll find out, and she'll be the one to pay the price," he warned us, voice low and dangerous.

I didn't believe Cease was bad, not in the way the System was bad. I knew he didn't enjoy what he did. He wasn't a sadist. But, I didn't think he regretted it or was troubled by it, either. He carried on after her interrogation like everything was normal. He was just doing his job.

It was this that broke my heart the most. More than seeing my old best friend in a System Water Forces flightsuit. More than watching seven of my fellow comrades draw their weapons on me. More than seeing Fair crumble beneath Cease's merciless blows. Nothing hurt as much as the fact that Cease was completely and utterly lost. When he comforted me after Apha's death, I allowed myself to hope there may be a trace of humanity left in him I could somehow salvage. But, I was wrong.

Why did this matter so much to me? Cease's icy detachment from his own brutality made him a more effective soldier. And, I wanted him to be a good soldier, because the alliance depended on it, and because he wasn't my friend, but my military commander. So, why would I want Cease to change? Why would I want him to develop a side of his character that wasn't obsessed with the war and didn't think the ends always justified the means? Why would I want him to be capable of regret, guilt, sympathy, compassion or attachment? Why would I want to weaken him in such a way?

I couldn't bring myself to admit the answer, because it ran contrary to my code of life—the code I developed when I lost almost everyone I loved, six ages ago.

* * *

Fair's intel changed everything. We finally knew the secret behind the absolute control of the System. I couldn't believe it.

Located at the bottom of the Conflagrian Fire Pit was a sort of magic-generator. This colossal 'Core Crystal' sustained the spectral web, and thus, the sources of each individual mage. Without the Crystal, my hair and eyes would be powerless. The further a mage got from it, the weaker his or her aura became. Yet, I was over three-thousand miles from the Crystal; why didn't my aura feel drastically depleted? I knew I was the Multi-Source Enchant and all, but I was no less dependent on the spectral web than any other mage.

Anyway, early on in recorded Second Earth history, the Crystal was discovered by a group of mages who soon became known as the 'System.' The Crystal's existence was a government secret, as the System became the keepers and regulators of its power and the overseers of the spectral web. The System managed to retain complete, unquestioned authority over the masses by manipulating the web so the thoughts of every mage stayed contained within specific boundaries. A typical mage mind thus became incapable of thinking a single rebellious thought against the System. It became a universally-accepted fact that the System was faultless. Eventually, however, the population grew too large for the System to quell absolutely and continually, and mages became able to break free from the spectral thought-control for up to seven minutes at a time. These blips were exhausting, uncomfortable and far too brief for anyone to organize or carry out an effective revolt. That's why there had never been a revolution in Conflagrian history.

I grew up under the spectral thought-control, like everyone else. But, I was able to permanently break free when thrust into an extreme situation that strongly challenged my loyalties to the System, because I alone harnessed a degree of the Crystal's energy that rivaled that of my oppressors. I harnessed so much spectrum, in fact, that if I were to just touch the Crystal with my flesh, it'd self-destruct. This had to have been a recent spectroscopic discovery—if the System knew that when they attempted to execute me, they wouldn't have tried to throw me in the Pit.

Now, the real question was what to do with all this information. It seemed only too obvious to me, but I was afraid of the implications of the idea.

Evening came, and I finished typing up the letter Cease asked me to write to the Trilateral Committee, Alliance Committee and the Ichthyothian and Nurian governments. I buzzed Cease's intercom.

"Sir, I have the completed letter, for your review."

He opened his door, face deadpan. I handed him the pages, wordlessly. He snapped on his visual band and read it quickly.

"It'll do," he grunted.

I turned to go.

"I haven't dismissed you, yet," he snapped.

I spun on my heel. "Yes, sir?"

"I have some ideas for our next strike, should our authorities permit us to continue the war," he said, peeling the band back off. "Come in; let's discuss."

My stomach twisted as I walked into his quarters. I sat stiffly at his desk, avoiding his penetrating glare and trying my best not to look at the cuts and bruises on his hands and face. Cease didn't sit. He folded his arms.

"I believe the best course of action would be an infiltration with the destruction of the Crystal as our objective," he began—my thoughts exactly. "Of course, that concept isn't without serious risk. For one, there's the possibility of divulging the war to the general Conflagrian population while their loyalties are still controlled by the System. And, there's the question of how exactly to destroy the Crystal, as we aren't familiar with its composition or what effect our tech could possibly have on it."

"Sir," I piped up, "maybe we shouldn't use tech, then."

There was a pause. Something in Cease's eyes flickered.

"If you're saying we should throw you in the Pit, Scarlet, you can forget it."

What was I seeing on his face, now...concern? Was he *concerned* for my life? Well, of course he was—he was a soldier, and we were taught not to leave a man behind, if we could help it. But, no, this didn't just look like a typical soldier's desire to preserve the life of his comrades in battle. This looked like something deeper. Stronger. I normally avoided his stares, but now, I couldn't look away or dare to blink. I hoped I wasn't imagining things.

"Actually, no, sir, that's not what I'm suggesting."

He visibly relaxed. "Explain."

The two of us spent the rest of the evening and a good chunk of the night developing our thoughts into a detailed, structured plan. For hours on end, I sat at Cease's desk, drawing diagram after diagram as he supervised.

"No, if the public entrance to the Pit is here," he said in Nurian, leaning way over my shoulder and pointing, "then our getaway ship couldn't possibly swoop in there." He slid his finger. "Change it to over here."

He hovered his nearsighted face only inches above the paper as I erased and redrew the vector.

"No," he insisted, "like this." He put his cold hand over mine and guided the pencil.

By two o'clock, we were very close to done. I tried to stay focused, but all the arrows, lines and numbers began to swim before my eyes. My head lurched forward…

"Scarlet!" I felt a hand shake my shoulder, roughly. "Scarlet, that's enough for tonight. You're falling asleep on the paper!"

I snapped my face up. "I'm sorry, sir!" I blurted in Ichthyothian. I started to gather the pages into a pile, but they kept slipping.

"Just leave them and return to your quarters," Cease said. "I'll finish up for us. Dismissed."

"Thank you, sir," I said stupidly as I drifted out the door.

I dropped into my bed without bothering to remove my uniform.

* * *

Cease forwarded me an email the moment the trumpet sounded. Overnight, the Trilateral Committee accepted our proposition to delay surrender, but only gave us until the end of July to figure things out. We had three days.

Everyone except Nurtic and his three closest friends here—Arrhyth Link, Dither Maine and Tose Acci—treated me with an aura of distant coldness at breakfast, obviously not quite over the events of the previous day, despite the explanatory meeting Cease held at dawn for everyone but me (Cease thought it better if I didn't attend). The most standoffish of them all was Inexor Buird. He didn't even acknowledge me when I looked him in the eye and greeted him by name. He just walked right around me and got in the serving line. I felt slapped for a moment, then realized what was probably going on, here; he was jealous. After being Cease's right hand for who knew how long, he was currently without rank. His best friend leaned on someone else, now. It made sense Inexor would be stony toward his replacement.

It was what happened right after we all got out of line that revealed there must've been something more serious going on between Cease and Inexor. Something far more personal than just a dispute over rank.

"Good morning, Inexor," Cease said as he passed Inexor, seated only two places away from me.

"Don't talk to me," Inexor retorted to Cease's back.

I froze in mid-bite. No one—and I mean, no one—addressed the Commander like that. Ever. Moreover, weren't they supposed to be best friends? Best friends who were just reunited after an age of separation, during which everyone thought Inexor was dead?

Cease swiveled around, bowl of oatmeal sliding noisily across his trey. "Excuse me?" he said, low tone slicing through the hubbub of the mess hall.

"Oh, you didn't hear me?" Inexor turned in his seat. "I said," he raised his voice, "don't talk to me, you—" and he proceeded to blurt a rather intense-sounding string of dirty Ichthyothian words I'd only ever heard from Amok's mouth.

Sitting on either side of Inexor was Illia Frappe and Quiesce Tacit, who both looked like they wanted to evaporate on the spot. The last thing any of Cease's subordinates wanted was to get mixed up in a personal dispute between the Commander and, well, anyone.

"What the hell did I do to you?" Cease growled, eyes like iron. The hand that wasn't holding his tray was balled into a tight fist.

Inexor stared hard at Cease for several drawn-out seconds before saying with solemn intensity: "Ask Fair."

Oh, Tincture, what was *that* about?

* * *

After breakfast, Cease and I stood before the fleet and presented our findings from Fair's interrogation along with our infiltration plan. Then, we opened the floor to input from everyone. Allowing even the greenest rookie to make suggestions was the best way to get fresh ideas. By mid-afternoon, our plan was refined and approved by all, and the divers who'd play a direct role were selected. Nurtic would be our pilot; that wasn't exactly a tough choice. And, Arrhyth—who had been taking off-hours, private pilotry lessons from Nurtic since we got to Icicle—would come along as our backup. Arrhyth seemed quite pleased to be chosen over Nurtic's second 'student,' Tose Acci, who had asked

Cease earlier this month to be reassigned from unit four to two, just so he could observe Nurtic in action more closely.

Cease and I constituted the core invasion force, of course. Which meant—

"Time to learn some Conflagrian, sir," I said, in the evening. The two of us were settling down in a small, empty seminar hall, for his first lesson. "On the island, you can't speak a single word of Ichthyothian or Nurian, in front of anyone," I reminded him.

Civilian mage society was male-dominant; the gatekeepers would expect Cease to be the one to request entrance to the Fire Pit. An illiterate man his age would draw a whole lot of attention.

Cease already had difficulty with Nurian, though Nurian and Ichthyothian shared the same alphabet and half the same words—the biggest difference between the two Nordic tongues was the accent. I had a hunch trying to teach Cease basic Conflagrian was going to be like trying to teach an Infrared to heal flesh with his hair.

How right I was.

Cease had absolutely no gift for language, whatsoever. It was unbelievable; the same man who was brilliant at everything else he attempted couldn't even remember how to say, 'hi, how are you doing, today?' in Conflagrian. He had a hard time just echoing a simple self-introduction, let alone understanding my slow, deliberate, over-articulated sentences.

"What brings you here today, mister?" I enunciated carefully.

"Yes, um," he began, his Ichthyothian accent already evident. "I would need… some two gallons… from that—uh, Scarlet, how do you say 'fire,' again?" Cease interjected in Nurian.

I sighed and told him. "Sir, you *can't* forget the most frequently used word on the island! For Tincture's sake, 'fire' is the first word mage infants learn!"

"Alright, alright!" he said. "By the way, what's with this 'Tincture's sake' and 'oh, Tincture' business? This isn't the first time I've heard you say that."

I shrugged. "It's a Conflagrian expression. Tincture is the name of our—their—Principal, as you know. I guess the Nordic equivalent would be 'for goodness' sake' or 'oh, gosh.'"

Cease nodded. "Interesting."

"Let's get back to the lesson, shall we, sir? You were asking me for something?"

"Yes." He cleared his throat and tried again, but this time forgot how to say 'gallons' and wound up requesting two 'gulps' of fire, instead.

"That was better, wasn't it?" he inquired in Nurian after laboriously constructing the question.

"Um, not quite, sir," I responded, in Ichthyothian. "You see, I couldn't exactly give you what you asked for unless I was a dragon."

Cease raised an eyebrow. I translated his sentence word for word and he actually chuckled, though without smiling somehow. It was the first time I ever heard him laugh, and I was startled by how the sound made my heartrate jump. It was like music. The first real music I'd heard, since Nurtic's viola.

But, I could tell Cease didn't really think his struggle was funny. His temples pulsed and his forehead shone with sweat. He was obviously frustrated with himself, worried about the looming deadline. He wasn't used to having difficulty learning anything. He was accustomed to being amazing at whatever he did.

"How long did it take *you* to learn Nurian?" he suddenly asked.

I couldn't lie; he could read me too well. I kept my head down, buried in the examples I was writing for him—phonetic Conflagrian phrases spelled out in Ichthyothian letters.

"A night," I said quietly, aware of how very cocky I unintentionally sounded.

"A *night?*" I could feel my face flush under the intensity of his astonished stare. "Who taught it to you?"

"I did," I replied, still not looking at him. "I snuck into the Order Chairman's home library in Alcove City and got my hands on a dictionary and some grammar books. I also soaked in a lot by just sitting in public places and listening to people talk."

Cease was dumbfounded. "What about Ichthyothian?"

"The academy taught me Ichthyothian," I half-whispered.

He narrowed his eyes into silver slits. "I bet you were already familiar with the language before going to the academy, right?"

I was stricken; how in the world did he know that?

"Am I right?" he insisted.

What could I say? Yes, sir, I snuck into a top-secret meeting and had my first exposure to Ichthyothian from *you!*

"Well, Ichthyothian is very similar to Nurian," I babbled. "It sounds like a dialect of Nurian—essentially, that's what it is—so, the patterns and sounds were pretty easy to pick up—"

"Ichthyothian is *not* a dialect; it's its own language!"

I waved my hand. "Sir, you know what I mean. Once upon a time, Ichthyosis was a Nurian colony, so, naturally, its origin had to be—"

Cease wasn't interested in a history lesson, right now. And, he was too sharp to be derailed.

"Were you or were you not already familiar with Ichthyothian before you entered the academy?" he interrupted, loudly.

"Yes, sir," I whimpered. "The first time I heard it, I was able to start understanding some of it."

"And, when was that?" he snapped, leaning forward.

"Right before I left for the academy," I said in a small voice.

Cease tapped his mechanical pencil against the metal table. "The Isolationist Laws make that pretty unlikely. How did you hear any Ichthyothian if you were living in southeast Nuria, at the time?"

I was silent.

"I'm aware of all your powers," he said. "And, I have a strong suspicion where you picked it up—or, should I say, from *whom*."

I didn't dare to breathe.

"You hid yourself with eye magic and snuck into the Alliance Conference."

What!? "Y-yes, sir."

It was dangerous to have someone know me *that* well. No one else could've guessed the truth, from so few clues. I waited for his loud reprimands to come, but instead he said something else that shocked me to the core:

"I felt it. I couldn't exactly *see* it—more like, I sensed it. I don't quite know how to describe it. I wasn't even sure what it was until I met you face-to-face in May and started feeling it again. It was your aura. It started about halfway through the meeting. And, when I passed near the door at the end of the meeting, it got really strong. That's where you were standing, right?"

I nodded. Cease, a Nordic of all Nordics, could *sense* my aura, like a mage?

"You looked right at me, sir," I breathed. "My heart almost stopped. How did you…?"

"I've always been unusually sensitive to the spectral web and no one here can explain why."

"Wow."

"Do *you* have any idea why?" he asked, looking a little on edge. No, not on edge. Afraid. Cease was afraid of his inexplicable connectivity to the magical world.

I furrowed my brows. How *could* Cease sense my aura like a mage, even when I put in a lot of effort into concealing it? How could I have a vision of him, despite the fact he didn't have an electromagnetic field in the visible portion of the spectrum? It was the same question, I knew. Because both scenarios implied twining. Typically, mages could only have visions of one another if they were spectrally twined. And, twining was a result of interpersonal relationship. It'd always been assumed only colored frequencies could twine. Infrareds couldn't. Until now. Somehow, Cease's infrared lifeline twined with my red one. Even before we had a chance to interact. How? I knew my aura had greater dominion over the spectral web than any in history. Did that explain it? Maybe. Possibly. But, I had no real way to find out for sure. I couldn't exactly research the issue. There'd never been a mage like me before. Not even the System Castle would have a spectroscopy book that'd cover this. I was venturing into uncharted territory here.

"I don't know, sir," was all I said. If the topic scared him and I had no real answers, there was no point in elaborating. My speculations would only frighten him, without actually leading us anywhere. "But, this is a good thing, right? Sensitivity to the web would be an asset for someone whose job is to fight mages. Like, you were able to blow my cover in a second, when we first came face-to-face. And, I was putting in some serious effort into hiding my aura."

Cease nodded. "It's an asset, yes, but I'd be lying if I said this didn't freak me out, a little."

I sat still as a statue, hoping my face also stayed stoic. I couldn't believe Cease would openly admit a fear. To me. I guessed he really did consider me a part of his inner circle of confidence. He trusted me not just with his men in battle, but with his personal weaknesses. His secrets. I was elated.

Cease folded his hands on the table, blinked, and abruptly changed the subject right back: "So, you were at the meeting. If you were living and working in Alcove City at the time, what brought you so far north?"

I swallowed. "I was curious about the war."

"How did you *know* about the war?"

"I figured it out. All I used to do back then was study. I read something in an early-seventh-age history book about a Nurian stowaway on a ship captained by a Terminus Lechatelierite, and it got me thinking." Maybe throwing out his grandfather's name would derail him?

Wishful thinking.

"No." He shook his head. "That could hint to you war once existed on Second Earth, but it wouldn't uncover the current conflict, nor would it lead you on a cross-country journey to the secret Nurian base on the northern shore. Is there a specific reason you're lying to me?"

I averted his eyes. Here it was. The stuff that freaked him out. The stuff I didn't even understand myself. I was going to have to dive into it, after all. "Sir, you know how spectrally-twined mages can have visions of each other?"

"Yes…"

"Well, for lifelines to twine, you, um, apparently don't have to both have frequencies in the visual portion of the electromagnetic spectrum… nor do you have to really… well… know each other, at least not yet. I'm not sure, maybe I'm an exception to the rule."

"What are you getting at, Scarlet?"

I inhaled. "Sir, I had visions of an underwater battle. I didn't know you or any Ichthyothian divers the first time it happened—for Tincture's sake, I didn't even know which nation was fighting which—but, I—"

"*First* time? How many visions have you had?"

I was taken aback. "Just two. Of the same battle."

"Which battle?"

I looked at my hands and answered in a small voice, "The one you lost, sir." I inhaled. "I saw it from your eyes. I could even hear your thoughts."

Cease didn't speak. He looked away. Was he embarrassed? His dying thoughts weren't exactly humiliating. There was nothing personal in them, at all—no desperate good-byes to loved ones, no flashing memories of his life. He thought of only his duty and how his death would affect the war. He cared about nothing but his job. I saw little difference between the Childhood Program and the System. Both indoctrinated their victims.

Cease's eyes met mine. "It was you who told me to let go," he breathed.

"What?" I blurted, forgetting proper salutations.

"The day I lost the battle. Right before the Underwater Fire hit my crystalline, a voice in my head—like my own thoughts—warned me of what was approaching and told me to let go of the handlebars. That was *you*."

I gaped; he was right. During the vision, I screamed at him—or, rather, at *myself*—to drop off or burn alive.

I saved his life.

We sat in stunned silence, for a moment. Then, Cease reached forward and placed his icy hand overtop mine, on the table. I froze.

"Thank you, Scarlet," he said, quietly.

I couldn't breathe. Could he feel my hand trembling beneath his?

"O-of course, sir," I stammered.

There was something odd about the way he was looking at me, now. His face was almost deadpan—but, only almost. What was I seeing in his eyes? Gratitude? Well, yes, of course. But, I could tell that wasn't all. Approval? Perhaps. Yet, that didn't quite hit the nail on the head, either. I'd seen gratitude and approval in his eyes before, and this was different. Greater.

Was I just imagining things? I sincerely hoped not. But, why did I hope not? Why did I want more from Cease than just the simple thankfulness of a comrade-in-arms?

At long last, Cease withdrew his hand and glanced back down at the pages spewed across the table.

I picked up my pencil and cleared my throat. "Al-alright, so where were we, sir?"

And, the evening wore on, long enough for Cease to fail four more times at conversation in Conflagrian.

"Okay, sir," I said in Ichthyothian, wrapping up the lesson. "That wasn't too bad for a first try," I lied, handing him a stack of notes. "We just need to work on your accent and your tendency to insert random Nordic words in the middle of your sentences." If you could even form a sentence, in the first place.

Cease looked dejected. He could tell my encouragement was empty. "If I use *any* Nordic words or speak with a *trace* of an accent in front of anyone there, our cover's blown," he said, flatly.

"We still have some time," I reassured delicately, getting to my feet. Right. Some time. A couple more nights.

Not for the first time since joining the fleet, I found myself doubting my legendary commander's abilities.

SCARLET JULY

It was seven o'clock on the thirty-first. Time for the inaugural Nurro-Ichthyothian infiltration of the South Conflagrablaze Captive. Cease had only set foot on the island once before in his life, if you counted his measly night as a prisoner, last week. I hadn't been there myself since I was ten, and I was sure the System wouldn't give me a warm reception if they recognized me.

So, yes, I was scared photon-less.

Dressed in full mage garb, I buzzed Cease's intercom. "Here you go, sir," I said as I handed him his new, black robe—I'd finished sewing it, last night.

Cease took it from my hands without even glancing at it—his focus was elsewhere. There was an indiscernible expression on his pale face as his eyes traveled up and down my body, like an elevator. My insides squirmed. I wondered what he was thinking when he looked at me like that.

"That's real, isn't it?" he asked. "Your robe—it's the one you actually wore back home?"

"One of them, yes."

"So, you brought it to Icicle," he said, sounding rather unsurprised. "Magically cloaked your cloak, huh?"

Did Cease just crack a joke? Well, it was the closest thing to a joke I'd heard from him, yet. I smiled, internally.

"Yes, sir."

"That's illegal, you know," he went on, voice miraculously void of anger.

A lot of the Nurians had illegal trinkets—photos of family and friends, pocket bibles, key-chains that had sentimental meaning, and so forth. The biggest offender of them all was Nurtic, who somehow, without any magic, managed to bring his viola to the academy and then to Icicle. Hmm, I still didn't know how he pulled that off…

Cease continued to stare at my robe, eyes intense. If I didn't know any better, I'd say there was some appreciation in his gaze. It was as though he actually liked what he saw. No. There was no way. He'd been taught all his life to hate mages, so the last thing I expected was for him to like it when I looked traditionally Conflagrian.

The last thing I expected was for him to like how I looked at all, no matter what I was wearing.

My pulse jumped higher than the Nurian Trade Centerscraper. Was it possible Cease was attracted to me? I certainly was to him—intellectually and physically. But, he was usually so cold, prickly and walled-off, I couldn't imagine him ever developing a romantic interest in anyone, let alone a scrawny, Conflagrian mage.

"Time to fix up your hair, sir?" I piped, more to break the silence than anything. What a strange question to ask my commander.

After considering various aspects of Cease's appearance, hair was the only possible 'source' we could come up with, for him to fake. His hair was convincingly thick and disheveled, but it wasn't quite wiry enough to look authentically spectral. For that, it needed gel.

"I'll put on the robe first," he answered.

I waited outside his quarters while he changed. When he opened up, it was my turn to stare. It was so strange to see Cease in anything but white, not to mention how very out-of-place he seemed in the robe's billowing folds; until now, I only ever saw him in a conforming diving suit or a crisp, ironed uniform.

And, his boxers, once. But, Cease and I were pretending *that* never happened.

I went inside and closed the door behind me. Time for hair.

"Your name is Nox Acherontic," I reminded him as he settled in his desk chair, facing away from me.

"Nox Acherontic," he echoed. "What does it mean, again?"

"Black Night." I shook the bottle, upside-down. "I chose 'Nox' because it's easy for you to pronounce."

"How very considerate of you," Cease replied, dryly. Then, after a pause, he added, "Black Night, huh? Sounds mysterious… and a bit evil."

I was silent. I didn't tell him I had my reasons to think an evil-sounding name suited him.

Fair would certainly agree. My chest tightened as I wondered for the umpteenth time how she was doing. I wished I could visit her. I hoped the hospital was taking good care of her.

I squeezed out a large lump of goop in my palm, put the bottle down and rubbed my hands together. Then, I hesitated, gooey fingers poised an inch above his head. Why was I so nervous? It's not like I could mess up. Cease's hair was always a mess—that was the point. I just needed to smear in some gel so the mess could be wirier and stiffer. There was nothing to it. And, yet, here I stood, hands frozen. Why?

Who was I kidding; I wasn't nervous because I was worried about botching anything. I was afraid to touch Cease because I was so strongly attracted to him, and the idea of running my fingers through my commander's hair seemed invasive and inappropriate in light of that chemistry.

I was being stupid. This wasn't inappropriate. Strange? Certainly. But, not inappropriate. Regardless of my feelings for him, there was nothing personal going on, here; this was still business. I wasn't playing with his hair for fun or giving him a scalp massage or doing anything sensual, I was helping prepare his disguise for a very serious mission on which the fate of the alliance rested.

I exhaled and dropped my hands into his hair. It was surprisingly soft and smooth. And, thick. I had to use three more handfuls just to cover it all. As I worked, I noticed, with a strange sensation in the pit of my stomach, that he'd closed his eyes, almost like he was soothed by my touch. I was relieved when I finished.

"All done, sir."

He retrieved a small mirror from his desk drawer and cocked an eyebrow at his reflection.There was a long pause.

"I look ridiculous," he finally declared.

Yeah, ridiculously handsome. "You look like a hair mage," I said, wiping my slimy hands on my robe. "Though, honestly, sir, if you were to have a source, it'd probably be your throat, not your hair. We just had to go with hair because it's easier to fake, visually." Plus, his vocal control faltered when he tried to speak Conflagrian. He had to put all his concentration toward just remembering the right words.

Cease put down the mirror, looking a little offended, now. "My throat, Scarlet?"

"Yes, sir," I insisted.

"I yell that loud, huh?" He smirked.

"You do have quite a set of lungs on you, sir," I laughed.

Throat mages could do a whole lot more than just shout loudly. They were masters of tone. They could manipulate their voices to compel, pierce, destroy, inspire—you name it. Cease was the first Nordic I'd met whose voice could practically capture and drug his listeners. I supposed it was one of the reasons he was such an effective leader.

"Well," Cease said, "when I was about to crash-land the manta ray and saw you still onboard, who could blame me for screaming at you to get the hell out. Kamikazes don't need co-pilots. Especially when that co-pilot is the best possible replacement a commander could ask for."

My heart hammered against my ribcage. I was floored by the magnitude of Cease's compliment. Did he really believe that? Me, the best soldier he ever had? No way. But, Cease wasn't a flatterer or a liar. He was always very direct and blunt. Brutally honest. He meant what he said. I hungered for his respect and approval since I got here. I lived in fear of letting him down. I guessed, I didn't disappoint, after all.

"If you didn't literally throw me out, I wouldn't have left," I said, refraining from telling him how badly it hurt to leave him behind, or how much I agonized over his presumed death, afterward. I knew, I could never reveal to anyone how attached to him I'd become. I had a hard time just admitting to myself: I'd broken my life code to pieces, despite my best efforts. "I guess you saved my life too, then, sir. We're even."

* * *

Just in time for today's infiltration, the Trilateral Committee was sure to provide us with a fresh-from-the-factory, mini, convertible vitreous silica, complete with diffusion shields. Cease, Nurtic, Arrhyth and I boarded it at exactly seven-thirty. The hours passed slowly as we traveled across the Septentrion Sea and the Briny Ocean, stopping to refuel at the Fervor Gulf.

Before our ship could come within eyeshot of the Conflagrian shore, I committed all my spectrum into hiding it from view. I cloaked it long enough for Cease and I to exit, and for the manta ray to turn around and clear the coast. The task was a real spectral drain.

"You okay?" Cease whispered as I squatted in the sand. We were in the deserted Northern Dunes. No one lived out here except for the occasional, passing gypsy tribe.

"Yes, sir," I breathed, peering up at the brilliant, orange sky. "Just give me a moment."

Cease waited with remarkable patience as I lay on my back for a several minutes, eyes and hair soaking in the wonderful, one-hundred-twenty degree sunlight. I stared directly at the sun. The bitter, Nordic frigidity that seemed to have seeped into my bones over the past six ages finally melted away. For the first time since the eighty-seventh age, I was warm enough to breathe freely. I got to my feet.

"Better?" Cease asked.

"Yes, sir," I answered, sheepishly. "Sorry for taking so long."

"That's fine."

"Stand still for a moment, sir. I need to give you your aura."

Cease's physical form couldn't just be black to the human eye. To really look like a mage, he needed an intangible, innate, acherontic air about him. He needed the appearance of a black electromagnetic field.

"Alright," Cease said, blinking repeatedly.

And, there it was again—fear, in his eyes. Fear of the magical. The same man who wasn't afraid to kamikaze into an enemy base was scared of letting a little spectrum flow into him. Incredible.

I inhaled and took a step toward him, gearing up to do it. Now, only inches from his face, I realized it wasn't just fear I was seeing in his silver stare. It was revulsion. He was disgusted. Disturbed. Just this morning, he called me, a Conflagrian mage, the best soldier he'd ever had. He had no trouble relying on me, working closely with me, trusting me with his weaknesses, and making use of my spectral gifts for the service of his country. He even thanked me a couple nights ago for using our spectral twining to save his life. I thought he was comfortable by *now* with me and my magic. And, yet, here he was, repulsed by the thought of having my aura affect his infrared frequency. I was surprised by how deeply that cut me. Even after all we'd been through together, he was still listening to his... his *programming*. His programming that taught him to hate all things magical. The Childhood Program sure did a number on him.

Well, for the sake of our cover, Cease was going to have to glow like a blacklight today, whether he liked it or not. I sent two locks of hair snaking down my arms, into my palms. Then, I placed my hands on Cease's shoulders and concentrated on sending a surge of spectrum into him. Slowly, a black mist began to form all around him, as though he really were Nox Acherontic.

I released him and took a couple steps back. He peered down at his glowing body in awe.

"Nice work," he said, though through tight lips.

I only nodded. Then, I scrunched my eyes shut, turned my vision inward and pictured my own red wavelength. Concentrating hard, I began to loosen the hard shell I built around it, six ages ago. Slowly, my scarlet aura began to seep from my sources, sweeping over my entire frame.

I opened my eyes to the sight of Cease gaping openly at me. He'd never seen me in my natural state before.

"You look..." he breathed, then bit his lip.

I looked what? I stared at him, in suspense. Why didn't he want to finish his sentence?

"You look... really, really red," he finally said.

Really, really red? I suppressed a laugh. Was it just me, or was that not what he was going to say, before he caught himself?

"Well, that's why they call me Scarlet."

Cease surprised me then by stepping forward and taking my hand firmly in his. I couldn't breathe. Our plan involved posing as a married couple, so this wasn't exactly outrageous. But, we were still in the Northern Dunes. Miles upon miles from civilization. We didn't need to start getting too in-character, *yet*. But, of course, I didn't dare withdraw. I just stood there stupidly, holding his hand, enjoying it, hoping he couldn't feel my pulse quicken.

His hand was very hot and sweaty.

That's when I noticed the perspiration dripping down the edges of his shiny, shellacked hair. His cheeks, usually so pale, had a rosy tint to them. Of course, while the heat was energizing me, it was killing him. I snaked a lock of hair back down my right arm and pumped a steady stream of spectrum into Cease's grasp, gradually reducing his fever.

Cease exhaled, relieved. "Thank you," he breathed, wiping his forehead with his floppy, black sleeve.

For the next couple hours, we walked silently, hand-in-hand. Mountains of sand rippled majestically, like water in the light wind. I hungrily drank in the beautiful sight of yellows, oranges, reds and beiges—colors never seen on the monochromatic, snow-covered nation of Ichthyosis. Cease probably found the vibrancy of his surroundings unsettling, but said nothing.

At last, we reached the outskirts of civilization—a small village called Cerulean, where, in exchange for a couple taro roots from our pockets and a "thank you," murmured by Cease in Conflagrian, we hopped aboard a crowded, wooden wagon with a tattered, burlap canopy, towed by a scabrous dragon. Conflagrian public transit. And, after a couple more hours and several more stops along the bumpy path, we arrived at Ardor Village—the capital of Conflagria, the city of my birth.

Things were exactly the same as during my childhood. Ichthyosis underwent more change and development in the last two months than Conflagria did in six ages. The System did indeed maintain a perfect, uninterrupted status quo.

It was our job to turn their world upside-down.

After pretending to be Nordic for half a dozen ages, it was tough to walk through my hometown again and see all the rickety, wooden cabins lining the dusty paths; scabrouses romping around in backyards, roped to wooden posts; taro fields filled with the bent backs of Uselesses; and colorful children running around with kites and fiddling with their untrained magic. Seeing all this proved my past wasn't just a nightmare I could escape by fleeing across the Briny Ocean and Septentrion Sea. Conflagria wasn't just an image on a classroom wall, a map in a textbook, or a memory in the back of my mind. It was as real as the sights and sounds before me, now.

We joined the winding line around the Fire Pit, where mages from across the island awaited their rations. After ninety minutes, our turn came. We stood before two mages I actually recognized from my Circle Trial, a decade ago. One was a dark-robed man with a goatee and a permanent smirk on his face, and the other was an aged woman with a low, raspy, mystical voice.

It was time for Cease to recite his big, memorized speech. I held my breath.

"I am hair-mage Nox Acherontic, and this is my wife, Ruby Ringlet," he said, sounding a little too slow and mechanical for comfort. "We come from the Seventh Dunes to pick up the ration for our community. The elders have chosen us to serve as Town Messengers, this week."

The gypsies of the Dunes didn't make daily treks to the Fire Pit like those who lived more inland. Because they were usually far from Ardor, they only came about once every week or two to collect vast amounts of fire for their entire tribe. According to the Ribald Briny Fire Safety Laws, these 'Dune Messengers' had to get special permission to enter the depths of the Pit, where they handled jumbo scoops.

"We need to verify your eye-hand coordination before authorizing you to use the flame-catchers," the goateed one said.

Cease stared at him, without comprehension. The man, murmuring under his breath about ignorant, teenage first-timers, groped for

Cease's left hand. Squeezing Cease's palm, he closed his eyes and furrowed his eyebrows.

"Here you are," he said gruffly, releasing his hold and holding out a glimmering net, woven from dragon mane-hair. Apparently, Cease passed the dexterity test. No surprise there. He took the net and we stepped forward.

"No, no, little lady." He caught my shoulder. "You have to wait out here until your husband returns."

"Seventh Dunes won't be able to send anyone for two weeks," I said, quickly. "He may need my help gathering an extra scoop."

The man laughed richly, at that. "*He* may need *your* help?" He gave my body elevator-eyes, and, unlike when Cease did that this morning, I found it extremely creepy. "The Fire Pit is no place for a woman."

I felt a surge of anger stream through my hair as I held out my hand.

"Test me," I growled.

His bushy eyebrows rose. "I can't while you're upset; it'll alter the results." He stroked his chin. "Maybe you should wait a few minutes, you know… to cool off."

I understood what he didn't say: He wanted to brush me aside for *seven minutes*—just long enough for my rebellious thoughts to get suppressed by the System's magical thought-control.

"Sit down for a while." He gestured to a wicker rocking-chair beside him. He turned to Cease and waved him on. "You can go in, now; she'll wait for you out here."

Cease probably didn't understand a word, but could figure out the situation well enough from his intonation and body language.

"Um, no… I, uh, would like to…" Cease looked at me, eyes pleading for help.

"Wait here with me," I quickly finished for him.

Cease nodded, vigorously. "Yes, I would like to wait here with me."

The mage blinked.

"Her!" Cease burst. "I would like to wait here with her!"

The man looked annoyed. "As you wish, kid."

He turned to the next people in line. And, as I expected, he returned to us exactly seven minutes later. I gave him what I hoped was a sweet smile.

"Would you like to test me, now?" I asked pleasantly, holding out my hand.

He was taken aback by my persistence, but no longer had an excuse to deny me the test. There was no actual law forbidding women from entering the Pit, it was just unconventional. The System discouraged it, and, due to the mind-control, that was all they really needed to do to get the masses to cooperate, for the most part.

He grasped my red palm and concentrated deeply. When he opened his eyes, he seemed all the more irritated.

"You passed, lady," he said. "Go on."

"Oh, *thank you*," I breathed, following Cease to the stone door.

My stomach knotted as we began descending the narrow, winding stairs. Cease left the flame-catcher on the ground, somewhere along the way. Soon, it was completely dark in all directions. As I felt my aura dissipate, I could no longer see Cease, just a couple paces ahead of me.

"Scarlet, why don't you use your eye-fire to give us some light?" Cease asked.

"I can't, sir. It's like a diffusion cell in here."

The temperature rose with every step we took. After half an hour, the path apparently came to an abrupt end—I heard the *slam* of Cease running into something solid, and the next thing I knew, we were thrown onto our backs, Cease on top of me. A sharp, stony clatter sounded near my head.

"Scarlet, are you okay?" Cease breathed in Nurian, quickly getting up.

His bony butt had landed right in my gut. I was glad I didn't have an appetite this morning, because my breakfast would've surely come up, right now. Bitter stomach acid burned my mouth.

"Yes, sir," I said, swallowing. "You?"

"You broke my fall; I'm fine."

"What was that sharp noise?" I asked. "It sounded like something small and hard bounced by my head."

"Is this it?" Cease asked, voice issuing from behind me. He somehow found his way back to me, felt for my hands and placed a rough object in them. My fingers traced the jagged, familiar edges.

"The crystal!" I whispered.

"What're you talking about? The Core Crystal is larger than a vitreous silica!"

"No, no, sir, I'm talking about *my* crystal." I touched my neck and found a jumble of wire there. The rock must've slipped from the coils. "A guard gave it to me the day I was deported."

"Yeah, okay," Cease said.

Sheepishly, I pocketed the fragment. Extending my arms out in the darkness, I touched what felt like a warm, stone wall. What Cease ran into.

"How are we supposed to get past this?" I wondered aloud.

WHAM!

I tasted blood in my mouth, and pain seared down my neck.

"What the—?"

THUD!

Cease groaned.

"Ichthyothian spies!" I recognized the voice of the goateed mage.

I fingered my utility belt, hidden beneath my swathe. But, I couldn't shoot a weapon in here, in such a tight space, when I couldn't see. What if I hit Cease?

A fist punched me in the stomach. Then again, and again, at evenly spaced intervals. Right when I expected his next strike, I jumped up into a backflip, kicking the man in the face. I heard his body hit the ground. Then, to the sound of Cease grunting, I heard a rip and a series of thumps, and it was all over.

"I took care of him," Cease said, shortly.

A chill ran down my spine. I was glad I couldn't see how.

I returned to the wall, now dripping with what must've been our attacker's bodily fluids. I slid my fingers across the stone, feeling several bumps and grooves. I slowly began to piece together a message, as the protrusions formed a string of archaic Conflagrian words.

"It's a riddle," I said, "requesting a password for us to get by. It says, the question changes according to who sees it, and it never asks the same one twice."

"Great. What's ours?"

"It wants us to speak the name, or the meaning of the name, of the 'Son of Nations.'" I folded my arms, feeling helpless already. "I don't even know what that means."

"Son of Nations," Cease echoed. "Is that a royal Conflagrian title?"

"No. We just call the executive leader, 'Principal,' and his cabinet, 'Throne Advisors.' That's it."

"What about mage mythology?"

I wrinkled my nose. "No, I *know* all those tales, but 'Son of Nations' isn't in any of them. Maybe it has nothing to do with Conflagria. I mean, it doesn't say 'Son of the Nation of Conflagria,' but specifically, 'Son of Nations.' Plural. It must be asking for someone born of more than one country."

Cease snorted. "Like that ever happens."

Well, it already did, but only a couple times on record. Arrhyth Link and his little sister, Linkeree, were Nurro-Orion. But, somehow, I didn't think the wall was asking for their names.

Cease was already growing impatient. "Now what?"

I wrung my hands. We didn't come this far to get stumped by a stupid guessing game!

"I don't even know where to begin, Lechatelierite," I sighed.

With a thunderous rumble, the wall began to move, and my spectrum returned to my eyes and hair with a sizzle. That's when I realized the barrier wasn't a wall at all, but a boulder. It rolled right over the mangled body of our attacker.

"What did I say?" I gaped. "Why's it opening?"

The stone stopped abruptly, and our sights were filled with bright, billowing flames. We were miles beneath the crust of the Earth, facing a fire that lashed all the way to the orange, Conflagrian sky. The crackle of the inferno roared in our ears. Enormous rock fragments intermittently dislodged from the cavern walls and came crashing down into the massive pool of bubbling, steaming lava. Straining my eye magic, I peered into the blinding base of the conflagration and looked directly at it—the sparkling, scintillating, colossal Core Crystal, framed by coursing magma. The two of us stood, staring in awe, for just a moment. Cease pulled his visual band over his eyes and the light danced across its silver surface.

Then, Cease nodded at the long, narrow, winding cliff before us and said in a firm, unafraid voice: "Who cares why it opened. Let's go."

He led the way, carefully but quickly, chin up and eyes forward. His steps were graceful and fluid. I followed closely behind, keeping my eyes on him so I wouldn't look down. When we reached the edge, Cease lassoed half a dozen massive stalactites with deadline from his utility belt, hidden beneath his swathe. I stood a foot in front of him, facing the fire. He shot two cables around me, binding my waist to his. We were bolted to the spot.

"Secure," Cease said. "Now, do it, Scarlet."

Do it, Scarlet. Just crush a magical rock ten times the size of a vitreous silica with your hair. No problem.

I took a deep breath, channeled my aura into my scalp, and sent all my hair through the flames and around the Crystal.

And, with that, I felt a galvanizing wave zip up my locks, striking my head like an electric mallet. My mind went numb with shock.

"Come on, what are you waiting for? Do it!" a faraway voice called through the crackling. "Concentrate!"

Where was that voice coming from? What did those weird words mean?

"Scarlet, what's going on? Why aren't you doing it?"

What was that obscure language? It definitely wasn't Conflagrian.

"Are you okay? Scarlet?"

Nurian? Ichthyothian? ICHTHYOTHIAN! It was the language of the enemy! There was an enemy of Conflagria, here! Powerful hatred as I'd never felt before pulsed like venom through my veins. I struggled to turn, but couldn't move—there were wires wrapped around my waist! The enemy had me trapped! I withdrew a single lock from the Crystal and used it to slice myself free. Without even turning around, I then whipped that lock behind me, where I'd heard the Ichthyothian voice.

There was a scream, followed by the sound of something hitting stone.

Only then did I turn and see the body of my enemy, writhing on the cliff, looking at me through a strange, silver strip across his face.

"Scarlet!" he yelled. "Scarlet, it's me! It's your Commander, Lechatelierite! Snap out of it!"

My frame shuddered violently, overwhelmed by the surges of spectrum coursing up my hair. My ears were filled with the deafening rumble of fire and tumbling boulders. His words meant nothing to me. I poised my free lock high above my head and prepared to deal my enemy a deathly blow.

But, the Ichthyothian rolled forward, narrowly escaping my hair as it crashed into the stone, creating a crevice too deep to cross on foot. We were stranded on this little oval of rock, now. Stranded in the heart of the Fire Pit.

"Scarlet!" the enemy called, again. "You're on the side of Ichthyosis, now, remember? Snap out of it! This is a direct order!"

I heard his words, but they didn't register. I ignited my free lock and launched it at him again. But, in a flash, he somersaulted through the air, right above my ringlet. His feet landed on my chest, knocking me clean off the cliff.

As I fell, I saw a wire lash toward me, from above. It coiled tightly around my waist, breaking my fall, but not without terrible whiplash. I screamed, dangling mere feet from the flames. I looked up and saw the white face of my enemy straining over the edge, holding the cable that saved my life with both hands. His whole body shook.

"Let me go!" I shouted, in his hateful, consonant language. "Let me go, now!"

He panted with an open mouth. "No!"

"Then, I'll cut myself free! I'd rather die than be indebted to the enemy!"

"Scarlet, don't! You'll fall in! You'll die!"

"What do you care, Ichthyothian?"

I slid a lock of hair between my body and the wire.

"Scarlet, NO!" he screamed, voice cracking. His hands were purple. "Scarlet, listen to me! Don't cut the wires! Let me pull you up!"

"Quit toying with me, enemy!" I hollered, legs thrashing.

"Scarlet, I'm not your enemy! I'm your commander! You're on the side of Ichthyosis, now!" he yelled again, visual band sliding to the end of his nose. He paused. "No, you're not fighting for Ichthyosis, but *with* Ichthyosis to liberate *your* people from the System." He inhaled, sharply. "Scarlet, this is Cease! This is Cease, remember me? Not your enemy, your friend!"

Friend. Not my enemy. Cease. That name was familiar. Cease… my friend…?

"Cease?" I whispered.

He shook off the visual band—it dropped to his neck—and he looked at me with his own two eyes.

"Yes," he breathed. "I'm here, Scarlet."

But, those icy eyes brought back too many unpleasant memories. Memories of violence and destruction and reprimands and harsh words. No, he wasn't my friend. Just my commander. Commander Lechatelierite. He didn't care for the Conflagrian people. All he cared about was the war. Winning the war for Ichthyosis. My life and my people were nothing, absolutely nothing to him. He just wanted to win.

If I fell into the Pit, the Crystal would detonate. It'd be the end of the spectral web. The end of the System's thought-control. The end of magic on Second Earth. The end of the war.

Exactly what this commander wanted.

"If I fell in, everything would be all over," I told him. "Your mission would be a success. Ichthyosis would be victorious. Isn't that what you want, Commander Lechatelierite?"

I wound my hair around the wire.

"*NO!* Scarlet, don't do it! Scarlet, please don't! I don't care about the war anymore; do you hear me? I don't care about winning! Just as long as you don't fall in! Please, Scarlet, listen to me!"

His words traveled slowly from my ears to my brain. Was this possible? Was the great Commander Cease Lechatelierite, Leader of the Ichthyothian Resistance, actually willing to give up the war? For me?

As I looked into his desperate, silver-grey eyes, I realized just how much I cared for him. I loved him. I probably already did before now, but I didn't recognize it until this wild, black moment. Until I saw him willing to sacrifice the purpose of his whole life... for me.

My hair released the Crystal. I lay still in the wire and allowed Cease to pull me up. As soon as I made it onto the stone, he wrenched me to my feet and threw his arms tightly around me. My second hug, in six ages—both, from him. We stood frozen in time, for just a minute.

"Don't you ever scare me like that again, Scarlet," he cried, face buried in my hair. "Let's get out of here. We tried our best and failed. Let's go home, to Icicle."

There was a long pause.

"No."

Cease's arms stiffened around me; he clearly thought I was turning against him again.

"What I mean is; no, we didn't fail, because we didn't finish trying." I took a deep breath. "I can do it this time, sir. I know what to expect. The shock took me by surprise, but it won't, now. I'll have more control."

Cease pulled away and gave me a long, hard stare. "Are you sure?" he demanded.

"Yes, sir, I am." I swallowed. "And, if I falter, you know what to say to make me come around."

He nodded, that maddening look of approval in his eyes. That look was enough to empower me with the strength of a hundred Core Crystals. It was the closest his face ever got to a smile.

I faced the flames and Cease shot new bindings around my waist and six stalactites. Repeating Cease's words in my mind, I reached back into the inferno with my hair and braced myself for the jolt. My locks raveled around the Crystal, and sure enough, electricity galvanized my every cell and photon. But, this time, I could take it. This time, I could focus through the pain and ignore the voice shouting lies inside my head. The Crystal slowly began to crumble as I increased my pressure. Lava squirted from the growing cracks, narrowly missing our faces. The cavern walls began to crumble and avalanche. My body shook as screams ripped through my throat. The last thing I remembered was a glorious rush of light and arms encircling my waist, before everything went black.

CEASE LECHATELIERITE

Scarlet's hair receded from the Crystal and her tiny body pitched forward. My arms caught her before the deadline could. A rumble sounded in my ears as I severed all the cables but one—wound around a stalactite, hundreds of yards above. I leapt off the stone island, swinging. When my feet came in contact with the other side, I cut the last wire and sprinted up the narrow, dark stairwell. I was still in the tunnel when I heard the final, deafening boom of the Crystal's detonation. Scarlet's limp body jerked in my arms, emitting irregular bursts of red light. She was losing her aura. Total diffusion. I felt my own black haze flicker and die. Without magic to control my body temperature, I suddenly felt hot, overwhelmingly hot—so much so, I turned my head and vomited right over my shoulder.

Dizzy, nauseous and sweaty, I emerged from the tunnel to the sight of mad chaos in the square. The sky changed rapidly from bright orange to dark brown—from early afternoon to late evening—as the island, no longer enshrouded in spectrum, visually adjusted to the Earth's thirty-six-hour rotation. Mages everywhere were scrambling about, screaming, as their colorful auras flashed and dissipated. Left and right, brawls were already breaking out between townsfolk and System officials, as the minds of the masses were freed from the thought-control. No doubt there'd be a big revolution, in the ages to come. The first in Conflagrian history. It was long overdue.

Clutching Scarlet to my chest, I pushed my way through the frantic crowd, the ground shaking beneath my feet. And, I ran right into a tall, muscular mage with copper-colored hair, alarmingly-huge hands and wide, amber eyes. Though he was much bigger than me, he was the one thrown onto his back. Fighting vertigo, I leapt over him and kept running, calling to Leavesleft through the microphone clipped inside my robe's collar.

"Now, Leavesleft!"

The vitreous silica dashed across the sky, pouring fire into the vacant Pit. Conflagrian society would always need fire—spectrum or no spectrum, it was an irreplaceable part of their culture. Then, Leavesleft swooped above me and dropped a ladder. Hoisting Scarlet's body over my shoulder, I flew up the rungs.

"Go!" I ordered as soon as I made it in.

Head throbbing and shapes spinning before my eyes, I passed Scarlet to Link and sank to my knees. Our ship shot into the distance, back home to Ichthyosis.

SCARLET JULY

I opened my eyes and stared at the white, metal ceiling. My whole body seared with pain, especially my eyes and scalp. It felt like thousands of ice-cold needles were simultaneously piercing my flesh. A large bandage was wrapped around my waist—where Cease's wire broke my fall into the Fire Pit.

I heard a creak and saw a blonde-haired, Nurian nurse in blue scrubs, Mrs. Insouci Raef, come in and approach my bedside. The lights seemed strangely dimmed, and it was actually a bit difficult to see the far side of the room. Normally, I would've been able to read the letters on the computer keyboard down the hall. But, now, I could hardly make out the individual, white buttons themselves. I blinked repeatedly, to no avail.

"Your eyesight isn't damaged, ma'am," Raef said, quietly. "We scanned your retinas. You have twenty-twenty vision."

I scrunched my eyes shut and only saw auburn—the inside of my lids. I willed a single strand of hair to move. Nothing happened.

So, we succeeded. The Crystal ended. Ichthyosis won the war. The spectral web diffused. My people were free. We did it. It was the moment of victory. But, I didn't feel like celebrating. I just wanted to fall asleep. Diffusion was such a major drain on my body, I felt like I barely had the strength to just keep breathing. I rolled over and saw a lock of my own hair—lifeless and limp—flop over my shoulder.

I peered out the window, at the snowflakes beating against the glass. I shivered, pulling the thin sheet to my throat. I could no longer spontaneously raise my body temperature. I was completely on my own, reliant on technology, just like the Nordics, for my wellbeing. How badly I wanted a fire, right now.

"The Commander will be happy to see you awake," Raef said giving me a mischievous smile. "He's been stopping by to check on you at least, oh, once an hour, every hour, since he himself has been discharged."

"Cease!" I gasped, somehow finding the energy to sit up. "Is he alright?"

The nurse seemed quite taken aback. "*Commander Lechatelierite* came home with fever of about one-oh-six. Heatstroke and mild spectral poisoning."

"Oh, Tincture!" I cried.

"Don't worry, ma'am; he's fine, now. We took good care of him. And, you know the Commander—doesn't matter if there's a lance sticking out of his back and blood oozing from his eyes, he'll still try to get up and return to duty." She folded her arms. "He actually *did* try, more than once, to walk over here to see you, when he himself was supposed to be bedridden and tubed up. He'll be very glad to know you're awake and well. Should I get him?"

"Oh, um, no, that's okay," I stuttered, floored by Cease's degree of concern, not to mention quite nervous to face him again now that I knew I wasn't just attached or attracted to him, but rather, I loved him. "I'm really tired; I think I'll just take a nap or something."

I lay back down. Pillow stiff and frigid under my head, I wondered what would become of me now that the Crystal ended. What do you do, after achieving everything you ever wanted? The Multi-Source Enchant fulfilled the prophecy and 'took from the fallen children of Second Earth what was no longer rightfully theirs'—the spectrum. I'd accomplished the purpose of my life. And, by winning the war, so did Cease. Was I just going to spend the rest of my days on this cold, isolated base, beating down generations of young men like Colonel Austere, repeating all the mistakes of the System by aiding in manipulating their lives and destroying their humanity?

No. I knew what I had to do. I knew what my next calling would be. There was no time to sit back and bask in the victory. There was still work to be done. My people needed me.

SCARLET JULY

August seventh.

I adjusted my robe over my narrow shoulders, surveying myself in the mirror of my military quarters for the last time. Yesterday, I briefly awoke from my coma, exchanged a few words with Raef, then fell right back asleep. Today, Fair and I would return to Conflagria. In a couple hours, we'd begin our trek across the Septentrion Sea, Briny Ocean and Fervor Sea, aboard a deck-ship, piloted by Nurtic. No longer bound by the Core Crystal, my people were now aware of the sixteen-age war and the thought-control that oppressed them for eras. I, the former Multi-Source Enchant, was now known as their liberator, the only Conflagrian strong enough to break free of the System's dominion while the Crystal was intact. My people called me home, to be their revolutionary leader.

I marched into the mess hall and faced my men. It was time for final farewells. They all looked at me now, dressed in my red Conflagrian robe, without a trace of hatred or distrust in their eyes.

"I'm sorry for calling you a spy and ordering the other officers to fire at you," Illia Frappe said, shaking my hand.

I grinned. "It's okay, Illia." I nearly killed Cease in the Fire Pit; I understood Illia's struggle better than he knew.

Arrhyth Link came bounding over next, Orion curls bouncing with every step. I never did get to hear the rest of his story—the story of how the Second Earth Order Chairman secretly denounced isolationism and allowed his own son to participate in an international conspiracy could get Nuria blacklisted, if the Order ever found out. He bowed deeply to me.

"You paid attention in mage culture class, I see," I chortled, returning the bow instead of shaking his hand.

"Yes, ma'am, I did. And, I think I knew, all along." He gave me a sly look. "You know, that you're a mage." Uh huh, sure he did. "I just didn't say anything about it 'cuz I didn't want to jump to conclusions or anything."

Arrhyth Link didn't want to jump to conclusions? "Imagine that," I chuckled.

Nurtic Leavesleft was next. My hand felt so tiny in his.

"I never imagined, when I met you at the train station, we'd both wind up here," he said, smiling his dimpled smile. "It's been a crazy ride."

No kidding. With Nurtic, that could be taken literally. The man could practically fly fifteen directions, at once. No one liked surface-riding on his crystallines.

"Riding on anything *you* pilot is as crazy as crazy gets."

"And, we've got one more trip together, so buckle up!"

I laughed. Then, I bit my lip. "It's been an honor, serving alongside you," I breathed, realizing that, after spending nine months feeling annoyed by his friendliness and constantly pushing him away, I was actually going to miss him. A lot. From day one, he was kind to me, when no one else was. Nurtic was my friend. "You're the most skilled pilot in the fleet," I said, honestly.

Nurtic's tan cheeks turned deep pink. "Yeah, well, I got some practice back at the arcade." He winked one of his large, hazel eyes. Then, after touching my shoulder for just a moment, he left the mess hall and disappeared down the corridors, off to get Fair.

I was surprised when Inexor Buird took my hand next, all prior hostility apparently behind him.

"I never really got to see you fight," he said. "But, from what the Commander tells me, I'm glad he chose you to fill my boots when I was MIA."

I noticed, with surprise, two cobalt blue bands were already on each of his arms. I guessed he and Cease patched things up during the seven days I was unconscious.

"Glad to return it to you."

After about thirty more minutes, the crowd abated. There was only one soldier left to whom I hadn't yet bid farewell.

Cease Lechatelierite stood in the empty hall with his hands clasped behind his back. His pale, sharp face and silver-grey eyes were set. I noticed a tiny, silver pin on his collar. He was an admiral, now. His country rewarded him well for his victory.

"Good-bye, sir," I whispered, in Ichthyothian.

"Call me Cease," he answered quietly, in Nurian.

Then, without another word, he walked up to me and placed his arms very tightly around my waist. I hugged him back, tears seeping from the corners of my magicless eyes and soaking into the fabric of his spotless uniform. It was all too easy to reach around him; he was so *small*. Small, yes, but also strong. The strongest, toughest, most brilliant man I ever met in my life.

Cease pulled back a little and stared at me intently, our noses nearly brushing. And, my breath caught in my chest when I saw something creep across his face that had never been there before, as far as I knew. A smile.

"You're not just really, really red," he said, smiling and stroking my hair. "You're beautiful."

And, with that, he touched my chin with his frozen fingertips, tilted my head up, and softly pressed his ice-colds lips against mine. I closed my eyes, a shiver running down my spine. Cease was usually so rough around the edges, so aggressive, I wouldn't have guessed he was capable of such gentleness. Then, he kissed me again. And, again. My memory wasn't perfect anymore, so it was hard to keep track of how long we went. Only once we were out of breath—quite a feat for a pair of divers—did he pull away.

And, he put his lips to my ear and whispered a phrase in Conflagrian I never taught him.

"I love you."

I knew, as I embraced him for the last time in my life, it was his attachment to me that salvaged the remaining traces of his humanity. By learning to love me—putting me above everything he was told he was born for, learning that ends didn't justify means—he recovered the small part of Cease the human that the Childhood Program didn't manage to extinguish when they forged him into the killing machine known as Commander Lechatelierite, Leader of the Ichthyothian Resistance.

But, I knew, it'd be unthinkable to stay in Ichthyosis when my people so desperately needed me. And, it'd be even more unthinkable to ask Cease to leave his military world and his icy nation to follow me to the Island of Fire where he'd never belong. I thought, when I joined the Nurro-Ichthyothian military, I'd found my new home. I thought, when I was deported six ages ago, I'd never willingly return to where my family died. But, I was wrong. As much as Conflagria needed me,

I needed it. The lives of Cease and I were simply cleaving in opposite directions. And, I knew our disparate paths could never reconcile, just as the elements of fire and ice could never unify. If they tried, they'd destroy each other.

We walked, hand in hand, to the exit, where I reluctantly let him go, drew my hood, and ventured into the furious snow. I boarded the ship where Nurtic and Fair were waiting, and we slowly receded from the frosted shore of Ichthyosis, where I knew I'd never willingly set foot again. From the vessel's dock, I peered back at Icicle to look at Cease one last time, but my magicless eyes were too weak to see as far as the doorway where he stood.

CEASE LECHATELIERITE

The war was over. Ichthyosis won. I was, as the media declared, 'the brilliant war hero who led his fleet to victory, once and for all, against the tyrannical South Conflagrablaze Captive.' The Trilateral Committee promoted me to admiral and awarded me the highest honor a diver could receive—a 'Silver Triangle' medal. It was everything I always wanted. But, somehow, this long-awaited moment just didn't feel as beautiful as I expected it to be, my whole life. The victory felt strangely empty. There was something missing from it. I knew, I didn't deserve to stand in the limelight alone. I wasn't the one who reached into the Fire Pit to destroy the Crystal. There was someone else who should've been standing beside me now, giving meaning to my success, giving my life a new purpose.

You see, something snapped in me when I saw Scarlet dangle from my wire, an inch away from burning to death in the Fire Pit. If she fell in, the Crystal would've ended and Ichthyosis would've won, just the same. I could've let it happen; it would've been so easy. It was what the Trilateral Committee and the Childhood Program would've wanted me to do in that situation, considering how unlikely it was we'd find another way to destroy the Crystal. But, hearing Scarlet speak the truth about me as she hung there—how I was too cold to care for human life as much as I did for winning—pierced me to the core. She helped me understand just what I was fighting *for*—a nation of people like her, people who lived to love one another. I never realized that before. All along, I just wanted to win for the sake of winning. Because the Childhood Program told me to. But, now, I realized ends didn't justify means. I never considered death and destruction as the necessary *evils* of war, just the necessities of war. Now, I felt guilty for what I did to people like Fair Gabardine, Scarlet's best friend. Since my release from the hospital wing, I tried several times to apologize to her. But, every time I went to her room and tried to speak, she started screaming at the top of her lungs in Conflagrian and wouldn't stop until I left. Not that I blamed her.

Now, every minute of every day, I felt like I was holding onto a live wire. Everything made me… react, internally. I felt so helpless. So out-of-control. I wasn't used to that. I couldn't think about the past without feeling literally sick inside. I mean, *sick*. Stomachaches, headaches, night-sweats, shaking. Because I couldn't live with myself.

The pain got worse when I thought of Scarlet, which was often. I supposed, on top of everything else, I was reacting to her absence. The Nurians expressed the same sort of anguish when they talked about their families. They called it, 'missing' someone. I wasn't used to this particular brand of agony, as I'd only attached once before to someone who disappeared so suddenly. And, missing Scarlet hurt more and hurt differently than missing Inexor ever did. I didn't know what to expect of *this* grieving process in the months and ages to come.

Scarlet was gone. Gone to fulfill yet another duty, gone to make one more sacrifice for her people. She found her next purpose in life, and it wasn't to be with me.

I had a new goal, too. I wanted to dismantle the Childhood Program. I wanted to reform the Ichthyothian military training system so soldiers weren't abducted and trained from birth, but allowed to independently enlist, as adults. I wanted soldiers to understand the sacrifice they were making and exactly what and who they were fighting for.

"Admiral Lechatelierite!" came a voice on my intercom. "Admiral, your presence is requested in the lobby."

I sighed, internally. Since I was discharged from the hospital wing early last week, not a day went by without having to endure either crowds of worshipful government officials or offsite interviews with overly-adoring civilian journalists and news anchors. The Trilateral Committee—which I was now technically a part of, since I was an admiral, though I still didn't know what my job with them entailed—welcomed the publicity with enthusiasm and pushed me into every possible spotlight. For a soldier out of combat, I had quite a full schedule.

The interviews were very difficult for me. The Trilateral Committee didn't want Scarlet's name or contribution mentioned. A Conflagrian serving in the Diving Fleet—moreover, a Conflagrian winning the war for Ichthyosis—was the biggest scandal of the Ichthyothian military world. Even after saving the alliance, Scarlet still wasn't one of them. She was a person of the fire, and we were people of the ice, and the

Trilateral Committee could look no further than that. This made me furious beyond belief, but whenever I ignored their orders and brought up Scarlet in an interview, it was edited out.

I trudged down the corridors with Illia now, to meet my mystery visitors. All my appointments were scheduled by my gatekeepers, the Trilateral Committee. But, oddly enough, they didn't inform me in advance of this one.

"Your guests won't be able to stay long, as they have business matters to tend to, back home," Illia said. "And, the Trilateral Committee thought it best to keep things brief."

"What are you talking ab—" My voice died in my throat when I caught sight of Leavesleft standing with a middle-aged couple, awaiting my arrival.

The woman had long, tousled, dark hair. The man had intense, silver-grey eyes.

I pulled my visual band slowly off my face.

"Mother?" I whispered in disbelief. "Father?"

"We're proud of you, son," said the father I never knew, face stoic.

My mother ran to me, tears streaming down her pale cheeks. "Oh, Cease, we didn't want to give you up, we really didn't," she sobbed in my ear as she threw her arms around me. "But, we had no choice!"

I stood there, stiff and uncomfortable, and she wept into my shoulder. It took a moment before it occurred to me that I should embrace her, too. I felt awkward as I did so, elbows out. I stared over her shoulder, meeting my father's oddly-familiar gaze. "Don't worry," I said, solemnly. "No other parents will have to go through what you've been through, handing over their newborns to the military. I'll see to that myself." I swallowed. "I promise."

SCARLET JULY

We were only about twenty miles from Conflagria's northern shore. Fair and I were almost home. I leaned against the railing and felt something hard bump my leg. I reached into my pocket and pulled out my crystal fragment. 'It'll keep you strong,' a System guard told me six ages ago, when he thrust it into my hand. Now, I understood. This was a fragment of the Core Crystal. The guard gave it to me in a moment of defiance, hoping it'd help sustain my aura when thousands of miles from home. That's why the distance didn't hurt me as much as it should've. All these ages, this little stone gave me life.

But, now, without spectrum, it was nothing but a rough, greyish, oval rock. Useless. I no longer felt even a hint of residual attachment to it. I pitched it into the water with all my might. It glinted in the sunlight as it soared through the air and dropped into the Fervor Sea.

A moment later, Fair joined me at the rail, smiling at the approaching landmass of Conflagria. She was happy to come home, plain and simple. She wasn't leaving behind anything or anyone she cared about. I now knew the mystery behind Inexor's odd behavior toward Cease when he returned to Icicle: somehow, during his months of captivity, he'd come to care for Fair. The prisoner fell for his captor. But, Fair didn't reciprocate. She wasn't bothered by leaving Inexor behind. As she told me just minutes ago, his broken heart meant nothing to her. To some degree, I envied her for this. I wished I could feel the same sense of freedom upon leaving Ichthyosis.

Fair was giving me an odd look, now. Despite my military training, I still wasn't very good at keeping a stoic stare. Whatever I thought or felt tended to show up on my face.

"You love him, don't you?" she asked. "Your commander."

My heart leapt into my throat. How did she know? No one was supposed to know. The truth could get Cease court-martialed, if it ever got out. I was planning on taking the secret to my grave.

"Nurtic Leavesleft and I were coming to get you from the mess hall, so we could all leave, when we...saw you two," Fair began.

Saw us. Holding each other. Whispering. Kissing. Oh, Tincture. Someone in the military witnessed Cease and I violating the Laws of Emotional Protection. But, Nurtic was my friend. I could trust Nurtic not to babble. He cared about me, and he wouldn't want to ruin Cease's career, either.

"Nurtic literally had to hold me down, or else I would've ran in there and pried Cease's filthy hands off of you. Nurtic made us take a backdoor and wait for you here on the ship, instead." Fair exhaled through her nose. "Scarlet, I don't see how you could love him, after all he's done. After what he did to *me.*"

I was already at capacity, as far as emotional pain was concerned. I wasn't in the mood to feel like a traitor to my best friend. I couldn't cope with it now, not when the ache of losing Cease was only hours old.

"I don't know how he got you under his spell, but I wouldn't be surprised if he was just using you," she went on, mercilessly, "because there's no way he actually loves you back. There's no way a person like him is capable."

How dare she! "Maybe that'd be true if he were the same person as when we first met," I said, defensively. "But, he's not like that anymore. He's changed."

"Changed," Fair spat. "Sure. And, how long have you known him, exactly? How fast was this so-called change?"

My insides squirmed. I knew *of* Cease for about an age now, but only started interacting with him since the end of May. "Two months."

Fair snorted.

"We've been through a lot together," I added, feebly. "It was a very intense two months."

"Right. Inexor told me all about the Childhood Program; you're telling me *two months* reversed seventeen *ages* of brainwashing?"

"Fair, when Cease didn't think I could destroy the Crystal and get out alive, he was willing to leave Conflagria without doing it. That mission was the last chance he had, to salvage the war for Ichthyosis—the Trilateral Committee would've forced us to surrender to the System, if we failed. The war is Cease's whole life, and he was willing to throw it all away. For me. If that's not love, I don't know what is."

"Well, *I* can never forgive him," Fair folded her arms across her chest, "for what he did to *me*. And, I can never forgive *you*, Scarlet, for loving someone who'd do that to your best friend."

Fair started to turn away, but I grabbed her shoulders. Hard. Her eyes went wide at my use of physical force.

"I see you've learned from your commander!"

"Fair, listen to me," I breathed, staring into her oil-black eyes. "What's the difference between the Conflagrian System and the Ichthyothian Childhood Program? One uses magical thought-control and the other indoctrinates kids from birth—they both produce the same results! I don't condone Cease's actions, but if there's no excuse for what he did, there's also no excuse for what you've done, too. You betrayed me to the System, on July twenty-fifth of the eighty-seventh age."

Fair stopped breathing.

"I forgave you for selling me out; I know you only did that because you didn't know any better," I went on. "So, I ask nothing more than for you to forgive me for loving someone who's also had to fight against mental shackles his whole life." I let go of Fair's shoulders and instinctively held out my hand, like a Nordic. "We need to be able to trust one another, if we're going to spend the rest of our lives working together to rebuild Conflagria. Do you accept my apology?"

Fair hesitated, temples pulsing. After a minute that felt more like an hour, she swatted my hand aside and pulled me in for a hug.

Her tears fell on the top of my head. "Only a true friend would forgive me for what I did," she cried. "It's tormented me for six ages, and now you finally lifted the burden. I'm sorry for making you feel guilty about Cease. If his memory makes you happy, then by all means, go ahead and love him."

The deck jolted beneath our feet; we arrived. Fair's words rang in my head. His memory. That was all I'd ever have of Cease. He'd be nothing more than a phantom in my mind, from now on. I adjusted my robe, stepped off the metal Ichthyothian deck and walked, barefoot, on the glimmering, Conflagrian sand. I was now the leader of a revolution. And, I no longer had two magic sources to set me apart from everyone. No, I didn't have a photon of spectrum anymore, but I had something better.

A smile. A single smile on a precious face.

That was the way I wanted to remember him. My memory wasn't perfect anymore, so I knew it'd take effort to keep that smile at the forefront of my mind. But, I'd do it. I'd remember a soldier who never had much to smile about in his life, whose face once glowed with happiness despite all the pain that came with being Cease Terminus Lechatelierite. Though he was three-thousand miles away on the icy nation of North Ichthyosis, a part of him would always live on in the fiery island of the South Conflagrablaze Captive, for I'd always hold him in my heart, whatever I did, wherever I went.

Made in the
USA
Lexington, KY